Hours later, it seemed, he struggled through a mist of pain and darkness to become aware that someone holding a lighted candle was kneeling beside him. Someone in white. Lynn opened his eyes wider. The pain in his head was intolerable. It must have been making him delirious, for there, kneeling over him, was a lady he already knew. The face floated before him, vague and pale, the only color in it the vivid lips. She had escaped from her dungeon, or she had walked out of her picture, for here, in her long white dress and Chinese red shawl, with her Chinese red earrings and vivid lips, was Lynette Carstairs. The Laughing Ghost . . . !

The Laughing Ghost

Dorothy Eden

ace books

A Division of Charter Communications Inc.
A GROSSET & DUNLAP COMPANY
360 Park Avenue South
New York, New York 10010

THE LAUGHING GHOST

Published in Great Britain by Macdonald & Co., Ltd.

An ACE Book,
by arrangement with the author.

CHAPTER ONE

BEYOND the chimneys and the rooftops and the spires the sky was yellow as a candle flame. At his high window Lynn sat dreaming over the elusive smudgy beauty of London at dusk. His writing pad was on his knees. At the top of a sheet of paper he had written, *Because Victoria was sad she thought that all life around her had grown old and sad and weary. The drab mourning dress of the Court ladies befitted this heavy joyless thing the world had become . . .*

But there his thoughts refused to be pinned any longer on his novel of the little fat old queen long dead. The girl in the leopard skin coat had walked into his mind. He could see her again driving gaily into the garage in the big battered Packard, the huge young man with the bandaged head slumped beside her. The girl had a smudge of dust across her cheek. She had lost her hat and her hair was windblown, her grave wideset eyes were big and strained, but her lips had a kind of imperturbable gaiety as she smiled at Lynn, beckoning him over.

"We've had an accident," she said. "Henry's

1

smashed up his car, and his head too, a little."

"A little," muttered the young giant, opening his eyes with an effort. "My God, I feel like death!"

"You'll be all right, darling," the girl assured him lightly, and turned again to Lynn. "So would you have a car sent out to pick up Henry's Bentley, and get the dents taken out of this before my my uncle sees them and has a heart attack."

She was so light-hearted and self-assured after what had evidently been a bad smash that Lynn stared in bewilderment.

"But you're sure you're not hurt yourself?" he asked. "Can I telephone someone for you or get you a taxi?"

"God, my head!" moaned the large young man.

"No, I'm not hurt in the least," said the girl, stepping from the car and swinging back her coat so that Lynn could see her fine slender body. "Only a bit messed up and grubby. Henry's not really hurt much either. Shock mostly, I think. I'll take him along to a doctor. Yes, I'd be grateful if you'd get a taxi."

Henry moaned again and struggled out of the car, holding his head.

"Felicity wanted the race," he complained. "She knew my car couldn't take corners as hers does. We might both have been killed. Say, when's that taxi arriving? I've got to get to a doctor."

Lynn put through the call and came back.

"Do you mean to say you were just racing when that happened?" he asked incredulously.

The lovely gaiety was back on the girl's lips.

"My family's notorious for chasing thrills. And Henry really can afford to smash a car or two.

Henry, don't be such a baby. You're scarcely hurt at all."

"Gosh!" said Henry weakly, sitting down.

In a few moments the taxi arrived, and Lynn, still extremely bewildered, escorted the two to the door. Henry was helped into the taxi. The girl, her foot on the running board, turned to Lynn.

"Someone will call for the Packard at the end of the week. My name's Valentine. Felicity Valentine of St. Simon. Thanks for being so kind."

And that was all. She had walked into his life and walked out again. That was all. It was incredible that the cataclysm that had happened to him could have happened in so brief a time.

Half an hour later Lynn was fired. He was dreaming, and neglected an important customer. And when Joe Rogers abused him, his quick temper flared up and in the course of five minutes he found himself in possession of one week's salary and without a job.

But he never could stand Joe Rogers anyway. He was glad to be quit of him and his damn garage. If it came to that he was glad to be quit of the job of touting cars. But one must live some way, even if it was by driving fools about in cars they didn't intend to buy, and in listening to the sneers of Joe Rogers about one's gentleman's accent and high-brow face.

So now he was one of the legion of unemployed, that drear, unhappy, crushed but invincibly optimistic legion whose literature was chiefly the "Wanted" columns of the daily newspaper and whose existence was as much a part of London as the Houses of Parliament.

The gold was fading from the sky. It was turning imperceptibly to a delicate clear green like cool water. But London smoked and stifled in heat. Below in the street the newsboys were shouting *Hottest day of summer. Big jewel robbery. Windermere neckless stolen. Hottest day of summer!* In tireless reiteration.

He ought to get a paper and look for jobs, Lynn thought, but made no move to go. It must be the heat that made him feel weary and dispirited and futilely angry with everything. That trickster Fate had twisted his life beautifully. Tonight even the memories he had of his mother were bitter. There were only two of them, the one vague, far-off, elusive as a dream—a sunny day, bees in a clover field, a slender girl in skirts like a shaken bluebell dragging at his hand, crying, "Lynn! See the butterfly!"—the other that was only a voice whispering with aching difficulty, "There's enough money— for Lynn's education. He's a—Carstairs. He's to go to—Oxford . . . ."

He was to have studied law as so many of the Carstairs had done before him, but there hadn't been enough money after all. Two years at Oxford and his education had come to an abrupt end. The next three years were spent in the varying occupations of wharf laborer, floor-walker, insurance agent and car salesman. It was depression times and jobs were almost as scarce as water in the desert. Lynn supplemented his Oxford education with a good deal of practical experience in human life, and today had come to one more painful realization—that the barrier existing between rich and poor was insurmountable.

At this unhappy stage in his reflections there came a violent knocking at the door. It was flung open and Polly Gay, his next-door neighbor, two bottles of lager beer and a packet of sandwiches clutched to her bosom, came running into the room shrieking realistically:

"Help! Thieves! Murder!"

"My God!" Lynn groaned. "That's not acting. That's purely exercising your lungs."

Polly grinned good-humoredly and repeated her performance.

"I've got to rehearse, honey. I've only got a week to rehearse in. I don't want to be unkind, and I'm awfully sorry for that poor kid Barnes, but she certainly did me a good turn by getting scarlet fever. You know, I've got a hunch that this is just the break I've been waiting for. When old Condell sees how good I am in that maid's part I'll bet anything I get a part in his next production. Or maybe Fran Leeds will be at the show and asking me to sign up with him—or maybe—"

"Polly, my sweet, I hate to disillusion you, but you must face the fact that there's very little scope for displaying your genius when you simply have to rush on the stage and yell three words."

"Yeah!" said Polly, unperturbed. "You don't need to worry about disillusioning me because it just can't be done. I'm on top of the world, and we've got a celebration right now." She dumped the sandwiches and the bottles of beer on the table.

"What's the celebration about?"

Polly looked impish.

"Well, it's because old Condell said today there was only one member of the company word perfect and that was me. Well, of course, you could hardly expect me to be anything else when I've only got three words to remember and I guess he was only being a bit sarcastic. But you've got to celebrate about something sometime. What kind of sandwich will you have?"

"Ham," said Lynn abstractedly, going back to his own problem. Surely there was something else he had inherited besides a half-finished education and the name of one of the oldest families in England.

"Polly," he said interestedly. "What would you say were my outstanding features?"

Polly stared at him.

"You're not going to become one of these introspective guys, are you?"

"No, no, honey. I'm merely summing up my stock-in-trade. Now my disposition, for instance. What do you think of it?"

"Well, you've got a crazy temper," said Polly frankly.

Lynn scowled, drawing down his dark uneven brows, then smiled. Yes, that was true. Hot tempers were a characteristic of the Carstairs family, his mother had said.

"Then," continued Polly, surveying him closely, "you dream too much and you're proud as the devil and too damn stubborn for words. But, on the other hand, you're good fun and you're good-looking—those eyes of yours do things to a girl—and you're a pretty decent friend to have. I think you've just about got what it takes. But what's it all about? Applying to be a big noise at St. James' Palace, or what?"

Lynn grunted and said no, he was planning to

join the ranks of the unemployed. Polly was right about his crazy temper. It had landed him in trouble again, and the best thing he could do was to buy a newspaper and study the employment offered column.

Polly was upset. She had the kindest heart in the world and was distressed by anyone's misfortune. She wasn't pretty and she was inclined to be a little too short and plump, and her eyes were china blue and she possessed a restless disposition that kept her endlessly chattering and jumping about, and her speech was a queer mixture of faulty grammar and carefully cultivated Yankee slang, but she had a finer understanding of human nature than anyone else Lynn had ever known. She didn't say: "Lynn, you idiot, what did you let yourself get landed into trouble for?" Her eyes looked distressed, and she said: "But I never could stand that old stick Rogers. I'm glad you're out of that. Maybe I could get a job in *Yours Truly*. Maybe Bill Hanley or Lee Martin will go down with scarlet fever, too."

Lynn grinned.

"You're a nice, kind well-wisher, aren't you. And maybe if I got the job I could act like Bill Hanley or Lee Martin."

"You don't know what you can do till you try," commented Polly sagely. "I guess you'd make a marvelous actor. Well, anyway, you'd look right, and that's all some actors do. They just look and smile. They can't act for nuts. Gosh, Lynn, you'd fill the part of a long-lost heir to an earldom or something perfectly." Her gaze ran approvingly over Lynn's tall, thin, wide-shouldered body, his face with its taut, alert look, his mobile brows ready to lift mockingly or to scowl, his eyes, oddly blue in his brown face, and young and pleasant and good-humored.

"Carstairs of Carstairs," he murmured mockingly. Then he said impatiently: "there's too much of this supposing going on. Maybe I'll starve or sell my book or steal jewels like the Windermere necklace. Or maybe I'll just sit and watch you become a famous actress. Anyway, there's a celebration on so let's get going."

"Oh, yes!" Polly exclaimed. "I nearly forgot that."

But the celebration wasn't a success in spite of Polly's chatter. Half-way through she said: "Say, what's the matter with you?"

"Nothing," said Lynn, munching gloomily.

"I'll bet!" Polly commented. "You look as cheerful as seven owls with the earache. Who is she?"

"She!" Lynn said exasperatedly. "She! Well, if women aren't the limit. See a man brooding because he's lost his job, and you instantly jump to conclusions. It's a girl."

"I've seen you lose jobs before and you haven't looked like this. You're goofy over a girl, that's what's the matter."

Lynn scowled and sighed.

"Polly, I don't know why I put up with you. I don't know why I don't throw you out. Well, can a man fall in love with a girl he's seen for about five minutes and will never see again, except perhaps when he's a shoeblack in the street and she goes past in her limousine? Can you tell me that?"

Polly looked at him, her mouth puckered rue-fully.

"Yes," she said at last. "If that isn't the sort of dame you would fall for. Here, have some more beer!"

As night approached the silhouette of Carstairs grew darker and more medieval against the sky, the fading light of the sunset blown into the windows, the dignity of three graceful centuries upon it. The trees surrounding it, oak and elm and cedar, looked as graceful with age as the house, and the wide gravelled drive sweeping in a curve from the high carved main gates was scored with the mark of carriage wheels and hoofmarks. As if modernity had not reached here. As if a spurred and booted cavalier might come galloping from beneath the blackness of the trees out onto the sunset road, or a messenger, with the borrowed imperiousness of his royal master, rap the heavy carved knocker on the big front door.

Inside the house, too, modernity was so subtle as to give an impression of comfortable exquisite age. In the library the warm blown light of the candles set at either end of the mantelpiece and on the table grew brighter as the dusk deepened. Soon there was no more than a wan yellow glow in the sky and the shrubs and clipped yews on the lawn had assumed their nightly dark crouching shapes. The windows were thrown wide open, for the night was close and still, but although no breeze moved the candle flames flickered continually.

The heat and the paragraph in the *Daily Mail* lying before him, and the unperturbed gaiety of

Felicity's face, were all combining to work old Lynnford Carstairs into one of his swift spectacular rages. His heavy eyebrows were drawn to the bridge of his mountainous nose. His fine old eyes flashed fire.

"What have you to say for yourself?" he was shouting.

"Speak up! Tell me whether this is the truth or not?"

Felicity's voice sounded very cool and quiet.

"I can't tell you whether it's the truth or not when I haven't seen the article, uncle. All the same, I daresay I'm to blame for whatever it is, and it's hardly fair of you to drag poor Henry out of bed."

Poor Henry, attired in dressing gown and pajamas, his large head still decorated with a proportionately large bandage, flung himself back in his armchair and groaned.

"Felicity, don't you think it's time I had my head dressed again?"

"No, of course not, Henry. Don't fuss so."

"This!" cried old Lynnford, stabbing at the paper with his forefinger. "This infamous article. Here, I'll read it to you:

"Greenslade's corner on the London road was the scene of a car smash this morning when a Bentley driven by Henry B. Higgins-bottom, son of a Chicago millionaire, overturned and was completely wrecked, and a Packard driven by Miss Felicity Valentine of St. Simon was damaged, but able to proceed. The occupants of the cars had a miraculous escape from injury,. Mr. Higginsbottom sustaining only a slight gash in his forehead and Miss Valentine being completely unhurt. Miss Valentine stated that the accident was the result of a bet—"

Old Lynnford paused. His brows were drawn together ferociously.

" '—was the result of a bet!' " he repeated, with emphasis, " 'as to which car could make the fastest time to London. But the Bentley skidded in some loose shingle and overturned, involving the Packard in the smash. Only Miss Valentine's skill as a driver saved her from complete disaster.' "

"That's true," murmured Felicity. "If I hadn't swung around as I did it would have been finis."

"Gosh!" Henry exclaimed, roused to indignation. "Do they say this horrible mess is a slight gash?"

"Damn your horrible mess!" shouted old Lynnford. "What about the mess my car is in?"

"Henry's is much worse, uncle."

"Henry's! What do I care about Henry's! He raced it, didn't he? And anyway he's got a father who can buy him a fleet of cars if he chooses. But you haven't. Your father's a good-for-nothing scamp fritting away his life shooting elephant tusks and expecting me to pay his daughter's bills."

"Not shooting tusks, uncle dear. Elephants."

Lynnford, purple in the face, banged his fist on the table, making Henry wince nervously.

"Tusks or elephants, it's all the same. He's a reckless scamp and it looks to me as if his daughter is the same. Racing to London for a bet. Smashing up cars for a bet. I tell you, it's not good enough. The next thing I know I'll be paying your funeral expenses."

"But I can't help being reckless," said Felicity earnestly. "It's a characteristic of the Carstairs family. You are yourself, you know. Just the same as you're famous for your good jokes and your bad temper."

"My—my hat!" spluttered the old man. "You're forgetting yourself, my girl. Next thing you'll be telling me how to behave." He paused a minute, breathing heavily. "Well I don't deny the Carstairs are partial to an adventure," he said more calmly. "But they don't rush about endangering the lives and limbs of people all over the countryside."

Felicity came and perched herself on the edge of the table smiling with sweet innocence at her uncle.

"Henry was bored, uncle. I had to do something to amuse him."

"Eh? Eh, what?" said Henry, starting up.

"Damn Henry!" exploded Lynnford. "Then why doesn't he go somewhere else to be bored? Why doesn't he go back to Mississippi or Missouri or wherever he came from?"

"But I'm not bored!" Henry protested, indignation written all over his big florid face. "Felicity, how can you say that? I'd just as soon be here as anywhere else in the world."

Old Lynnford's swift temper was dying. His face looked old and tired, but his eyes remained remarkably shrewd.

"Then if that's the way of it," he murmured, glancing from Henry to Felicity, who was perched negligently on the table swinging a velvet-slippered foot, "God help Carstairs. A rag-a-muffin and an imbecile!"

"What did you say, uncle?"

"I said that you can't blame Henry for what happened if he wasn't bored after all. So you're to blame, and I sent for you to tell you that it gives me great pain to think that Carstairs is going to fall into such careless hands as yours. First thing you know, your rascally father will have elephant tusks all over the place and you'll be smashing up cars in the rosebeds."

"Uncle, you're joking."

"Not this time, my dear. Carstairs isn't entailed, you know. You're next in the line of succession, but I can leave it to whomever I please. If I thought you were going to do nothing but make scatter-brained bets—"

A look of pain flashed in Felicity's eyes.

"But, uncle!" She shook herself and laughed lightly. "You couldn't do that, uncle. You couldn't leave Carstairs to just anybody like a—well, like a motor mechanic."

"No, you couldn't do that," Henry put in. "You couldn't leave a fine old place like this to a motor mechanic and you don't know what anybody is nowadays."

"I guess I can't help being a gambler," went on Felicity. "But where Carstairs is concerned— Anyway, the ghost wouldn't let anyone else live here. He'd be scared out of his wits in a week."

"I don't know so much about that," Lynnford muttered. "I'm not proposing to make a motor mechanic my heir. But you'll have to watch yourself, my dear. Be a little less irresponsible." He rubbed his hand over his forehead. "Now be off with the two of you. I'm tired. Send Mark to me."

When the valet came, however, old Lynnford sent him away again.

"I'll ring for you presently," he said querulously. "I don't want to be interrupted just now."

Alone again he stood at the window staring at the fading yellow glow in the west. That familiar tightness was in his chest again, making it difficult for him to breathe. One of these days, he reflected, he'd find he couldn't breathe at all. And then—Carstairs in the hands of sweet Felicity with her rag-a-muffin ways. And with that great hulking Yankee come to visit England and to stay at Carstairs because he was some sort of second cousin of Felicity's, and because he thought he ought to know how to fox hunt, b'gad! Following her like a shadow. Not for her money, of course. He had enough of his own. But for one of England's oldest names, if he possessed enough sense in that great frame of his to realize that such a thing was an asset. The two of them would be racing cars all over England. God knew what would be the end of them and of Carstairs. Felicity was a good girl. Plenty of spunk, and that was what he liked. But she hadn't come to her senses yet. She didn't want to be left too much money and responsibility for a year or two. What she wanted at present was a good sharp lesson.

And by Jove! thought old Lynnford, by Jove! I've a mind to teach her it. Yes, she said I was famous for my good jokes. Perhaps she won't think this a very good one—but, by Heaven, it's going to be the best of all!

Mr. Edward Burke, attorney, didn't approve of clients ringing him at his house after office hours. But old Lynnford Carstairs was the exception to the rule. Mr. Burke would willingly have got out of his bath to speak to Lynnford Carstairs on the telephone. But this evening he listened in amazement to the crisp autocratic voice at the other end of the wire.

"Trace other branches of the family? Yes, Mr. Carstairs. Certainly, Mr. Carstairs. It must be a Lynnford Carstairs. Yes, I see. Your father had a cousin Lynnford who went to South Africa. Yes, I understand perfectly. It may take a little time. You'd like it done urgently? Very well, Mr. Carstairs. I'll attend to it at once and let you know as soon as I hear anything. Yes, Mr. Carstairs. Good night, Mr. Carstairs."

Mr. Burke replaced the receiver and rubbed his brow.

"Whew!" he murmured. "Well, I daresay there'll be a good fee in it. But the old chap's crazy. Clean crazy!"

The silver bell of the clock had struck seven times and the minute hand had slid on to five minutes past seven beford Green arrived with the evening paper.

"You're late, Green," said his employer in his soft emotionless voice, glancing up at the clock.

"I'm sorry, sir. The boy was late, sir. It's only five minutes past seven."

"Five minutes late or an hour late, you're still guilty of unpunctuality. I don't approve of it. You may go."

"Yes, sir. Thank you, sir," said Green with a scared backward glance at his employer. Gawd, if it wasn't for the wages he'd quit! Cold-blooded, that was what Kiffin Pope was. Cold-blooded as a frog and finicky as an old woman. But the wages were all right and so were the grub and the living conditions. One could put up with a few lectures on unpunctuality and a few glances from those deadish-looking eyes when one lived and ate like a lord.

It didn't occur to Green that Kiffin Pope treated his servants well because it didn't suit him to have to change them too often. But that was exactly the case. Pope led an extremely retired life, and he had a distinct aversion to strangers. Few of his neighbors ever saw him, and those who did had no wish to enlarge their acquaintance. He was a thin, peculiar man with a nose like a beak and his skin was the color of a corpse.

Pope could have told them that it was fifteen years in jail that had given his skin that unpleasant tinge. Fifteen years of too little fresh air and too few changes in diet. Still, he was lucky it hadn't been the rope. For a franic three weeks it had been, and then, although the man dead by his hand had not returned to life and nothing in his crime had materially changed, his petition for a reprieve was granted and the death sentence had become a life sentence.

But those three weeks had left their mark. The man had fiendish nightmares. A hundred times the noose had closed around his neck, and the hand that jerked it tight was the hand of the man he had slain. Nor was he ever quite alone, for frequently a voice that no one else could hear spoke in his ear, a form invisible to others stood at his shoulder, sometimes in the night the face of a murdered man looked down on him.

That, of course, was nothing but nerves bred of long weeks of solitary confinement. Pope had thought that life in the outside world would cure it. It hadn't. He was hag-ridden. He was beyond salvation.

So, having nothing to lose, he became at once the friend and the enemy of many a desperate and frightened criminal. It was more or less of a game to him and it helped his income and fed his craving for luxury—another trait bred of fifteen years of forced austerity. It helped him to forget that little chant that had been sung about him in prison, *Kiffin Pope is afraid of the rope* . . . .

But tonight Pope had found something in the newspaper that promised to be his biggest scoop of all. His eyes had skimmed over the headings, *Tension in Europe. Son of Chicago Millionaire in Car Smash. Big Jewel Robbery—Windermere Necklace Stolen*, and the last one had drawn his eyes like a magnet.

The Windermere necklace! My God! He'd stake his entire possessions on the fact that that was the Kitten's job. How many years ago was it—five, ten?—that the Kitten had confided to Pope one morning during exercise in the prison yard that it was his greatest ambition to steal the Windermere necklace. The Kitten was something of a fanatic about that particular piece of jewelry. His big face had glowed as he had whispered to Pope about his plans. Pope was a safe man to talk to, and anyhow he was a lifer. The Kitten would be out and have the job done long before Pope breathed free air again. The Kitten had scooped his two great hands together, gazing at them gloatingly as if the necklace already lay there. Of course it would be the devil's own problem to get them out of England once they were stolen, but if only he could get possession of them he would be content to lie low for years, if need be, until the opportunity to get rid of them came along.

Why, it would be like having a handful of stars, real shining stars, in his hands.

The Kitten was an extraordinarily clever burglar. Even Pope recognized that. The man had no brains for anything else, he was foolish and as easily led as a child, but when it came to burgling he was the slickest thief in England. He had an uncanny flair for finding entrances to houses, avoiding burglar alarms and opening the most intricate locks; but his most uncanny gift was his ability to move absolutely without sound. He was big and ungainly with a heavy, stupid, child's face, but one could be less aware of him in a house than of a shadow. It was this soft-footedness that had given him the title of the Kitten.

Now Kiffin Pope read and reread the paragraph relating the tragic tale of the shattered lock and the empty safe. Usually Lady Windermere left the necklace in her safe deposit box in the vaults of the Bank of England, but the previous night there had been a big and distinguished gathering at Windermere Hall. Lady Windermere had worn the diamonds and because it was too late to return them to the Bank that night had locked them temporarily in her private safe in her own bedroom. In the morning the door of the safe hung open; the necklace was gone.

And now, thought Pope, no flicker of expression on his face save a faint twitching of his colorless lips, he'll want to get them out of England. This is where I come in.

His next actions were methodical. He locked the door, pulled the heavy curtain across the windows, switched on the lights and unlocked the safe in the corner. From the safe he drew a slim black book and, taking it to the light, ran his fingers down the names listed in the index.

Scotland Yard, had it known such a book existed, would have given a great deal for it. It contained a list of all the criminals with whom Pope had associated, a record of their crimes, their personal description and methods, and habitual haunts. It was a valuable volume, for Pope had associated with a good number of criminals more to his own profit than theirs. As the Kitten had an uncanny flair for moving soundlessly, so he had an uncanny flair for detecting criminals and getting them within his power.

The Kitten had half a page devoted to him. Pope glanced at it briefly merely to confirm his memory, for he knew already the Kitten's habitual haunts. There were three of them. If the Kitten were not at any of them a least there would be news of him.

Before replacing the book in the safe Pope turned up the name of Claus Jensen, Swedish seaman, and read the half dozen lines devoted to that person. Then, smiling faintly, he locked the book away, unlocked the door, and rang for Green to get his hat and coat and call a taxi. Pope was in a good humor. He spoke almost genially, for he had another of his brilliant, crafty cold-blooded schemes up his sleeve, and if it didn't work someone would suffer. Badly.

It was but half an hour to midnight. At midnight Constable Diver could go off duty. Another half hour and he could get home to Katie. But how the hands of the clock crawled. The thing could start happening in half an hour and there was Katie all by herself with no one to help her. It made the sweat break out on Constable Diver's forehead to think of it. Certainly Katie was the bravest little woman in the world. She had refused absolutely to have help in the house. There was the telephone, she said, and that was as good as a person. The moment the pains started she could ring the doctor and nurse. But just think of her stumbling to the telephone—

Constable Diver shook himself out of his reverie and began leisurely retracing his footsteps down the cobbled street of St. Simon. He was getting balmy about the business, but he had never been waiting to be a father before, and this night duty, with nothing to do but wander about and think, made him exaggerate things. Pity St. Simon was such a quiet orderly town. Nothing happened except an occasional disturbance by a drunk. There wasn't much chance for a man to earn promotion in a town like this. No thieves or murderers to catch. Now if the Windermere necklace theft had happened here instead of in London there would be some chance of distinguishing oneself by tracing the thief. And Constable Diver earnestly wanted promotion now that there was going to be a kid in the house. Nice to have the little beggar admiring one's stripes, thinking what a fine father he had.

But nothing ever happened in St. Simon. Only a car smash on the London road, and wild young Felicity Valentine bringing that large American with a bandaged head back to Carstairs. Old Lynnford would haul his niece over the coals for that. But there was no subduing Felicity, the lovely minx, and if it came to that old Lynnford had been a wild hot-tempered young scamp in his day. High spirits seemed to run in the Carstairs family. They had been notorious smugglers in Elizabethan days. And there was one old villain who had murdered a whole batch of people including his wife and had finally been banished from England.

But Carstairs looked innocent enough in the moonlight tonight. Constable Diver's footsteps were taking him past the wrought-iron gates three times as high as himself, and through them he could see the lovely dim shape of the house. It was an inheritance any man would be proud of. The rooms contained some of the finest paneling in England. It was said, too, that the Princess Elizabeth, daughter of Anne Boleyn, had stayed there as a child, and once, not so many years ago, a fat little girl named Victoria, daughter of the Duke and Duchess of Kent had scrambled up and down the stairs. Two little girls destined to be the *greatest* queens in English history. Funny, thought Constable Diver in a rare flight of fancy, if their ghosts should meet. Indeed, there was reputed to be a ghost at Carstairs, not that of one of the little princesses, but of one of the Carstairs ladies. The Laughing Ghost, it was called. Servants were scared away sometimes, but the Carstairs themselves didn't seem to take much notice of it. Family business, so to speak.

Anyway it was quiet enough around here tonight, with only the call of an owl and the drag of shingle on the beach. Constable Diver decided he would take a turn on the beach and have a look at the caves which were accessible only at low tide and which were reputed to have run beneath Carstairs until falls of rock had blocked the way. It was rumored that smuggling had been carried on there during the middle ages, the smuggler anchoring off the beach and the contraband being taken through the caves to the cellars beneath Carstairs.

But the sea was empty tonight. No white-sailed vessel rose and fell with the waves, and anyway the days of smuggling were long past. The beach was a lonely deserted place. Few people ever went there. At any rate, it wasn't the place to go looking for promotion, Constable Diver reflected, turning back toward the Police Station to report and go off duty. Already all thoughts of Carstairs had left him. There was room in his mind for nothing but the image of Katie with her soft patient face and precious body.

Half past twelve of a summer's night and all was well.

Constable Diver, large and ludicrous in pink striped pajamas, stood staring down at the sleeping form of his wife. Then he climbed with clumsy caution into the bed beside her.

In spite of his caution she awoke and whispered sleepily.

"Hello, Thomas."

"Hello, Katie."

He slid his arm around her and they lay snuggled together in the warmth.

"Everything all right, Katie?"

"Just fine. I wish you wouldn't worry, dear."

Constable Diver drew a deep breath.

"Katie, I thought to myself tonight, I thought I'm going to get promotion some way, for the sake of you and the kid. I'm going to get it if I die in the attempt."

Katie's hand touched his cheek.

"Don't die, Thomas," said her soft amused voice. "That wouldn't be much use to me or the baby."

The silk curtains of Felicity's bedroom swayed in and out, and moonlight polished the floor. Felicity lay with her hand thrust under her head, staring at the ceiling.

"Uncle, I'm not really as reckless and irresponsible as you think I am." She didn't realize she was talking aloud. "I didn't mean to smash the cars, but I just had to wake Henry up some way. I wanted to see if he could be awakened because maybe I'll marry him. I'll have to do something. It's dreadful to know that your existence is quite aimless. It's dreadful knowing that when you're twenty-two. Maybe I should fall in love. But who is there? Rudolph, Cam, Henry. They're all decent scouts, but you just don't fall in love with them. Maybe I'm the sort of person who doesn't fall in love."

That thought caused Felicity to lie quite still staring unhappily out of the window. Then she tossed impatiently, calling herself an introspective idiot, and wondered if she would ever sleep.

Five minutes later she was asleep. The anxiety had gone from her face. It looked small and pale and peaceful, and her lips were solemn and innocent, like a child's.

Something stirred heavily on Lynn's feet and Lynn sat up wrathfully.

"Buddy! You disgraceful little scamp! Off you get!"

The shaggy white Sealyham looked up and blinked and stared off on the journey over deceptive hillocks and hollows of blankets toward Lynn's face. Half way, discouraged by the forbidding look on the face that was his goal, he sat down and lifted a tentative paw.

"It's not good enough," said Lynn severely. "If I've told you once I've told you fifty times you're not to get on the bed. Shoot!"

Precipitated by the violent upheaval of blankets behind him Buddy tumbled onto the floor and resignedly stretched himself on the mat, jaw resting on stubby forepaws.

Lynn twisted and sighed.

"Damn!" he said presently. "If I can't sleep I'd better work."

He switched on the light, reached for manuscript and pen, and sat staring at the last words he had written. *This heavy joyless thing the world had become* . . . .

"It's a nice sort of name—Felicity," he said aloud. "What do you think, dog?"

This heavy joyless thing the world had become . . . .

But there would always be laughter in the world for Felicity. . . . So Polly thought he was in love. How women harped on that subject. Only sons of Chicago millionaires could afford to be in love with girls like Felicity Valentine.

"Buddy!" said Lynn explosively, to an instantly attentive dog. "Do you realize I mightn't even be able to pay your license fee next month? Just chew that thought over, will you."

The atmosphere was blue with smoke. In the center of the room a girl danced and swung short red skirts. The orchestra played and a crowd of men sprawled over tables and chairs watching the dancer. But Kiffin Pope and Claus Jensen sat isolated at a table in a corner of the room. No one took any notice of the pallid thin man or the big colorful golden-eyed Swede who smiled all the time.

"But why refuse me this time?" Pope was saying in his soft insinuating voice. "You've done other work for me. It's not safe for you to refuse, you know. I know too much about you. I can get you a five year stretch if it suits me."

The Swede chuckled good-humoredly. Nothing, it seemed, could disturb his complacency.

"You try, my frien'. You try."

Pope glanced around.

"Listen," he said softly, "there's five thousand in this for you. Just to take a handful of diamonds out of England. Christ, man, that's child's play to you! A handful of diamonds when every month you land loads of liquor."

"How much are the diamonds worth?"

Again Pope glanced around with his casua'. air.

"Twenty thousand. I get five, you get five, and my friend gets the rest."

The Swede's big body shook with colossal mirth.

"You lie, my frien'. You pull the wool over my eyes. The diamonds are the Windermere diamonds and they are worth one hundred thousand pounds. You get eighty your frien' gets fifteen and I get five. Is that not so?"

Pope's heavy eyelids flickered. He smiled for the first time and looked strangely repellent.

"I give you facts, Jensen. The diamonds are worth more than twenty thousand, but you are being fanciful about the Windermere necklace. My friend and I are not so ambitious as to touch it. What about seven thousand?"

The Swede shook his head.

"No, no, it is too risky. Small things like brandy and tobacco, yes. But not this. It is too big."

"Ten thousand, then. It's a fortune, Jensen. You can retire."

The Swede was thoughtful.

"Yes. Yes, that is so. My wife, she would like me to retire. Ten thousand. But it is risky."

"Good God, man, you thrive on risks."

"Yes, that is so. I will think about it. No, let me see. You go and see old man Carstairs. You know the property Carstairs in a little place called St. Simon. You go to him and ask him about the Laughing Ghost. If he will do anything for you then maybe I will, too."

The Swede got ponderously to his feet. His fat face was shining with mirth. Pope sprang up to detain him.

"But, Jensen, that's not enough. My God, I give you facts and you give me fancies. What's this about a Laughing Ghost?"

"You go and find out," the Swede returned, and, shaken with roars of laughter, he made his way out of the cafe leaving Pope to fume over his defeat. Claus Jensen, petty smuggler, sending Kiffin Pope on a wild-goose chase. Laughing ghosts! Bah! The man was mad.

CHAPTER TWO

It was halfway through the second act that Lynn had an uneasy feeling that the play *Yours Truly* was going to be a flop, and halfway through the second intermission that he saw Felicity Valentine. He was on the pavement ouside the theater smoking a cigarette, and she came down the steps in her silver dress and green velvet shoes to lift her face to catch the slow-falling rain. She looked radiant and remote, and her silver dress had the luminosity of a new moon. Lynn had a sensation of ecstasy until it was changed to wild rage by the sight of the large young man with the piece of adhesive tape on his forehead taking Felicity's arm and telling her not to be so dumb as to stand in the rain.

"Who's going to catch a chill in this lovely rain?" The girl laughed and said in her low eager voice, "Henry, after the play's over let's have supper at the Black Cat. It's just around the corner. It's a most intriguing place. Checked tablecloths and tankards of ale and things like that."

Henry said, "But, gosh, Felicity, I've booked a table at the Savoy."

"And I don't feel a bit Savoyish," said the girl, turning to go in. "Henry, do let's go to the Black Cat."

Their voices had come to Lynn quite clearly. His extraordinary luck in seeing Felicity at all was incredible enough without the luck of knowing where she was going for supper. If she had been going to the Savoy he, with a recklessness similar to that that had led her to race high-powered cars to London, would have gone, too, even though it meant deliberately forgetting to eat for a week afterwards. As it was, she was simply going to the Black Cat, where he frequently supped himself. The last act passed practically unnoticed by Lynn. He didn't mean to forget that he had promised to take Polly home. He had just forgotten that Polly existed.

He left the theater and strolled into the Black Cat and ordered a sandwich and a tankard of ale, and sat on a stool at the bar chatting with the barman who was an old acquaintance. He was blissfully happy in the thought that he had discovered one thing he had in common with Felicity Valentine—a liking for old cheerful low-ceilinged taverns with checked tablecloths and tankards of ale—which thought reminded him to finish his ale and order another tankard.

He drank that, too, and still the girl in the silver dress hadn't come.

"I think I've made a mistake," he informed the barman, and gloomily ordered another drink, and gloomily drank it.

A moment later Felicity, with a flashing of her skirts beneath her white fur wrap, entered.

"I think Dinah Gale's marvelous," she was saying to her escort, the large and lugubrious Henry.

"It must be lovely to be so lovely that it doesn't matter if your name is Dinah. But all the same, I don't think it was a terribly successful first night. You could feel the atmosphere. Let's sit here, shall we? Isn't this a delightful place? Henry, what's the matter?"

"I was just thinking, honey," said Henry heavily, "that it wouldn't matter if your name was Martha or Abigail or something."

"Oh, *Henry!*" said Felicity.

Lynn was slightly drunk and blissfully happy. He leaned across to the barman and said confidentially, "The lady is beautiful," and turned to survey Felicity with a bright-eyed impudent stare.

"What shall we have?" Felicity asked Henry. "I'm as hungry as two hunters."

"I wonder," said Lynn to the barman, "if she knows how bewitching green shoes and a silver dress are. But probably she does, don't you think?"

"Yes, perfectly," said Felicity to Henry. "Henry, I wonder if they know what hamburgers are. You know, the things you have in Chicago. All the same, the gentleman is offensive, don't you think."

Henry looked extremely bewildered, and seized on the only thing that made sense to him.

"Well, I guess they wouldn't know what language you were talking if you talked about hamburgers here. Eh, honey? What gentleman? Oh, that guy over there. Well, I told you I'd got a table at the Savoy. That's where we should have gone."

Lynn, meeting Felicity's frank gaze, smiled. His smile was young and shy and gay, and it altered his long lean face with its prominent cheek bones and slightly arrogant brows unexpectedly. It made

Felicity's lips tremble with their lovely gaiety, too, then abruptly she straightened them, frowned and reached for her wrap.

"This place is too noisy for you, Henry. It will be giving you a headache. We'll go to the Savoy after all."

Lynn watched the two go out. His smile had vanished, his brows were lowering.

"And that," he said savagely to the barman, "is what they call the laws of civilization. To him that hath shall be given. He'll get his moneybags and the loveliest girl in the world as well. Though what she can see in that tame elephant—What's my bill, Charlie? God help me, I'm drunk."

His hands thrust in his pockets, Lynn tramped the streets fiercely for an hour, then, with a sober thought as to the value of shoe leather, turned home.

A little dark form sat curled up at the foot of the stairs. Lynn stumbled against it, and Polly cried,

"Ouch! You clumsy brute! Can't you see where you're going? Oh, it's you, Lynn! If it interests you, I've been waiting an hour."

"Oh, no!" said Lynn ruefully. "Polly, you'll never believe I forgot all about you. Honestly, I did."

"Yeah," said Polly wearily. "I believe you all right. You're the sort of guy who goes around forgetting things like girls. Never mind. I forgive you. I'm locked out, otherwise I wouldn't have bothered you. Left my bag with the key in it down at the theater. I can get into my room along the balcony from yours."

"You poor kid, sitting here in the dark. Honestly, Poll, I'm frightfully sorry. How was the play?"

Suddenly Polly began to laugh. She rocked herself

backward and forward until her laughter sounded suspiciously like sobs.

"How was the play? I'll tell you. That play only had one leg to stand on from the beginning. In the second act it lost it, and what happens when you lose both legs? You fall down. That's what's happened to *Yours Truly*. It's fallen flat. And then I sit in the dark for an hour and you walk in and say, 'How's the play?' just like that. Honest, Lynn, it's so funny I could die laughing."

Lynn slid an arm around her.

"Yes, it's funny, all right," he said gently. "You're in the dumps and I'm one of those fools who goes around crying for the moon, and—oh, here's Buddy left alone all evening. That's three of us. Yes, it's funny as hell!"

The Kitten's heavy lower lip hung down foolishly. His little dark eyes were popping with astonishment. The finger that supported his cigar, the thick, spatulate, hairy finger ludicrously adorned with a large ruby ring, trembled visibly. The whole gigantic body of the man sitting tensely in one of Kiffin Pope's luxurious chairs was suggestive of fear.

"But, Kiff," he was saying piteously, "you can't pin this on me. That little business at Corrington's maybe, but not this. Why, the Windermere necklace is way above me. I wouldn't be going into that dame's bedroom after she was in bed, not a big hulking fellow like me. Why, I'd be knocking something over, a what-not or something. No, I stick to places where there's no one around."

"Come off it," came Pope's soft remote voice. "If you didn't pinch the diamonds, who did?"

"But I wouldn't know that," the Kitten protested eagerly. "How would I? Some slick guy, maybe, but not me."

"Oh, no," said Pope mockingly. "Someone's the thief, but not the Kitten. Not the quiet harmless little Kitten. Now, listen! I want you to throw your mind back to a certain day eleven years ago in a certain prison yard where certain prisoners took daily exercise." His voice had changed. It had become slow and drawling. The Kitten's small popping eyes stared at him hypnotically. "One of these prisoners, a big harmless-looking fellow, but the slickest thief in London, had an ambition. He was so full of it that he had to talk about it. To be sure, he was cautious and only talked to a poor lifer who probably wouldn't live to see freedom again. But he talked. He was going to get the Windermere necklace. It was his life-long ambition. He said it would be like owning a handful of bright shiny stars. He had his plans made then. They were good plans and the sort this fellow could carry through successfully. And mark this!" Pope struck his clenched fist in his palm and the Kitten jumped convulsively. "Those plans were exactly the ones the thief of the Windermere necklace carried out!"

The Kitten rubbed his palm over his wet forehead. When it came to physical danger and he knew where he was he could stick it, but the dead eyes of this man, the cold remorseless voice, the diabolically clever methods he had used in running the Kitten to earth, reduced him to a craven coward. Why had he been such a fool as to talk of his ambitions in jail? Why hadn't he been more careful to whom he talked? And why hadn't he remembered he had talked at all? This Kiffin Pope was a man to be afraid of. He was like the devil. There wasn't a crime committed that he didn't know of.

"Well," said Pope softly. "Halves or I'll squeal."

"But you've no proof," the Kitten protested feebly. "I've never seen the damn diamonds. I don't want to see them. I—"

A negligent hand was waved at him.

"That'll do, Kit. You know, you are by way of being a human tragedy. Given great brilliance as a burglar, but not sufficient brains. No, not sufficient brains. I know you've got the diamonds. And I also know you'll go halves with me or do a ten year stretch. That's as clear as daylight."

The Kitten's lip dropped still lower. He looked on the verge of tears. He didn't know that the memory of his meeting with the Swede, the only man who dared to laugh at him, still rankled in Pope's mind, and this torturing of the Kitten, this ability to make a big burly man writhe with the sting of his tongue, was necessary to his self-esteem.

"But, Kiff, you can't pin this on me," he protested. "you haven't got a shadow of proof."

"No! How does this speak?" With a quick movement Pope moved his hand from under the desk and the Kitten found himself gazing into the barrel of a revolver. "I'm not afraid to use it, you know, Kit. But of course you'll know that."

"Why you—you— It'll make you a murderer!" gasped the Kitten.

"That's what a British jury has already decided I am. I've nothing to lose." This was Pope's strongest card and one he played frequently. It gave his victims the impression he wanted them to have—

that he was ruthless and cold-blooded and desperate, and would stop at nothing.

The Kitten mopped his brow.

"What do you want me to do?"

Pope smiled and lowering the revolver produced a sheet of typewritten matter.

"Just sign a little confession. Just so as I'll have some security over you. I can't be letting you run loose over Europe with fifty thousand bucks that belong to me. Just a little confession that you are the thief of the Windermere necklace. And you have my word of honor that it will be destroyed the moment I get my share."

The Kitten's fingers shakingly took the proffered pen. His heavy lips were trembling like a hurt child's.

"God, Pope, you're a devil!" he whimpered. "Where must I sign this damned thing? Why should I do all the dirty work while you sit safe at home and get half the dough? Doesn't make sense to me."

"You're not doing all the work, Kit. But at least you're starting to talk sense. Now, here's where I come in. I can get these pretty jewels out of England for you, and almost immediately. I'm an influential man, Kit. If you're wise, you won't risk offending me."

The Kitten's face cleared a little. That did sound more like sense. Those damned jewels, hidden away behind a loose brick in the wall of his room, were giving him nightmares.

"Well, that's better," he said in a happier tone. "I don't mind admitting the sooner those jewels leave merrie England the more pleased I'll be. What are you going to do?"

"At the moment you do the things," Pope said

suavely. "There's a little preliminary work that you can do far better than I."

"Well, shoot," said the Kitten impatiently.

"I want you to go to St. Simon—it's a village on the coast about fifty miles away—and find a man called Lynnford Carstairs. When you've located him, which shouldn't be difficult as I believe he's a pretty big bug in those parts, ask him about the Laughing Ghost. Tell him Claus Jensen sent you. He'll come across. Find out all you can an report here to me—let me see—say a week tonight at this time."

Pope got to his feet and went to the door, indicating that the interview was at an end. The Kitten stood staring at him incredulously.

"Say!" he demanded. "What do you think I am? A kid listening to a blooming fairy tale? Laughing Ghosts, my hat! You'll have to tell me a better one than that."

But Pope, his temper worn thin by the rankling memory of Jensen's treatment, shouted angrily:

"Do you question my orders? If you don't want to spend the rest of your life in a cell you'll do as I say and do it quick. Now, get out!"

A minute later the Kitten, guided by Green, stumbled into the street.

"He hasn't got a thing on me," he was muttering to himself. "Not a thing. Laughing Ghosts! Laughing fiddlesticks! He's not a cold-blooded devil after all. He's just clean crazy."

The hedges flashed by like a dark taut ribbon. Trees sprang up by the side of the road and banished. The needle of the speedometer crept to sixty and then, quiveringly, to seventy.

35

"Say, Felicity!" Henry protested.

Felicity's head was in the air, her hair flying. "Scared?" she asked airily.

"No. No, sure I'm not scared," Henry replied uneasily. "But there might be a hen or something on the road. Anyway what's the hurry about?"

What am I running away from, wondered Felicity to herself. Myself? My thoughts? Yes, it must be my thoughts, because one can't concentrate on anything but driving at this speed. But what's the use, anyway?

"There's not any hurry," she said aloud, slowing down to a crawling thirty. "I just enjoy speeding. Makes you feel powerful, like a shooting star. You haven't lost your nerve after the smash, have you, Henry?"

Henry looked uncomfortable and self-conscious.

"No, but I like to go slowly and sort of look at the stars and things. I guess I'm feeling sentimental."

"Don't, Henry," said Felicity firmly. "It's a foolish state of mind. It's not about me, I hope."

"Well, yes, honey, it is."

Felicity withdrew her hand from the large warm one that had been placed over it.

"Don't do that, Henry. Don't interfere while I'm driving."

"Well, let's stop, then."

"No, I want to get home. I'm a bit worried about uncle. He hasn't been himself this last day or two. Henry," she said suddenly, "there was something remarkable about that young man in the Black Cat."

"Remarkable! Huh!"

"Yes, he's most awfully like some of the faces in the portait gallery at Carstairs. There was a

Lynnford Carstairs who went to South Africa gold-mining, and was never heard of again. And another one who fought with Prince Rupert of the Rhine against Cromwell, and fell on Marston Moor. Those dark uneven eyebrows of his were really remarkably like that portait. And his cavalierly air. He had a cavalierly air, hadn't he?"

"I didn't notice," said Henry sulkily.

"Well, he had. You know, the Carstairs nowadays aren't very true to type. They used to be so lean and fine. Uncle's inclined to be too stout and his brothers weren't very prepossessing either. I could have sworn that young man was one of us."

Henry grunted.

"Skip that young man, will you?" he said. "A nice night like this and you've got to talk about a cavalierly young man."

"Sorry, Henry," said Felicity sweetly. "What shall we talk about then?"

"Well, I can't think of anything better than you."

"Oh, Henry! This isn't going to be another proposal?"

"Well, as a matter of fact it was," said Henry, abashed. "If you felt about me as I do about you—Felicity, you're about the sweetest kid this side of heaven."

Felicity negotiated a corner, passed a slow and laden truck, gave chase to an alarmed rabbit for a few yards, and felt profoundly bored. She turned her lovely innocent face to Henry.

"Yes, darling. What next?"

"What—what next? Honey, I'm asking you to marry me!"

"Yes, I gathered that," Felicity murmured, then

suddenly exclaimed. "Oh, I know now where I've seen him before. He was the man in the garage when we took the Packard in. What an odd thing. I knew I'd seen him before." She reflected, and added in a despondent voice, "It's rather tragic, isn't it? I mean, uncle would harldy approve of my marrying a motor mechanic. It would be almost as bad as leaving Carstairs to one."

"Say, young lady," Henry said wrathfully, "who are you talking about marrying? Not a guy you've only seen once in your life! Are you crazy?"

"Perhaps," said Felicity gloomily. "Quite probably. Anyway, I'm not talking of marrying him. I'm only thinking aloud."

"Well, I've had enough of it. Here I'm asking you to marry me and you're miles off thinking of a guy in dirty overalls." Henry's tone was indignant and surprised. He had been insulted, and the sweetest kid on earth or not, she wasn't going to get away with insulting Henry B. Higginsbottom.

"I tell you it's not good enough," he said in an injured voice. "I'm giving you your last chance to marry me. If you say no this time, I warn you there won't be another time. What have you got against me, anyway?"

Felicity reflected, appearing to give the matter deep thought.

"Well, for one thing, you say 'gosh' too often." Henry looked bewildered.

"I—but, that isn't important."

"And for another thing, uncle doesn't approve. Oh, it's not you yourself, Henry, but your nationality. He wants me to marry an Englishman. He's rather a feudal lord, you know. He thinks a great deal of carrying on the Carstairs tradition, and that sort of thing." Felicity was frowning. She said wearily, "But let's not talk about it. All it amounts to is that I'm saying no again. Sorry, Henry, but I can't help it. And now, do be nice and don't mention the subject again. For tonight, anyway."

Although it was after midnight when they arrived home, there was a light in the library and in old Lynnford's bedroom, and as Felicity entered the hall she met Mr. Edward Burke preparing to leave.

"Good evening, Mr. Burke," she said in a surprised voice. "Has uncle been bothering you at this late hour?"

Mr. Burke's habitual smoothness had vanished. He looked flushed and agitated.

"Oh, just a little matter of business. He sent for me rather unexpectedly. I believe he wanted to see you when you came in. I think I'd go up right away. He seems not quite himself."

I'll go right up," said Felicity. "I do hope he's not going to be ill. Good night, Mr. Burke. Don't wait up for me, Henry. I might stay with uncle for a while."

Old Lynnford Carstairs was a big man, stout and florid and boldly handsome. But tonight, in the big four-poster bed, he looked oddly small and shrunken. Or perhaps it was the blown light of the candles that cast shadows over his face and made it seem drawn and unfamiliar and possessed of a strange quiet composure.

"Well, my dear," he said quietly, as Felicity entered the room.

She crossed quickly to his bedside.

"Uncle, is anything the matter?"

39

"No, no. I'm just a little tired, that's all. I wanted to see you. Play good?"

"Not very. We had supper at the Savoy. I drove home. No more smashes, uncle."

The old man's lips twitched humorously.

"You're a spunky kid, Felicity. That's how I like 'em."

"You've got plenty of spunk yourself, uncle."

"Yes, yes, maybe. But I'm getting old. And that Henry of yours is a fool. Don't know why we ever had him here. Relationship's too distant to matter, and as for making a fox hunter of him, I'd as soon teach one of your father's elephants. Light another candle, Felicity. Mark's only left two. Don't know what he thinks he's economizing for. We're not poor people."

Felicity obediently lit more candles on the dresser. The soft light wavered and grew. She stood with her face bent over the flames, the glow making a dim ring of light about her hair.

"I'm not proposing to marry Henry, uncle. The candlelight's lovely, isn't it?"

"Yes. But it's out of date. Carstairs should have electricity. I don't suppose the next owner will love these lights as I have. Like yellow moths, aren't they?"

Felicity looked up sharply.

"The—next—" she began.

But the old man went on as if he hadn't heard her.

"I'm glad you're not proposing to marry that Yankee. But all the same you'll have to think about marrying someday. Anybody in mind?"

Felicity sat on the side of the bed, shaking her head.

"No, she said, then was thoughtful, remembering suddenly the arrogant lift of the dark young man's head. "I've just got a picture of what I want him to look like. I daresay I'm foolish. Romance went out with your generation, didn't it?"

The white old head on the pillow was shaken vigorously.

"You're wrong there, Felicity. Romance won't go out while human nature remains the same."

Felicity clasped her hands around her knees, smiling.

"You're a queer mixture, uncle. Adventurer, humorist, autocrat, romantic, all mixed. But I still love you."

Old Lynnford smiled.

"Yes. We've been good friends, Felicity. I'm happy about that. Even if I do lose my temper with you sometimes. But you're still too wild. You'll have to settle down. That's why I want you not to be surprised at anything that may happen after I'm gone. I want you to understand. Do you think you will?"

"Of course, darling," said Felicity, puzzled.

"Pray God it will work out all right," murmured the old man. "It's my last gamble—or my last joke. I'm not sure which." He raised his voice. "And still be friends with me, Felicity. I'd hate to have my dead bones hated."

"But, uncle—"

"No, don't be shocked, my dear. One must talk of death sometimes. It's only another adventure, after all. But a damned crowded one," he added with a flash of his old humor. "Every Tom, Dick and Harry takes it. Come and kiss me good night, and then be off with you."

But when Felicity had obeyed, kissing his forehead gently, he commanded her to stand back so that he could look at her.

"Yes," he said to himself. "Good carriage and figure, nice eyes, mouth too red," Felicity rubbed it guiltily, "small hands, wilful chin. You look a fine lady, my dear. Always feel one."

"Thank you, uncle," whispered Felicity.

"Now blow out the candles and pull up the blinds. Is it a fine night?"

"The stars are out," said Felicity from the window. "There's a new moon scarcely as bright as the candles. It's so still you can hear the sea. Listen!"

The slow distant surge of the sea filled the room. In a quiet remote voice old Lynnford began to quote,

"The sea is calm tonight,
    The tide is full, the moon lies fair
    Upon the straits...."

"Go on," whispered Felicity.

"Listen! You hear the grating roar
    Of pebbles which the waves draw back and fling
    At their return, up the high strand,
    Begin, and cease, and then again begin,
    With tremulous cadence slow, and bring
    The eternal note of sadness in ...."

His voice trailed off.

"Uncle, are you all right?" asked Felicity, bending over the bed. "Can I get you something?"

The old man stirred. His white hair shone faintly in the gloom.

"Some of the Napoleon brandy, eh?" he suggested, chuckling. "You know, my dear, I think that very soon I'll be settling accounts with His late Majesty, King George the Fifth." He gave his deep rich chuckle again, then sighed. "I'm all right, Felicity. Only tired. Good night."

But Felicity was perturbed. When she went to her room she got out writing materials and did what she had intended doing for the last two days. She wrote:

"Dear Father,

"Uncle says you're a scamp and a scallywag and I say so, too, honest and truly, daddy, you've deserted your daughter for long enough. There's a big Yankee hanging around handing out proposals of marriage every half day or so, and I'm tired of it, but I suppose I shall have to get married some day. Honest, daddy, need your advice. So please come home.

"Also I'm worried about uncle. He has been tired and strange lately. And he is talking as if he is going to leave Carstairs to a stranger. I know I don't deserve Carstairs, but I think I would die if I had to leave it and it went out of the family. I confess I have been behaving badly lately but I can be better and it will help immensely if you come home, daddy dear. So leave your old elephants for someone else.

"Uncle and I had the loveliest talk tonight. Whatever happens, I shall always be grateful for that. Please come, daddy!"

"Love—from Felicity."

But that letter was never sent, for old Lynnford Carstairs died in the night.

Death, taming at last his violence and his immense vitality, had left him very serene and content. The white-faced quiet old man upstairs bore little resemblance to noisy, joking, hot-tempered Lynnford Carstairs, and Felicity, almost as white-faced, sent frantic cablegrams for her father, and could think of nothing but the terrible finality of death, and of her own overwhelming loneliness.

Lynn had spent all the afternoon in a queue waiting to be interviewed for the job of sales manager in a commercial firm. He earned the contempt of his fellow applicants because he stood apart from them and scribbled occasionally about Queen Victoria in his small notebook. They didn't understand that the prudish little queen was the only thing that enabled Lynn to stand there all afternoon with a tired body and a mind full of bitterness. His notes had reached the Empress of India stage when at last his turn came to be looked over and rejected. He walked two miles home, still thinking rigidly of the brilliant dark-faced eastern princess bowing before the stout complacent old lady, and met an exuberant small dog on the doorstep.

"Hello, beautiful," Lynn said cheerfully, because

Buddy was a sensitive and sympathetic animal whose spirits rose and fell in almost exact imitation of his master's. "I'm still sober, which you may wonder at. Any visitors or anything happen today? No, of course not. Well, come on. I'll race you upstairs."

As a result of the noisy scramble that followed (which Lynn won unfairly on account of his longer legs) Lynn dropped panting into a chair in his room, and Buddy leaped on his lap to lick his face.

"That's another of my good points," he murmured. "I'm kind to dogs. I'm the sort of whimsical idiot who talks to dogs. Aren't I, Buddy? Yes, all right, don't agree quite so enthusiastically. Oh, for the Lord's sake, there's a letter! Now who do you imagine might be writing to me, The King of England?"

The address was typewritten and the envelope bore the postmark of St. Simon. With suddenly eager fingers Lynn tore the envelope open, extracted the letter, and read.

His first perusal was hasty. His mouth fell open and he gave an exclamation of incredulity.

"Hold on, Buddy. Excuse me, will you? I've got to read this again. Someone's having a colossal joke on me."

On the second reading, however, it appeared that the colossal joke might not be a joke at all. It might be reality. The address of St. Simon was clear enough, and also the printed name of Edward Charles Burke, attorney, and also the elegant signature of the same Edward C. Burke. It was the contents of the letter that were incredible.

"Carstairs," Lynn murmured. "Carstairs of Carstairs. Oh, but I say!" And suddenly, as full realization dawned on him, he went wild, flinging open the door, tearing along the passage with Buddy scampering madly at his heels, and hammering with both fists on the door of Polly's room.

"Hey," Polly shouted. "If it's you, you can come in, but if it's a herd of elephants, stay out. What's biting you?" she asked, as the door burst open. "Got a job, I suppose. Well, I've known that to happen before."

"But it's not a job, you thrice-confounded idiot!" Lynn was yelling. "It's a legacy! It's the most amazing, incredible—it's—honest, Polly, I might be dreaming, but it seems to me I've come into that earldom!"

CHAPTER THREE

FELICITY could see the people in the room reflected in the long mirror on the opposite wall. There was her father, with his gay red face, his stiff, straight, light hair, his stocky body, listening to James seriously, but with no real concern, because scarcely anything ever disturbed his good humor; there was Henry, sprawled inelegantly over the settee—Henry never could sit up straight if there was anything to lean on—his cherished adhesive tape still adorning his forehead and an expression of dismayed sympathy on his face; there was she, rather fragile in her black frock, rather somber and childish looking, with her drooping mouth and wide unhappy eyes; and there was James, standing unsteadily before them, saying in his trembling old voice that now the master had so kindly left him an annuity he would like to retire if Miss Felicity didn't mind, because he had grown too old to do his duties well and to try to serve a new master.

In the mirror Felicity saw herself move as she said, "Oh, James! Not you, too, as well as Uncle

Lynnford. Why, it won't be Carstairs without either of you"—and then she stopped abruptly, remembering that after all it was none of her business. She wouldn't be here either. And at the same time the strange little thought was in her mind that none of these things happening were any more tangible than the reflections in the mirror. They were dreams, visions, nightmares, not reality. Presently she would wake up . . . .

But she had been waiting for a whole week to wake up, and the nightmare persisted. If only she had someone to turn to for advice and comfort things would be a great deal easier. For father was proving disappointing, being too jovial and light-hearted, and not having had any affection for Uncle Lynnford anyway, and what little mind Henry had he required to devote solely to himself. He was about as useful in a crisis as a sheep.

"All right, James," she said. "I'm glad my uncle left you the annuity, and I know Carstairs will miss you terribly. But I can't ask you to stay."

James thanked her and went out, his long slightly bowed legs a little unsteady, and Felicity said to the reflections in the mirror:

"So that's another problem. Am I expected to engage a butler for the new owner or do I leave him to find his own?"

"The point is," said her father, rapping the table noisily, "what have you been up to to get yourself in this mess? Oh, I know old Lynnford was eccentric, but he wasn't eccentric enough to leave Carstairs to a complete stranger for no reason at all."

"He said I was irresponsible," Felicity murmured.

"Well, why?"

Felicity said wearily, "Oh, I don't know. Perhaps it's because I'm your daughter. He never did approve of you, daddy."

"No, the old criminal. He spent all his time grumbling at me for wasting my time big game hunting, but there was never a word said about his private activities. Oh, no, never a word."

"Father!" said Felicity sharply. "I won't have you saying anything about uncle. I just won't have it. He and I, the night he died—we talked about things I'll never forget. He said I was to try and understand, no matter what happened. We were good friends . . ." She rubbed her hand over her brow and said unsteadily, "If you ask me any more questions, father, I'll just weep and then we won't get anywhere."

"Felicity," Henry said, "you don't need to worry. You seem to forget that I'm here."

Felicity looked at him thoughtfully. Her lips curved faintly.

"No, Henry. I really haven't forgotten that you're here. At least, there's always you."

"That's what I say," Henry declared contentedly.

Guy Valentine eyed the two of them. His brows went up ruefully.

"And to think I left a perfectly good spoor to come home to this."

Felicity forced back her tears.

"Father, we've got to make some plans. Yes, James, what is it?"

The old butler had come in again and was saying apologetically:

"There's a gentleman wanting to see Mr. Carstairs.

He says it's important. He—well, to use his words, Miss Felicity, he said he's come to find out about this ghost business."

Felicity looked startled, and Guy Valentine, with a low whistle, got to his feet.

"I'll see him, James. Show him into the library."

"Gosh! said Henry, as Felicity's father went out. "There's that ghost again. What *is* it all about? I've been here a month and haven't seen a trace of an apparition, not even a bit of floating drapery. And yet you have strange men coming to the door asking about it. Say, Felicity, you might tell me about it."

"Oh, there's nothing to tell," Felicity said wearily. "Carstairs is supposed to be haunted, as mostly all old houses are. Our visitation is called the Laughing Ghost. People have been known to hear it. Maybe you will sometime."

"I've heard that part of it," Henry protested. "Everybody knows that. What I want to know is, why is it so important that strange people come asking about it?"

Felicity answered a little impatiently, "That's what I'd like to know," and at that moment Guy Valentine returned, looking highly diverted.

"Gad, Felicity, I believe it's as well old Lynnford is gone. That guy was a blackmailer if ever there was one. Big fellow with a ruby the size of a plum on his finger. Stolen, I'll be bound. Though how he'd make a successful burglar I can't imagine. The fellow's as corpulent as an overfed elephant."

"But what did he want to know about the ghost for?" asked Felicity breathlessly.

"Yes, what did he? I didn't quite gather that.

Gave the fellow no satisfaction at all. I tell you, he's on to something, Felicity. But he hasn't got the finesse of a bumble bee. Said he'd been sent by Claus Jensen to ask about the Laughing Ghost. Blurted it out like that."

"Claus Jensen!" Felicity gasped, looking startled. "What did you say?"

"Oh, don't worry, my dear. I sent him off with a flea in his ear. Told him someone had been having a joke on him. Pulling his leg. Perhaps that's true, and it's Jensen who's been doing it. *But why the hell is he doing it?*"

"Who's Claus Jensen?" demanded Henry, sitting up.

"Oh, Lord!" moaned Felicity, her head in her hands. "First James gives notice and we've got to find a new butler, then a strange man with a ruby ring comes asking conundrums, and now Henry wants to know who Claus Jensen is."

"We've got to decide something definitely," said her father, looking serious at last. "We'll talk about this later."

"I'll tell you one thing, father," Felicity said firmly, "and that's that I'm having nothing further to do with this business. Nothing!"

Guy Valentine stared at her.

"Are you proposing to marry this—this interloper who's coming to Carstairs?"

"Save me, no!"

"Then how do you propose living for a year on a hundred pounds."

"I can do it," Felicity said stubbornly.

"Yes. You can do it all right. You try it, sweetheart. You'll soon find how easy it is. Why, you'd spend that much on stockings alone, probably."

"I can do it, daddy. You'll see. And it's only a year till I get the twenty thousand."

"A year's a mighty long time to starve in, my dear." He hesitated and looked pointedly at Henry. "We'll talk about this later."

Henry raised his large bulk out of the chair.

"Okay!" he said in an injured voice. "I'll go if you want me to. Next thing you'll be spelling words so I can't understand."

"Sorry Henry," Felicity said. "Don't go. Daddy enjoys being mysterious. That's absolutely all there is to it."

"Oh, I'll go. I want to go down to the links and practice some shots, anyway. You might find me there after you've finished entertaining mysterious visitors."

"There, you see, daddy," Felicity said indignantly, as she went out. "Now, you've made him curious."

"Curious nothing," said her father with his imperturbable light-heartedness. "He hasn't got enough energy to be serious about anything. He's completely wrapped up in Henry B. Higginsbottom and the Higginsbottom dollars."

"And me," added Felicity wearily. "You know, daddy, the simplest way out of this mess might be for me to marry him. He's asked me often enough. He's organized a sort of high pressure campaign to wear down my resistance. And that way I'd get Carstairs because this Lynnford Carstairs, whoever he is, would forfeit it simply by not being able to marry me."

Her father looked at her.

"Would you like to marry Henry?"

"Frankly, daddy, I'd rather do anything. But I must have Carstairs. I can't let it go."

"Then we'll try the other game."

"But with a stranger here—" Felicity looked troubled.

"We'll get around that," her father said confidently. "You've got a parent with an ingenious brain, my dear. Fortunately we can get tonight's lot over before this fellow arrives."

"Yes, said Felicity doubtfully. "But honestly, daddy, I'd much rather keep out of this."

"Nonsense, child! Where's your spunk? You're not going to give up so easily."

Spunk! Why, that was what Uncle Lynnford had said. That was what he admired about her. He would want her to go on doing this. Indirectly, that was what he had expressed in his will. A masterpiece of double meaning, Uncle Lynnford's will. Then she couldn't let him down. She would have to go on being spunky, taking absurd and senseless risks for a year until Carstairs became solely hers.

"All right, daddy," she said resignedly. "I'll do it. But you'll have to think of a plan."

Lynn was in something of a dilemma as to what to pack for his first visit to his inheritance. Mr. Burke's letter had been remarkably uninformative. Lynn hadn't the faintest idea whether Carstairs was a mansion or a poverty-stricken fifteenth-century ruin. Nor was he aware of the income that went with the place.

Polly suggested wisely that he go and see this Mr. Burke and find out what was what, but Lynn was in a fever of impatience to take possession of his inheritance. So, after some cogitation, he packed his gray flannels and his dinner suit, which looked remarkably good in spite of its age, and an assortment of underclothes and his manuscript of Queen Victoria, half a dozen books, a photograph of Polly and an inordinately excited scrap of an animal who made super-human efforts to chew up his lead.

Polly went down to the station to see Lynn and Buddy off. Lynn joked all the way, because Polly was looking unwontedly serious, and had forgotten her rouge, which was a sign of great emotional upset.

"Next time I call," he said, "it'll be in my limousine. Probably with a chauffeur, but don't let that scare you. How'd you like to drive all over London with me and a chaffeur?"

"Well, I think probably I could dispense with you, honey."

Lynn laughed and hugged her in the privacy of the taxicab. And then hugged her again on the railway station.

"You've been a pal, Polly. I won't forget."

But he wasn't really thinking of Polly so much as of that girl called Felicity Valentine who lived in St. Simon. He'd be bound to meet her. St. Simon was only a village and too small to hide lovely girls like Felicity Valentine. In fact the whole thing looked remarkably like fate, if one believed in fate. But Polly was looking peaked and wistful. Her mouth was drooping and her eyes looked unusually large. So Lynn resolutely put Felicity Valentine out of his mind.

"But I expect it's all a hoax," he said. "These things don't happen, really. They'll find I'm not the right person, or else I'll find Carstairs is a junk heap or has to be sold to pay death duties."

Polly said thoughtfully: "I guess it's as well we're saying goodbye. We were good pals while we were both lame dogs, but now you're one of the landed gentry you're way above me. I always knew that was the way it should be with you but you've been pretty swell to me." She stopped and blinked. "I guess I'll find another lame dog. Say, can't you look more cheerful?"

Lynn took Polly's square little shoulders in his hands and said:

"Now listen, lady! Because I've had a lucky break doesn't mean we part forever. St. Simon is only fifty miles from London, and you'll be seeing me pretty often. And if the luck doesn't hold you're to come straight down to Carstairs. Understand?"

"Oh, no, Lynn. That's just what I couldn't do. Imagine me—"

Lynn shook her fiercely.

"Understand?" he repeated.

Polly nodded, giggling unsteadily.

"Gosh, Lynn, what would you do with an actress down there?"

"And don't look wistful!" Lynn said angrily. "If there's one thing I can't stand, it's a girl looking wistful. Well, don't *do* it!"

It was strange, though, how the thought of Polly's round, unusually earnest face went out of Lynn's mind as the distance between them increased. Polly had been a good friend. She was warm-hearted and absurdly generous and usually flowing over with high spirits. When one was in a high-spirited mood Polly was fun, but on the other hand her exuberance and scatterbrained impulsiveness could be definitely wearing. No, Polly was a good friend, but not one's ideal. And anyway there was a new life beginning . . .

St. Simon was a straggling village with a crooked main street, a cluster of shops, an old gray stone church with a clock tower, a profusion of elms and beeches, and a family of blue-breasted pigeons that fluttered out and circled around the church tower every time the clock chimed. Lynn found it quiet and sleepy and rather enchanting. He left his luggage at the station and, taking Buddy on his lead, set out to find the office of Mr. Edward Burke. The information in Mr. Burke's letter had been meager, and it would be a great deal wiser to find out the exact conditions of his inheritance before he barged in on family life at Carstairs.

Mr. Burke's office, being the most modern in the street, was not difficult to find. Lynn found that Mr. Burke was not engaged, and only too ready to see him.

"This affability," thought Lynn to himself, as he shook hands with the smooth plump little man, "apparently means I'm a valuable client. He looks like a downy bird."

Indeed, Mr. Burke's affability was not assumed but genuine. He found this long lean young man with the steady eyes and shy youthful smile definitely to his liking. In fact, he was pleasantly surprised. He had been afraid of some dissolute weedy young fool arriving from nowhere to take possession of Carstairs, and Mr. Burke was sufficiently sentimental to realize the tragedy that would be. But this man was different. He even spoke as if he were educated. Perhaps old Carstairs' joke wasn't so crazy after all.

Perhaps even that headstrong young Felicity Valentine wouldn't think so either when she met this unknown relation of hers.

"Well, Mr. Carstairs," Mr. Burke began. "I consider myself remarkably astute in having found you. In fact, it's the astutest thing I ever did. And just in time, too, upon my word."

"In time?" Lynn repeated, puzzled.

"Yes. Before the old man died. He made his will the night he died, you know. I had been working hard tracing you before that, and I believe he only made himself live until this business was settled. He was very old. Human machinery worn out. But no doubt you'd like to hear the terms of the will. I think I should prepare you to find it a little—shall we say, eccentric?"

"Oh, I expected that, of course," Lynn replied. "Old gentlemen delight in making eccentric wills, don't they? Well, as long as I don't have to marry the spinster daughter or anything like that I daresay it will be all right. Go on."

Mr. Burke hesitated and looked uneasy.

"I'm afraid, Mr. Carstairs, you've just about hit the nail on the head."

"What?" Lynn sat up. "Good lord, you don't mean to say it's true about the daughter! Then, look here, I'm not being dragged into any mess like this."

"Now, wait a moment, Mr. Carstairs. Wait a moment. She's not a daughter, she's a niece, and if I may say so, remarkably attractive though rather headstrong. And you don't have to marry her. It's merely a suggestion, although it is definitely to your interests to carry it out."

"Well, I don't like it," said Lynn emphatically. "I don't like these nasty match-making suggestions. I'm not marrying any headstrong young lady even if she is remarkably attractive. I don't like the business at all. It's odd. What made the old blighter leave me the place anyway?"

"Because, as far as we could discover, you are the only living member of the Carstairs family bearing the name of Lynnford. That's the family name, you know. The old man had conceived the idea that he'd like the place still to belong to a Lynnford Carstairs. His niece was next in line of succession, but of course she has a different name, and in addition is—er—rather headstrong."

"I see it all," Lynn muttered, pacing up and down. "Old man wants family name carried on and niece is wild and headstrong and likely to play ducks and drakes with the estate. So distant relation is hunted up to take the responsibility. And that's me. I'm the mug. I knew this would be a hoax. Why didn't you tell me all this in your letter and save me the trouble of coming down?"

"Perhaps," said Mr. Burke nervously (this tall young man with his black Carstairs scowl was a little disconcerting), "it would be as well if you read the will."

An hour later Lynn walked down the cobbled street of St. Simon again, with Buddy at his heels. The clock in the tower struck five and the pigeons whirled into the air like blown leaves. It was almost closing time and people bustled in and out of the shops, some of them pausing to turn and stare with unconcealed curiosity at the long young man, his black brows drawn together in a preoccupied frown, striding down the street, followed by a shaggy short-legged and dusty dog.

Lynn noticed neither the whirling birds nor the glow of sunset that gave the village a mellow and heightened charm, nor the unveiled curiosity of the villagers. His mind was in confusion. Indignation and amusement and disappointment and interest were all mingled. What had possessed old Lynnford Carstairs to make such a curious and absurd will? It seemed to be nothing more than a colossal joke. Lynn could not remember accurately the legal wording, but the provisions concerning himself were clear in his mind.

Old Lynnford had wanted an heir of his own name, a husband for his niece and a sane and responsible person as owner of Carstairs. So, being a born gambler, he had staked everything on this unknown relation of his whom Mr. Burke had traced from Lynn's grandfather who had died in a South African mining town. But this shrewd gamble was only for one year. If, within that time, Lynn did not marry the niece and become reconciled to the family ghost, known as the Laughing Ghost, he was to forfeit all right to Carstairs, which was to go to the niece, and old Lynnford's fortune, comprising something like forty thousand pounds, was to be shared equally between Lynn and the niece. During the year, Lynn and his unknown cousin were to receive the sum of one hundred pounds, "in order that they may learn economy," the will read. There were other provisions in the will apart from the one which ordered that the household expenses of Carstairs for the test year were to be paid out of the estate, and some directions as to legacies for the servants.

On the whole, Lynn reflected, he stood to make a good deal, as even when he gave up Carstairs at the end of the year, as he assuredly would, he would receive twenty thousands pounds. But the will was fantastic. What was the Laughing Ghost? How become reconciled to it? Who was this wild extravagant headstrong niece whom he was expected to reform? Probably, anyway, Carstairs was a huge drafty badly ventilated moth-eaten place. Mr. Burke said that there wasn't even electricity installed, and that old Lynnford used to drive his four-in-hand up to the last week of his life. It sounded like something out of the Victorian age, Lynn reflected gloomily, and then suddenly his interest was awakened. The Victorian age, candles, ghosts, landaus. Where could he find better atmosphere in which to write his book? A year at Carstairs would finish it, and by that time he would leave the place, collect his legacy and be free. Decidedly, on reflection, things were a good deal better than they had seemed. Anyway, there was no harm in having a quiet unofficial look at Carstairs.

And, reflected Lynn, swinging off in a rapid stride down the winding briar-hedged lane that Mr. Burke had told him led to Carstairs, it would be strange if in the course of a year he could not find in so small a place as St. Simon a girl as lovely as Felicity Valentine.

The first glimpse of Carstairs enchanted Lynn as nothing had done before in his life. He stood for a long time at the high elaborately fashioned gates looking down at the old graceful house with the sunset lighting its windows and turning its walls to a soft rose-red. Long shadows lay across the lawns, the high old trees were dappled with sunlight, it was so still that the birdsongs echoed and the wind running through the grass sounded like silk-shod feet. Far off there was the dim surge and drag of waves on the beach.

Lynn's footsteps crunched on the gravel drive. He went a little way and stopped again involuntarily. Yes, the place would be haunted. If one gazed long enough the shadows on the lawn would become the swaying graceful forms of ladies, the sound of the wind would turn to low sweet laughter. The ornamental lake with its still dark gold water and the cherub bestrewn fountain would reflect the silken plumage of a lady's gown, that green-shaded sward between the shrubbery and the elms, peopled now with pink-tipped daisies, would echo to the swift thrust and parry of swords. It's ageless, thought Lynn. Time doesn't touch it. It probably looked the same to some young gallant of Cromwell's day as it looks to me now.

And suddenly the exultant thought that one day it might all be his swept through Lynn. He forgot the wild and unmanageable niece, the mysterious ghost, the eccentric conditions of the will. For a moment he visualized only the great and unimaginable delight of owning and living in Carstairs.

A cawing flight of rooks circling over his head aroused him. He shook himself free of fancies, called to Buddy who was investigating the exciting darkness of the shrubbery, and proceeded up the drive to the house.

The front doors stood wide open. Lynn rang and waited. Nobody came. He rang again, impatiently. Still no one came to answer the door. He thought, "Hang it all, it's my place. Why do I have to wait to be admitted? It must be the butler's day off," and walked inside.

His footsteps noiseless on the thick carpet, he walked the length of a high lovely hall, looking with delight and approval at the dark golden gleam of the paneling, the tall windows and the shadowy carved ceiling.

Apparently no one was at home. Lynn stood at the foot of the curving staircase, then called softly to Buddy, and the two of them went stealthily up it, like a pair of thieves. At the top he stood listening again. Still no sound. A door along the passage stood ajar and as Lynn passed it he saw a white bed with a rose-colored silk dressing gown lying over the foot of it. There was a vase of yellow roses on the dressing table and robins on the wallpaper. It was a girl's room, he thought, passing it hastily with the uncomfortable feeling that he had been spying. And then came the thought that it must be the niece's, and that she must like pretty things. After all, a girl who liked roses on her dressing table and dainty expensive clothes could not be altogether unattractive. But wasn't there anybody at all alive in this house?

As Lynn hesitated again there came the sound of a piano played softly from a room at the end of the passage.

Lynn went to it quickly and stood at the open door looking at the girl sitting at the piano. He nearly cried out then, in surprise and delight. But he restrained himself in time, and stood instead watching unobserved the face of Felicity Valentine as she sat absorbed over her music.

This was the ultimate and transcending charm of the afternoon. It was little short of a miracle. The breathless loveliness of finding Felicity, wistful over the keys of the piano in the long sunlit room, was almost unbelievable. Lynn thought impulsively that if hearts were transferable his was no longer his own. It had been given to Carstairs and Felicity Valentine.

The girl was playing thoughtfully and with skill. The slow gentle beauty of the Chopin étude was part of the quiet evening and the fading sunset and the irrefragable charm of Carstairs. But Lynn was not so much aware of the music as of the player. She wore a dark red dress square at the neck and short-sleeved. Her face was small and slender. There was no gaiety on her lips now, but they drooped with a wistful sadness. Her hair, brushed smoothly over her head and curled on the nape of her neck, had a kind of autumnal brightness. It was the color of November leaves. She played the piano softly and slowly as if all the world were sad.

This then, thought Lynn, with dawning wonder, was old Lynnford Carstairs' niece. This was the girl who had had a motor smash because of some wild bet, who was headstrong and wilful and was going to play ducks and drakes with Carstairs.

But she doesn't look it, thought Lynn, looking at the bowed head, the lovely drooping lips. She looks unhappy and very much alone. She—why, God in heaven, she's the girl I am to marry!

And suddenly he could not control his exultation. "Wow!" he yelled, grabbing an astonished Buddy and tossing him into the air.

The girl's hands stiffened and her head shot up in startled fright. She saw Lynn and her face became, if anything, more startled.

"Heavens!" she whispered. "You again!"

Lynn came forward, Buddy tucked under his arm. He was feeling distinctly ashamed of his outburst now, for the girl's eyes were dilated, and her face had the pallor of a magnolia flower.

"I'm most awfully sorry," he said. "Did I frighten you?"

"I should think that's fairly obvious," the girl returned, her composure coming back. "I'm not accustomed to having people come in on me whooping like wild Indians. Perhaps you'll explain why you overlooked the doorbell, and what you are doing here anyway."

"I didn't overlook the doorbell, but your butler overlooked answering it. Or else he's deaf. So I came right on in."

A flash of annoyance passed over the girl's face.

"Didn't Peewee answer the bell? I'm sorry. I'll have to speak to him. He's just new here and not very satisfactory. But that doesn't explain your intrusion."

Lynn looked at the girl standing there erect and dignified, yet for all her dignity looking very young and unhappy and alone. He wondered how he was to tell her that he was the interloper who was to take Carstairs from her. But before he could speak she said, quite calmly:

"You're Lynnford Carstairs, aren't you?"

For a moment Lynn gaped.

"How on earth did you know?"

A flicker of mischief showed in Felicity's eyes.

"No one but a Carstairs would have the impertinence to walk in unannounced and yell like a wild Indian. Incidentally, why did you yell?"

Lynn looked embarrassed.

"I was overcome. Private thoughts. I'm afraid I can't explain." Then he smiled, and, as always, his lean dark face was transformed with shy youthful gaiety. "You're Cousin Felicity, aren't you? I'm delighted to meet you."

The girl gave him a cool handclasp.

"How do you do."

"Lynn," Lynn added anxiously. "That's my name. It doesn't wear out with using. And this is Buddy. I can feel him seething with indignation because he's been overlooked."

"Like the doorbell," Felicity murmured. "Does he shake hands?"

Lynn set Buddy down and he obligingly placed a stubby and dusty forepaw in Felicity's outstretched hand. She laughed and said delightedly:

"Oh, he's nice!"

Lynn found himself staring at the soft color in her face, and thinking how her lips, curved and gentle now, were like a red blossom.

"Now you're human at last," he said.

Felicity got to her feet. The light had gone out of her face.

"I'm beginning to wonder," she said distantly, "if you have any manners at all. I suppose you can't help it, but please try to put up a better show in front of the servants. If you'll come with me now I'll introduce you to the housekeeper and Peewee. What about your luggage?"

"It's at the station."

"You can have it sent for, then. And I'll get Peewee to show you over Carstairs, otherwise you'll probably get lost. It's a tremendous place. If you got shut in one of the secret passages you'd probably die there before anyone heard you calling for help. And by the way, I'd speak to Peewee about his carelessness. He just seems not to hear doorbells. He hasn't had a great deal of experience, but James, my uncle's butler, retired after uncle died and I had to get someone for you. You won't mind making allowances for Peewee for a while, will you? I really think he will turn out all right."

"Is that all?" Lynn inquired gravely.

"All what?"

"All the instructions you have for me?"

Felicity looked impatient.

"It's not my place to give instructions. If you'll come now, we'll get these introductions over and I'll go."

"Go?"

"One doesn't usually stay uninvited in someone else's house."

"But, good God, Felicity!" Lynn exclaimed. "I'm not turning you out! Because an eccentric old gentleman chose to make a crazy will you don't have to leave Carstairs."

"Thanks, Lynn," said Felicity. "That's very hospitable of you. But I'd really prefer to go. I have a room in the village and I'll go there until I decide what to do."

"This is the sort of thing," Lynn declared violently, "that makes me mad. A man like me coming and turning a girl out of her home because the law, directed by a crazy old man, says he must. Will you believe me when I tell you that when I left Burke's office I fully intended renouncing my inheritance."

"And what made you change your mind?" asked Felicity, looking at him with interest.

"I saw Carstairs," said Lynn simply. "And then I came upstairs and heard you playing Chopin's Etude in A Major."

The girl looked faintly surprised.

"You like Chopin?"

"He makes all those delicate little eighteenth-century ladies with their high-heeled shoes that you can almost see on the lawn dance," said Lynn slowly, then added, in some embarrassment, "I'm sorry. I'm a fanciful fool. I was just trying to explain how I feel as if the place is a little bewitched."

"Yes," said Felicity softly, gazing at him. Then she started up. "Well, come and find Mrs. Mell."

Mrs. Mell jingled. Her earrings, her bracelets, her necklace and the keys at her waist kept up a little tuneless jangle all the time she talked. She was a tall gaunt woman and her array of cheap jewelry gave her a slightly macabre appearance, as if a statue of forbidding appearance had been bedizened. Lynn discovered, in the first few minutes of conversation, that she suffered from a weak heart which did not hinder her at all in the performance of her duties, but which made sudden shocks highly dangerous for her. For instance, she always had a "turn" when the Laughing Ghost was heard. One of these days, she predicted ominously, the Ghost would be the end of her. She would have a turn from which she would not recover. But for all that she was prepared to stay and serve Lynn as faithfully as she had served the late master and Miss Felicity.

To this rapidly delivered speech which was accompanied by a distracting and continual jingle Lynn replied politely, but with some bewilderment, and when Mrs. Mell had jingled out of the room he turned to Felicity in genuine amazement.

"She's an excellent housekeeper," Felicity said gravely, anticipating his question. "I know she's a little odd, but she's really splendid at managing."

"H-m," said Lynn dubiously. "She'd need to be something. She'd mutilate one's nerves. Who's next? That rascal Peewee?"

Peewee, his stiff light hair straight on end, his face flushed and irrepressibly jolly, entered confidently.

Felicity said, "Peewee, this is Mr. Lynnford Carstairs, your new master." And without waiting for the man's acknowledgement of the introduction she went on sharply, "Why weren't you there to answer the doorbell?"

"The doorbell, miss?" Lynn thought how easily that round jolly face could express guilelessness. "But I didn't hear it. I was down in the cellar going through the wine list."

Felicity sniffed suspiciously.

"Yes, I thought so," she said reproachfully. "That's the second time I've caught you. You've been drinking again, Peewee."

Peewee shook an unrepentant head.

"No, miss, not what you'd call drinking, miss. Just sniffing the aroma, so to speak."

"Well, don't sniff it again," ordered Felicity. "Mr. Carstairs may not be as lenient as I am. Now you may go."

Peewee went out briskly, showing a surprisingly cheerful back.

"I say," said Lynn wrathfully, "does that fellow drink your uncle's liquor? I'd sack him for that. What sort of a household is this, anyway? A house-keeper who's been left over from the Romanies, and a drunken incorrigible butler."

"Mrs. Mell's all right." Lynn was surprised at Felicity's earnestness. "She's been here for years and she's absolutely all right. As for Peewee, I know he's a scamp and liquor is his weakness, but I promised to give him a chance. Keep him on for a while, please, it's frightfully hard to get a really good butler nowadays. If you catch him drinking again punish him as severely as you like, but please don't dismiss him. I'd feel as if I were partly responsible," she added, "because I gave him the job."

"Very well," said Lynn, a little puzzled by her earnestness, though realizing already that he would find it extremely difficult to deny anything this girl asked. "But if I find the beggar drunk I warn you, out he goes. I suppose your uncle has a good stock of liquor."

"Oh, very well. There's some genuine Napoleon brandy. Uncle would have been delighted to drink it with you." The glow in her face died to wistfulness. "Oh, well. I must be getting along."

"You're not really determined about going?" Lynn asked. "I mean, I can't stay here and see you go. I'll clear out—"

Felicity shook her head.

"I'm really adamant."

"Then at least you'll stay to dinner?"

As the girl hesitated, Lynn pressed his advantage.

"You can't leave me to my first dinner here alone with that rogue Peewee hanging over my shoulders, and maybe Mrs. Mell having a turn. Please stay, Felicity. We'll have up some of the Napoleon brandy."

Felicity looked at him gravely. Suddenly she smiled. It was her first spontaneous act of friendship.

"Very well. I'll stay."

On the days that his nightmares rode him, Kiffin Pope hated sunlight. Then the blinds were drawn or heavy curtains huddled across the windows. If a ray of sunshine crept in it was a stealthy fugitive visitor that was quickly banished. In the semi-gloom of his luxurious apartments, Pope, pallid, heavy-eyed as an owl, sat brooding. If, he reflected sardonically, the Almighty kept a debit account against him and every other criminal who walked the earth He'd need a host of bookkeepers and receivers of bankrupt souls. But perhaps that silent unseen form that haunted him would be his sole judge. Perhaps even death would not free him from that whispering implacable voice. Perhaps for all eternity the mocking chant would go on, *Kiffin Pope is afraid of the rope.* . . . The dead man, Godfrey Vinson, had learned that while Pope was in prison.

With the supernatural powers of the dead he had discovered Pope's private fear, and ever after the voice in Pope's ear, instead of whispering quietly and patiently of revenge, had chanted with diabolical glee *Kiffin Pope is afraid of the rope* . . . . Sometimes, while in the midst of conversation with someone else, Pope would clap his hands over his ears, to the astonishment and fear of his companion, who invariably supposed that the cold-eyed man was mad. But usually, when in his worst mood, he contrived to be alone in the sanctuary of his gloom-ridden rooms.

It was unforunate that the Kitten should have chosen such a day as this to come and report to Pope of his failure to elicit any information from Carstairs as to the manner, form, or reason of the Laughing Ghost. He came into the dark room, blinking like a cat, all the bravado he had worked up on the way utterly vanishing as he looked at the pallid silent heavy-eyed man watching him from across the room.

"God, it's dark in here!" he burst out uncomfortably, stumbling against a chair leg, and finally settling his corpulent body in a chair.

"Well," said Pope uncompromisingly.

The Kitten mopped his brow. His fat red face was puckered into innumerable creases.

"God, it's hot! You haven't such a thing as a drop of whisky, Kiff?"

Pope sat unmoving.

"What did you find?" he asked in his expressionless voice.

"Golly, Kiff, give a man a chance," the Kitten protested. "I nearly broke my neck to get here in time and my throat's as dry as a desert. A drink would help with the tale."

"You've failed," came the uncompromising voice from the other side of the room.

The Kitten's nerve broke.

"What else did you expect?" he shouted. "Pulling my leg like that. Sending me on a wild goose chase half across the country. You wanted to get down on the jewels while I was away, that's what you wanted. But you didn't manage it," he declared triumphantly, a smile of childish glee on his great fat face. "You couldn't do it because I guessed your game and took them with me. I've got them with me right now, in a wallet around my neck. I'm one up on you this time, Kiff."

Pope leaned forward. His heavy-lidded eyes flickered.

"Do you mean to say you're running about England with those diamonds on you?"

"Why, sure," said the Kitten boldly. "They're safer with me than where guys like you can pinch them. The cops think I'm a slick thief, but they don't think I'm slick enough to deliberately keep the goods on me instead of dumping them."

"You're a fool," said the quiet deadly cold voice of Kiffin Pope. "You're running your head into a noose. But never mind that. It's your head."

"Why, it'll be yours, too," put in the Kitten indignantly. "You're in this as well as me."

The room was too dark and Pope already too pallid for the Kitten to observe how, at those words, his face became ghastly. But all he said was:

"You'd better tell me the whole story."

"There isn't anything to tell except that someone's

been pulling our legs. Honest, there isn't. I found the place called Carstairs and asked for the old man and what do you think they told me? Why, that the old blighter had been dead a week."

"Dead," muttered Pope to himself.

"It's not so strange, of course," the Kitten reflected. "There's more people dead than alive."

"Spare me your philosophy. What happened? Whom did you see?"

"I saw a guy who was brother-in-law or something to the old blighter and he laughed in my face. Yeah, laughed in my face, he did," the Kitten repeated sullenly. "Said he'd never heard of Claus Jensen. Said the Laughing Ghost was just the private family ghost that didn't interest anyone except the Carstairs family and people like curates and spiritualists. Said I didn't quite look to him like a spiritualist nor a curate neither."

"I'm inclined to agree with him," Pope murmured sardonically. "The amazing thing to me is how you ever came to be a successful burglar. Haven't you any finesse?"

"What's that mean?" the Kitten growled suspiciously.

"Tact," said Pope gently. "The ability to find things out without anyone knowing what you are finding out."

"Well, I can do that all right. I tell you one thing I found out, and that without asking for it neither. I asked a cop the way to the nearest pub— I mightn't have what-you-may-call-it, Kiff, but I do know it pays to keep friendly with the cops. Well, I got to talking with this bloke. He didn't seem to have much to do. I don't suppose there's much crime in a village that size. Probably not a decent burglary in five years. Well, I asked him a few discreet questions about the Carstairs family—"

"Discreet," murmured Pope. "Go on."

"Are you laughing at me?"

Nothing further from mirth than the long somber countenance of Pope could be imagined.

"No. Go on."

"Well, this cop said that Carstairs was pretty famous for its ancient history and that a century ago it had been a hotbed of smugglers. It's got cellars and passages that run right out to the sea-shore. That's interesting, don't you think, Kiff? You know, I'm fond of old history. Sort of gets in my blood. On a moonlight night you could just about see those smugglers landing with their cutlasses and kegs of rum. No, I'm wrong, it's pirates what have cutlasses, not smugglers. Say, is anything wrong?"

Pope was sitting up very straight, his lips drawn back over his teeth in what might have been intended for a smile, but which was only a grimace.

"You're incredibly stupid, Kit," he said slowly, "but it's conceivable you may be useful. You'll go back to St. Simon and find out—discreetly—all you can about what goes on at Carstairs, including the Laughing Ghost.

The Kitten stumbled to his feet.

"Go back there again! Go back and be taken for a damn fool curate! Are you in your senses? A joke's a joke, but this has gone far enough. You said you'd help me get the jewels out of England, and here you do nothing but send me ghost hunting. Well, I'm getting out of this. I'll take the jewels to the continent myself."

Pope said languidly, "Even without your signed confession which I would see they received at once, the police have their eyes on you already. You haven't earned your reputation for slick thieving for nothing."

The Kitten's eyes bulged.

"Say, is that true?" he whispered. "About the police? Do you think that cop at St. Simon had anything on me?"

"I shouldn't say so. He sounds like the village idiot. Go back tonight and pump him some more."

"I thought I told you—" began the Kitten.

"And one more thing. Don't carry the diamonds about with you. It's dangerous."

"Say—" the Kitten began again, but Pope had his hands clenched against his ears and was whispering out of his dreadful grinning mouth:

"Are you going? Are you going?"

The Kitten stared and mopped his forehead again.

"I'm going, all right!" he muttered, stumbling out.

CHAPTER FOUR

NIGHT WAS so near that the sky was ashen. Owls were calling in the shrubbery, the sharp sweet wooing call and the liquid answer. And within the ticking of the big clock on the stairs made the seconds of this enchanted evening as solemn and portentous as they had been on evenings ten, twenty, fifty years ago.

"It's nearly dark," said Felicity, looking out into the garden where the reflected candlelight hung in a dozen slender blooms, like yellow broom flowers.

But Lynn was looking at the shadows and the soft radiance that the light put in Felicity's hair.

"You don't need to go yet."

"I must soon."

"Marvelous stuff this wine is. It must have been in the family for generations."

"Perhaps it has. The Carstairs have always been famous connoisseurs. You'll have to keep up the tradition."

"On a hundred a year? And for one year only. Can one make traditions in twelve short months?"

Felicity looked thoughtful. She suddenly said fierce-ly:

"Whatever you think of what uncle has done I won't listen to *anything* you say against him."

"I'm not going to say anything against him. I'm immensely grateful to him."

Felicity said nothing.

"If only for this evening," Lynn went on. "It's bewitched, isn't it. The candlelight, the shadows, the owls calling, a lovely lady to dine with—"

"There's one thing I ought to tell you," said Felicity. "That's that you mustn't think of the other provision in uncle's will. About your staying here after the year is up, I mean. I couldn't marry anyone under conditions like that. Uncle's only done it for a joke, and it's not a terribly good one."

"I admit," said Lynn wickedly, "that a headstrong wife rather frightens me, too."

A pair of accusing eyes were on him.

"Who said that about me?"

"Oh—old Burke, I believe."

"And what do you think?"

"I've hardly had time to form an opinion yet. But you play Chopin exquisitely, and one can't play Chopin and be headstrong at the same time."

The girl smiled down at her hands lying in her lap.

"No, that's true."

"You must be meditative for that. May I put a problem to you? Supposing we fall in love. Would you still object to carrying out that provision?"

Felicity looked at him, her wide eyes guileless.

"I shouldn't worry about that, if I were you. It isn't at all likely." Her eyes remained grave, but now there was a curve of laughter on her lips. "I feel you should know my headstrong qualities far exceed my meditative ones."

Lynn matched her coolness with his own.

"That's a pity. Do you feel it's quite impossible to reform? Carstairs blood, I suppose. Well, I'm a bit that way myself. We'd probably fight like the devil." (God, how lovely she looked with the candle light in her dead-leaf hair and the soft hollow at her throat.) "Then we had better discuss the other provision in the will. The ghost part. It may make sense to you, but it doesn't to me. What is the ghost?"

Felicity did not answer at once. She got up from the table.

"Let's go out on the terrace. It's so warm. You can smell the jessamine out there."

The night wind was soft and perfume-laden, and the first stars were out. Felicity's gown made a faint hushing as she walked, the same sound as the wind made in the chestnut tree. Where the light from the windows shone across the ground there were quaint and fantastic shadows, a sword, a spread fan, a battlemented tower. Again, to Lynn's heightened imagination, it seemed that forms moved over the darkened lawn, that the pale reflection of a hooped skirt lay in the darkly glimmering waters of the lake.

"Do you believe in ghosts?" Felicity asked.

Lynn listened to the faint sigh of the wind in the chestnut, saw the candles blinking out of the windows like watching eyes. Unwillingly he felt himself enchanted, his mind receptive for even the most impossible tale.

"I think you've brought me out here so that I'll believe whatever fantastic story you have to tell me. I'd believe almost anything here."

"We once had an ancestor," Felicity said in her low sweet voice, "whom every generation of Carstairs since has tried to forget. His name was Rollo Carstairs. He lived in the Middle Ages. He had all the vices of the Carstairs, was arrogant, hot-tempered, lawless, brutal and a sort of petty but complete sovereign of his domain. There's a story that once he hanged three men in a row in one of the dungeons because they hadn't carried out some trifling order of his. I think the story's true enough. He was a swaggering, boastful, brutal fellow, and there are three hooks in the roof of the dungeon still. They're so deeply embedded no one can get them out. Old Rollo was very thorough in his methods of torture."

"Lord, I hope it's not his ghost that prowls," Lynn murmured.

"Rollo had a wife," went on Felicity. "Her name was Lynette. She was very gentle and lovely. There's a portrait of her in the gallery. She's wearing a white dress with a Chinese red shawl."

"How did she come to marry the beggar?" Lynn asked.

"Who knows. It would be one of those marriages of convenience—the sort Uncle Lynnford is trying to resurrect. Anyway one night old Rollo had an important visitor, an earl, and they were gambling and Rollo was drunk, as he mostly always was. He cheated and the earl saw him and accused him of it, and Rollo got into one of his murderous rages and drew his sword and ran it through the earl's

80

body. Rollo was used to killing men, and one more or less didn't make much difference, but this was an important person, and there was bound to be a hue and cry. He began to get rather frightened, so he planned to get rid of the body."

"Well?" said Lynn, as Felicity paused.

"His plans didn't work because, just as he had committed the murder, Lynette had walked into the room. She hated her husband and was splendidly brave, and threatened to tell the whole story. So Rollo, scared for once, had her locked in one of the underground dungeons. He kept her there for several weeks and then one day when he went down to see her she had gone."

"Good for her!" Lynn applauded. "How did she do it?"

"No one knew exactly what happened, but there must have been a secret door in this dungeon which Lynette found and went through. By doing this she got lost in some hidden passages that no one has ever discovered. She was never seen again."

"Poor creature," said Lynn. "So she's the ghost. But why the Laughing Ghost? She'd hardly be merry about it."

"No," said Felicity, in a low voice. "She was dying of starvation and mad with fear. She went insane and laughed and laughed. For nearly a week they could hear that wild laughter coming from behind the walls but they couldn't find their way in to her. At last it stopped. But it's been heard at intervals ever since."

Lynn stopped short.

"Truly? Is this gruesome story and its outcome really true? I hardly believe it, you know."

Lynn was going to laugh again and jest at her solemnity, but they were within the lighted square of the window and he caught sight of Felicity's face. It's gravity sobered him. Good God! She really believes it, he thought. She's heard some bird calling and thinks it's that poor mad woman.

"You know," he said gently, "you've lived here too long. You've been brought up with the legend. Anyway, it's not a pleasant story. Let's skip it, shall we? Cigarette?"

Felicity took one, holding up her face to the cupped flame of the match he held. Laughter was lurking about her lips again.

"I've depressed you," she said.

"Both of us, I think. Let's talk of something else. How do you propose living for a year on a hundred pounds?"

"Oh, I shall do things," said Felicity evasively.

"Such as? Forgive my curiosity, but I feel such a damned usurper."

"You don't need to. You're not responsible. To be explicit, I was planning to take music pupils."

"Oh!"

"At least I'm grateful you don't laugh at me. The others do."

"Who are the others?"

"Oh, my father. He—he's in South Africa elephant hunting. He's dead keen on collecting tusks, and skins and things."

Lynn scowled.

"Don't you think he ought to come home and look after you?"

"Oh, daddy knows I can take care of myself."

"And the others you mentioned?"

"There's Henry." Felicity smiled faintly. "Henry's the most kind-hearted and singularly helpless person you'd ever meet. But, honestly, I'm not badly off. I've got a grand piano, a car and a wardrobe full of expensive clothes. My hundred pounds from Uncle Lynn will pay a year's board and lodging. I'll earn pin money with my music pupils. It's rather an adventure. I think Uncle Lynn knew it would be that. He always said that if you didn't make life an adventure you might as well pack up and leave it."

"That's true," Lynn agreed. "Like my own never-let-it-get-you-down complex. By the way, what are you doing with all those clothes of yours? You can't store them in a furnished room. Will you at least do this much for me and leave your room exactly as it is now? Come up and get anything whenever you want it."

"For instance," Felicity murmured, "making up for my black velvet evening frock and then finding I've got to run half a mile in my petticoat to get it. Still, it might work. Thanks, Lynn, for the offer. I'll only take a dressing case tonight, anyway. And now I really must go."

Lynn followed her back into the house and waited in the hall while she ran up for her things. His thoughts were in confusion, and the sight of Felicity coming down the stairs, a fur coat wrapped around her, the color bright in her cheeks, did not lessen their confusion.

"I'll take you down to the village," he said.

But to his intense disappointment Felicity flatly refused his offer.

"No, please, Lynn. Not tonight. No, I insist.

Good night. Thanks for being so charming."

With that lovely lingering gaiety on her lips she turned and left him, running down the steps and across the garden. Lynn strolled after her, enjoying the mildness of the night, thinking this was the most enchanting spot in the world, and reflecting on how completely he had fallen in love.

Then suddenly he was surprised as a large figure emerged from behind the shadow of the garden gate, went toward Felicity and took her arm through his.

"Gosh, Felicity, you've been a deuce of a long time," Henry complained. "You can't tell me he took all that time to settle in."

"We've been dining," said Felicity lightly. "One must eat."

"Don't be flippant. You can't be flippant about losing a fortune and seeing a damned—"

"Usurper is the word," Felicity supplied. "But I haven't lost a fortune, Henry. It's only postponed. And the usurper is—well, rather nice as usurpers go."

"Hell!" said Henry violently.

Felicity could not feel despondent in company with Henry. She could not even feel sorry that she had deliberately kept him waiting half an hour later than the time appointed over the telephone before dinner. Her chief emotion in regard to him was a slight annoyance that he had insisted on meeting her and taking her down to the *Duck and Drake Inn* where he too was staying temporarily now that he was no longer a guest at Carstairs. But even that sensation scarcely affected her mood of sweet unreasonable elation. Why should she be elated when she had to leave Carstairs and face a year of drudgery and poverty and unwilling nefarious enterprise? Because the night was heavenly, warm and duskily lighted by a half moon, because the sweet-briar hedges were in flower and the blossoms, colorless in the moonlight, gave out the most delicately sweet scent imaginable, because she was young and lovely and life had a way of showing just a flash on one of the jewels it held in store for her; because a brown-faced young man had strolled on the terrace at Carstairs, had lifted slender uneven brows and smiled with an absurd youthfullness . . . .

"Henry, you couldn't imagine who the new owner of Carstairs is. You'd never guess it in a lifetime."

Henry, slouching along with his shoulders humped, said peevishly:

"Then you'd better tell me because I haven't got all that time to waste guessing."

"You remember that impertinent young man in the Black Cat, the one I said was like a Carstairs."

"Hell!" said Henry again, explosively. "It's not that guy!"

"Well, it is," siad Felicity, with childlike delight. "That's almost the sort of thing you'd call Fate, isn't it?"

Henry humped his massive shoulders more than ever, and said nothing.

"Henry, he feels the enchantment about Carstairs, too. You've always laughed at me for feeling it and said all places were alike, just bricks and mortar, but there *is* something about Carstairs."

"Yeah!" growled. Henry. "Maybe. But I'm not one of these ultra-sensitive guys who feels things like that. I'm just an ordinary human being. And a damned worried one at that. But I couldn't expect you to notice that. Your head's full of this guy with the funny eyebrows. I wouldn't expect you to even notice that I was worried!"

"Why, Henry!" Felicity exclaimed, coming out of her maze of enchantment. "What's the trouble?"

"Trouble," Henry said, a little mollified by her solicitous voice. "I've trouble enough to sink a ship. I got a cable from the old man this afternoon."

"What's happened? Is he ill?"

"Ill? Hell, no! I wish it was as simple as that. He's gone broke, that's what's happened."

"He—but, good heavens, Henry! I thought he was wealthy enough to buy half the States."

"Yeah, so did I," said Henry gloomily. "But he's busted it all in some Wall Street smash. It'll be in all the papers tomorrow."

"But, Henry—" Felicity fell silent, grasping the meaning of what she had just heard.

"It means I haven't got a dime," said Henry. "Except the bit I've got left from my last allowance. One minute I'm rolling in cash, the next a bit of yellow paper arrives telling me not to expect any more remittances. Funny, isn't it? It just happens as quickly as that. One minute I'm wealthy, the next I'm broke." Henry's voice was shaking suspiciously. In the half dark Felicity could see his heavy underlip trembling.

"It might not be as bad as that," she said, thinking that he was no more than a great big baby. First sign of trouble and he was in a panic. "There'll be something saved, surely. And anyway, I'm broke too."

"Not a dime," Henry was muttering. "A fellow's got to live some way, and you can't live without money."

"You'll have to get a job," said Felicity practically.

"Job! Me!"

"Why not? You could be a football coach or a car salesman. There are lots of jobs you don't need any special training for."

Henry stopped suddenly. He stood towering over Felicity in the dark lane. Felicity couldn't see his foolish placid face very clearly, but his big looming form was vaguely alarming.

"Tell you what I'm going to do, Felicity. I've been waiting here tonight to tell you. I'm coming in with you in this business at Carstairs."

Felicity was genuinely startled. Was he bluffing, or what did he know?

"What are you talking about?" she asked. "What business?"

"Don't come over all innocent," Henry said. "You know as well as I do what I mean. There's smuggling going on at Carstairs and I'm coming in on it and sharing the profits."

"Henry, what *are* you talking about? There used to be smuggling a hundred years ago. Carstairs was notorious for if. But now—"

Henry took her shoulders in his big hands. All at once he ceased to be the amiable indolent person she knew and had become aggressive and a little frightening.

"Now listen, honey, you're wasting time bluffing because I know. That rascally father of yours made me curious yesterday and last night I knew by the way you were acting there was something in the wind. You can't fool me, honey."

Felicity was just beginning to realize that. Daddy's temper when he found out that big foolish Henry of all people had discovered their secret, would be worse than the famous Carstairs one.

"Well, what did you do?" she asked sharply.

"I followed you down to the cellars after you were supposed to have gone to bed." Henry's voice was triumphant. "I saw everything. Gosh, Felicity, you've got a gold mine there. You might have trusted me enough to tell me. As it is, I'm coming in with you."

Felicity gave up bluffing and became really alarmed.

"But, Henry, you can't do that."

"Why not?" inquired Henry truculently.

"But daddy will be absolutely furious. He won't let you come in."

"How can he stop me? I know all about it. What's to prevent me from going to the cops and telling them the story?"

"Oh, Henry! And you said just now that we could trust you."

"Well, you can still trust me. Only I'm coming in with you. I want some of the profits and I might start a line of my own. Silk, for instance. Maybe a little dope. You can make four or five hundred per cent profit on dope."

"No, Henry!" Felicity said sharply. "I won't have it. You're not bringing dope through Carstairs. I don't care what you tell the police. Smuggling for adventure is one thing, but no one is going to start doing it criminally at Carstairs. Do you hear?"

"Hell!" said Henry. "Smuggling's smuggling however you look at it. Even if you only do it for an adventure, they'll still call you a criminal."

"Yes," said Felicity in a low voice. "I hate it. Oh, how I hate it all. But there's father, and now you. And Uncle Lynn said I was spunky."

"Course you are, honey. Spunkiest kid I know. Okay then, I'll give up the dope idea. May have been a bit ticklish anyway. But the liquor and silks are a deal, aren't they? I'm coming in, aren't I?"

"Oh," said Felicity weakly, wondering where the enchantment of the night had vanished to. "I suppose so. I'll have to ask daddy. But for heaven's sake, learn discretion."

"Good!" said Henry. "You can count on me to be as discreet as they make 'em. Gosh, we'll have a time! Come and let's celebrate. I'll get a table at the *Duck and Drake*."

"You don't get a table at the *Duck and Drake*, you stand at the bar. And besides you haven't got any money, and I'm tired and am going straight to my room. And Henry, you're still saying gosh. Before long you'll make me scream."

"Gosh!" murmured Henry, staring wonderingly at Felicity's retreating form.

Felicity was a queer girl, Henry reflected, standing alone at the bar of the *Duck and Drake*. You would have thought that she would appreciate some help in that decidedly ticklish business that went on at Carstairs. She would have enough trouble as it was, with a stranger in the house prying about. But, no. There she was, independent and proud as the devil. And after all the sympathy he had given her during her misfortune she had scarcely a word for him in this appalling financial disaster that had overtaken him. Not a word for him, Henry reflected gloomily, finishing his drink and ordering another. After the way he had hung around in this tin-pot village waiting to be of help. She had just about turned him down flat. Wrapped up in that strange guy at Carstairs, that's what she was. But he'd show her she couldn't play fast and loose with him. (The drinks were restoring to Henry his colossal self-confidence.) He'd show her he was coming in on this business and making some money out of it, same as old Lynnford Carstairs had, or else spilling the whole story to the police. Why, if she had only some sense she would see that by their both making money they would soon be able to get married.

Gosh! thought Henry suddenly. I didn't ask her again tonight if she'd marry me. I clean forgot.

"You all alone?" queried the fat man next to Henry at the bar. "Have one on me?"

So engrossed had he been in his thoughts, Henry had not observed anyone else enter the barroom. But now he stared at the stranger, scarcely remembering to thank him for the drink, so surprising was the man's appearance. He was enormously fat. Three chins ran one into another, the last one appearing to spread right around his neck and hanging in a soft pink fold over his collar. His small eyes were round and bright and had the appearance of popping out of the continent of flesh surrounding them, his mouth was a ridiculous moist red button, and his body, encased in a tweed suit, was colossal.

"Come and sit down," said this mammoth of a

man cordially. "Nice little place, this. I want to talk to you."

"Why, yes," said Henry bewilderedly, as usual taking in and answering the first remarks before the last had registered their meaning. "Who, me? Why do you want to talk to me?"

The Kitten seated himself happily at the table opposite Henry. This was the most amazing piece of luck he had encountered since heaven knew when. To come across Henry Higginsbottom in St. Simon while on a damn-fool chase after a ghost, was scarcely credible. The stage was all set for as pretty a piece of blackmail as the Kitten had ever done. In addition, the twisting of this big stupid fellow's tail would ease a little the rankling feeling of his own injuries at the hands of Pope.

Henry had finished his drink and was sitting staring at the fat man.

"Have another," the Kitten said genially. "Dry work, talking."

"It's you who wants to do the talking," Henry pointed out.

"Yes, that's right. I do want to talk to you, Mr. Higginsbottom."

Henry stared.

"You know me?"

"Yes. I know you. It's not hard to know a familiar figure like you. Specially out Chicago way." The Kitten sat smiling at Henry with his popping eyes.

"Oh, of course. Yes, yes," said Henry uneasily. "Didn't know you'd been in Chicago. Yes, I suppose I am pretty well known there. You'd know my father, too."

"Nope. Didn't know your pa. Only you. Happened to be in Chicago last year. January of last year."

"Did you then?" said Henry, pleased with the nonchalance of his voice, and repressing a desire to tramp on this fat slug-like man. But his foot, even his large foot, size twelve in shoes, wouldn't be big enough to make much impression on that gross bulk.

"Yes," said the Kitten pleasantly. "Say, you're not drinking. Let me fill your glass. That's better. Yes, I was in Chicago just at the time the newspapers were full of a little scandal. Your picture was published quite a lot. I couldn't help recognizing you from it. You've got a memorable sort of dial, so to speak."

"Yeah," said Henry thickly, swallowing his drink.

The Kitten crossed his legs and lit a cigar.

"Interesting story that, you know. Real drama. Husband finds millionaire playboy in bedroom with wife. Fires revolver at playboy but wife springs in front and gets hit. I suppose your pa, being an influential sort of guy, thought it wise to get you out of the States until the scandal blew over. Is that so? You know, the thing that puzzles me is how a dame would cotton to you at all."

Henry gulped and swallowed.

"That's priceless, that is. Some other guy with same name and same looks, but not you. Why, I'd take an oath there isn't another guy in the world who looks like you."

Gosh, thought Henry, this is awful! What does he want, anyway?

"Say, aren't there any more drinks?" he asked desperately, pushing his glass forward.

"Sure. Sure. Go ahead." The Kitten refilled Henry's glass, thinking that nothing would suit him better than to get the guy a little drunk.

"What is it you want?" he demanded truculently. "Even if the story is true you can't do anything about it."

"Sweet little lady you came in with tonight," the Kitten said thoughtfully. "Real top notcher, she looked. I'm sure she'd be interested to hear that story. You know, you didn't come out of it in the best light."

"Felicity!" whispered Henry, the sweat starting out on his forehead. "You can't tell her that."

"No?" The Kitten leaned back contentedly. This was good. This was better than anything Pope had handed out to him. The guy was in a sweat already. "Why not? I've got a tongue that can talk and I haven't heard of any law that's to stop me from telling the truth."

"Malicious slander," muttered Henry.

"But that's what it's not. The truth isn't slander. Couldn't be."

Not Felicity, thought Henry desperately. Why, if she heard that story she wouldn't marry him, not if he begged her to every day of his life. And she was the sweetest kid. He was just sick with love for her. If she heard that, why—Henry began to giggle helplessly, then that dreadful cold feeling of disaster seized him. He stopped giggling and tried to pin his eyes on the face of the man opposite him. But curiously enough it wouldn't stay still. It kept floating about like a large pink moon.

"Wha'—what is it you want?" he asked.

"My price is low," said the Kitten magnanimously. "Only five thousand bucks. That's nothing to a guy like you. And I'm not being hard on you. I'm giving you a week to get it from your pa."

Five thousand bucks! His pal Well, at least that made sense. Henry leaned forward eagerly.

"Listen to me! You think I can get that from my old man. Well, I can't. Because he's gone broke. Went broke today."

The Kitten didn't even look interested.

"Have another drink. Now stop pitching yarn and let's have a spot of truth."

"But it *is* the truth!" Henry protested. "My old man's gone bust. Look, here's the cable I got today. That's clear enough for anybody."

The Kitten glanced negligently at the crumpled bit of paper, then his jaw dropped.

"Course it's true. Think my father would send me that if it wasn't right? I tell you, I haven't got a dime."

There were tears in Henry's eyes, his heavy lip hung down and he looked like a scared defiant child. In a minute he'd be blubbering like a kid, and the Kitten felt that he could have wept, too, for sheer disappointment. If this wasn't too bad. All that sound preliminary work only to discover the fellow hadn't got a bean?"

"Well, what are you doing here?" he shouted angrily. "What are you hanging around a swell dame like that for if you haven't got a bean?"

"I've been staying at Carstairs," Henry said in an injured voice. "To learn hunting. I'm a sort of relation of the family. I've been there a couple of months. But the old man died and a new guy's moved in, so I'm staying here for a while seeing Felicity over the worst of things. We're going to be married—or at least—gosh, why can't you leave me alone?" he demanded petulantly.

"Carstairs," the Kitten was saying to himself, a very alert look in his little eyes. "The old luck holds after all. See here," he said to Henry. "I want you to tell me all you know about Carstairs."

"All I know," Henry repeated bewilderedly.

"All of it, including any little titbits about"—the Kitten shot a bow at a venture—"about smuggling and about that damn apparition they call the Laughing Ghost."

Henry's jaw dropped. He looked terrified.

"Smuggling!" he whispered. For a moment his voice deserted him. Then he got out convulsively, "I can't tell you anything about that."

"Can't you, now? Well, I think you can." The Kitten, toying with his cigar and trying to look negligent was a humorous spectacle to anyone in the mood to appreciate it. Henry definitely wasn't in the mood. He felt sick and dizzy and scared to death.

"Honest to God, I can't!" he repeated in his convulsive whisper. Then, hypnotized by those bright popping little eyes which never left his face, he burst out, "How'd you know about it, anyway?"

"Well, now, because I happen to be interested in things like that. It happens to be in my line. What about telling me ways and means."

"But I couldn't," Henry protested piteously. "Felicity would never forgive me."

"Felicity will never forgive you if she hears that little Chicago scandal."

"But you wouldn't tell her that! Not when I haven't got a bean!"

"I'll tell her, sure as you're alive, if I don't hear all about this smuggling racket. What's Claus Jensen got to do with it?"

This was another bow at a venture, but, miraculously, it too hit its mark.

"Say!"breathed Henry. "Are you a wizard?"

The Kitten grinned fatuously.

"Surprising the things I know, ain't it? Well, are you going to come across or do I tell the dame?"

Katie Diver, feeling extraordinarily well, had begun to grow impatient of Thomas' constant solicitous manner. Gracious, you'd think no woman had ever had a baby before. You'd think he, the big silly, was having it himself. So she said, with a trace of impatience in her soft voice:

"Thomas, I do wish you'd stop mooning about. Can't you find something to do?"

"I am doing something." Thomas said, scrunching up the newspaper indignantly. "I'm reading the paper."

"You don't look as if you are. Why don't you sit down quietly with it? Any news?"

"Not a thing. Wall Street crashed and a few Yankees lost their wad, that's all. I wish they'd put something about that diamond theft."

"What diamond theft?" inquired Katie innocently.

Thomas cast a quick pitying look at her. To him there was only one diamond theft, but you couldn't expect everyone to take the absorbed interest that he, as an upholder of the law, took in it.

"Why, the Windermere necklace of course," he explained patiently. "Worth a cool hundred thousand. Golly, if I could catch that thief I'd be a made man. No need for you and the nipper to worry then, Katie. But, damnation, nothing ever happens here."

"Why don't you go out for a while?" Katie suggested. "I'm all right. You want a bit of amusement. Why don't you go along to the *Duck and Drake* and have a glass of beer with somebody?"

"I believe I will," said Thomas. "No harm in me doing that in plain clothes. I'll just pop out for an hour or so."

There were none of Thomas' more intimate acquaintances in the *Duck and Drake*. He spoke a few words to the landlord, then took his mug of ale to a table and sat down. The room was unusually empty, with only a farmer or two at the bar, and in a corner that big Yankee, Henry Higginsbottom, and an extraordinarily repulsively fat man, sitting over their drinks. Young Henry looked a trifle worse for drink. His eyes were heavy and bloodshot, his lower lip hung down and his face was a mottled red. He seemed to be in a temper about something because every time the fat man spoke he scowled and muttered sullenly and looked scared.

Always knew he was like that, Thomas thought complacently. Drinks too much and gets unpleasant. He's not half good enough for Felicity Valentine. It's to be hoped she doesn't marry him for his money now that she hasn't got any.

The fat man seemed to have a good many intimate things to say to Henry. He leaned across the table, talking in a thick urgent whisper, and all the time Henry was growing more alarmed.

At last he stumbled unsteadily to his feet, and gripping the edge of the table, said in a loud childish voice:

"I won't do it! Whatever it is you want me to take, I won't do it!"

One or two people glanced casually around. Thomas sat unmoved, his legs crossed, his eyelids drooping. Whatever happened, he mustn't let them know he was watching. They were hatching some plot, and if only it were bad enough—and God! if only he were smart enough to unmask it. . . . Why, it might even be as important a plot as that hatched to steal the Windermere diamonds. Now, the thing to do was to look totally unconcerned. Don't even look their way, except under your lashes. Drink your ale. Look stupid. How did you deliberately look stupid?

Under his half-closed eyelids Thomas saw the fat man seize Henry's wrist and pull him down to his seat.

"Sit down, you fool!" he hissed. "And shut up!"

Henry's lip moved but no sound came. Perspiration shone on his forehead. He looked scared to death.

The fat man, with a surreptitious glance around that wouldn't, Thomas thought, have deceived a child, leaned across the table and talked again in a low voice. Then he chuckled in a fat unpleasant way and refilled Henry's glass and his own. Either the drink went to his head, or he thought there was no need for discretion, for he said quite audibly:

"Cheer up! If anyone takes the blame it'll be the new guy at Carstairs!"

At that, Thomas had difficulty in maintaining his air of indifference, but he contrived to be intent over his drink while watching the fat man get ponderously to his feet and smile genially down at Henry.

"Just one more word, old son, and that is if ever you've got anything valuable to hide never let it out of your possession. Never!"

Fascinatedly, his discretion vanished, Thomas watched the fat man's plump hand fondling his shirt at the breast. Then he called to the waiter, paid his bill and sauntered out of the room, waving expansively to Henry when he had reached the door, while Thomas sat manfully controlling the impulse that urged him to rush after the fat stranger and demand to see what lay hidden beneath his shirt front. Why, it might even be the Windermere diamonds! Nothing seemed too fantastic to imagine tonight.

Polly said piteously, "But, Mrs. Miggs, can't you wait just one more week? I promise you I'll pay something then. I promise!"

Mrs. Miggs' lower jaw was granite. She stood, arms folded, on the threshold of Polly's room and delivered her ultimatum.

"Not this time, Miss Gay. You've promised once too often. There's six weeks' rent owing and if I don't have it by tomorrow morning I'll have to have the room. Yes, I know times are hard, but I've got to live as well as you. Pay or quit. That's my last word."

"But, Mrs. Miggs, I haven't anywhere to go. I haven't any money. You'd have got your rent all along if I'd got my salary, but there's six weeks owing to me and now the show's closed down. If you'd only wait—"

"You've said that before, Miss Gay," was the unyielding answer. "You've said it once too often."

"But how'd I know the show was going to close

down?" Polly wailed. "First time I get a break this is what happens: show a washout, company bankrupt. But I'm practically certain I can get a job with Fran Leeds. If you'll only give me a week—"

"I'm sorry, Miss Gay, but I'll wait no longer. People's got to look out for themselves. I've got a crippled husband to keep and I've got to get my money in. Six weeks' rent by tomorrow morning or I'll have your stuff taken out."

The door banged behind Mrs. Miggs.

"Oh, hell!" said Polly.

Now things were in a mess. She had been in tight corners before, but it looked as if this one was going to be too tight altogether to squeeze out of. Six weeks' rent by tomorrow morning. One might as well ask her to catch the thief of the Windermere diamonds. If only she hadn't been such a fool as to say nothing to Lynn. Letting him go off to his earldom this morning thinking she was happily at work when the show had closed down a couple of nights ago, and no salaries paid. But when she had known the show was closing down Lynn had had his own worries, and she couldn't foist her own on him. And when he had heard about his fantastic inheritance—well, you couldn't begin immediately to sponge on a new-made earl, or whatever he was. Besides, she hadn't known Lynn for a year without catching some of his stiff-necked pride. She wasn't going to start out an acquaintance with an earl by telling him a hard-luck story of a show that failed and six weeks' salary, which was to have paid rent and sundry other accounts, that had vanished into thin air. Not even when she had known the aforesaid earl when he was in just such dire straits himself. Maybe it was foolish of her, but she couldn't bring herself to spoil Lynn's pleasure this morning. It wasn't as if Lynn was under any obligation to her. There was nothing like that about their friendship. Certainly she herself would have been agreeable. Lynn was lonely and she was lonely, and—well, when a boy and girl get together— But Lynn hadn't felt that way. He was an idealist. He dreamed shining dreams of one perfect girl. It was all rather tragic from Polly's point of view. She hadn't realized quite how dreadfully lonely she would be tonight with no Lynn along the passage to come look her up. Queer how she kept seeing those funny uneven eyebrows of his, that lifted when he talked, his hesitant charming smile that made something turn over inside her . . . .

"Snap out of it, Polly!" she said aloud, jumping up impatiently. "You can't sit here brooding over a guy you'll probably never see again. You've got to get out and earn your living."

She wasn't in love, of course, Polly reflected sagely, as she made her way on foot to the Criterion in the hope of finding Fran Leeds. Oh, no, she wasn't in love. She was just terribly fond of Lynn Carstairs, and as a companion in both good and bad times she was going to miss him dreadfully. Of course, if things came to the worst, there was her promise to go down to Carstairs. But she didn't intend to do that. Not under any circumstances.

No, not even when Fran Leeds turned her down flat. She had waited two hours to see him, only to be told that he didn't want an extra of any kind whatsoever.

"I've no doubt you'll get to the top of the tree, Miss Gay," he told her sardonically. "If perseverance does it, you will. But not through this present show of mine. Sorry. Good night."

So that was that. Don't be a fool and let a little thing like that cast you down, Polly told herself. After all, you expected it. But you wouldn't have waited two solid hours and made enemies of the whole damn company if you'd known what you know now. Gosh, hasn't anyone in the whole world got some spare cash? How did you go about meeting a wealthy American, one of those playboys?

It was difficult to walk gallantly when she hadn't had anything to eat all day but a twopenny bun. Nevertheless, Polly contrived it—until somehow she lost her handbag containing her remaining half-crown. That ended it.

She cried herself to sleep that night, in lucid intervals taking herself to task for her childishness and lack of courage.

Polly, you great big goof! You great big cry-baby! Lynn, I'm sorry. Truly I didn't intend to come to Carstairs, but now I've got to—if I can find somebody to lend me enough money to buy my railway ticket. Things are just too damn tough for this child!

CHAPTER FIVE

THE MOON had swung low over the elms and its light had grown dim, patterning vaguely the diamond-shaped windows on the floor. A rising wind stirred in the branches, its sound mingling confusedly with the sound of the sea. It seemed to have got into the long passages at Carstairs, too, for there was a subdued rushing and whining that was decidedly eerie. But it was only the wind.

Lynn, staring into the gloom at the bedposts of the ridiculous immense four-poster to which Mark the valet, had solemnly conducted him two hours ago, knew that what had awakened him was not the sound of the wind. But what it was he could not have told. He had started up from sleep with what had seemed to be an indistinct high-pitched scream ringing in his ears. Now, apart from the wind, there was utter silence.

What had it been? The Laughing Ghost? But that was absurd. Haunted and bewitched as the atmosphere of Carstairs was, the thought of a lost lady who laughed through centuries was pathetic but quite impossible. No, he couldn't believe in the ghost, but all the same something may be wrong. Perhaps Buddy was crying. Anyway, he had better go and see.

Lynn fumbled for matches on the night table, and finding them, lighted the candle in the tall elegant candlestick with which Mark had lighted him to bed. First thing tomorrow he'd buy himself a powerful electric torch. This absence of all lighting except candles was the last word in eccentricity, although the candlelight was delicate and lovely, and a little eerie in this tall old room, with the shadow of the bed leaping monstrously across the ceiling, and the wavering jack-o'-lantern flame reflected in the paneling.

Lynn put on his dressing gown and slippers, reflecting on their shabbiness in comparison with the rich hangings of the bed. Nice down-at-heel person he was to be master of this dignified old place. No wonder Felicity—sweet Felicity—had gaped politely.

The unsteady candle flame lighted him down the wide staircase into the hall, and along the passage leading to the servants' quarters to the small storeroom where an indignant Buddy had been imprisoned. A gentle unhappy whining behind the closed door led him to open the door in haste, and a dusty white object catapulted into his arms.

Lynn rubbed Buddy's head affectionately.

"Did you scream, old man? No, of course you didn't, and your whining wouldn't reach my bedroom, so it wasn't you. Jove!" Lynn's eyes were resting on the door at the other side of the storeroom. "I believe that leads down to the cellars. Let's explore shall we?"

Buddy, quivering with excitement, signified his assent. Lynn went across to the door, reflecting on Peewee's refusal to show him the cellars that evening. Peewee, who, with his bland amused face, was the last person one would imagine to be superstitious, had reported himself reluctant to go down to the underground passages after nightfall. No, it wasn't the ghost, he assured Lynn. But the passages were dark and drafty and maze-like. If your candle blew out ten to one you wouldn't find your way above stairs until morning. If by then, he added ominously. And, strange as it may seem, there didn't appear to be any electric torches in Carstairs.

He intended purchasing one the first opportunity he got, as it was what you might call spooky going down to the cellar by candlelight to fetch up the wine for dinner. Besides—no, he didn't believe in the ghost, but if you should be lost in the dark in those passages and should hear anything, why you'd most likely be scared to death.

All the time Peewee had been talking, his chubby face and wide light eyes as solemn as an owl's, Lynn had imagined he was laughing up his sleeve at Lynn's gullibility. He was a plausible rascal if ever there was one. All that talk about candles and ghosts was a blind. There was some reason why he didn't want Lynn to go down to the cellars.

But in spite of it all Lynn was going down to the cellars alone, at midnight, and by candlelight.

He opened the door and a gust of cold damp wind came up from the narrow stairway beneath him, causing the candlelight to waver perilously. There was a faint exciting odor of perpetually damp walls and the sea. Lynn went down the flight of steps,

Buddy at his heels, and found himself in a long narrow intensely dark passage. A door ajar on the left hand side led into the wine cellar, superbly stocked, as the candlelight showed Lynn. Old Lynnford had certainly been a connoisseur in wines. Those rare old vintages, shelf on shelf of them, must have cost a fortune, or the family had laid down their stock for generations. Well, he would sample a few bottles this year, but after that—

Lynn's thoughts were broken off by Buddy, who was beginning a low grumble and standing with ears pricked at the door.

In a second Lynn was beside the dog, holding his collar and peering down into the dark passage.

"What is it, Buddy? Quiet! There's someone coming."

Rapid footsteps approached. A glimmer of light showed on the far wall. Lynn snuffed out the candle and holding tight to the trembling dog stood in the shadow of the doorway as someone bearing an electric torch came around the corner at the end of the passage. Someone who walked jauntily and who was singing under his breath, absurdly, the dwarfs' song from *Snow White and the Seven Dwarfs*.

A jovial ghost, thought Lynn grimly, and as the man came level with him he sprang, knocking the torch to the ground and seizing his victim by the scruff of his neck.

"Damnation!" yelled Peewee. "Let me go, you fool, whoever you are!"

Peewee! thought Lynn in amazement, and tightened his hold on the man's neck.

"So you were scared to come down into the cellars after dark," he said scathingly. "There were no electric torches in Carstairs and candles blew out. The Laughing Ghost might scare you or you might get lost in the passages. Well, I tell you this, and that is that you'll get *locked* down here if any more of this midnight prowling goes on. Got a match?"

"Yes, sir. I think so, sir," came the totally unperturbed answer.

"Well, strike one, you scoundrel, and light my candle. Your precious torch will be smashed."

Obediently Peewee struck a match and the light illumined his bland face with its secretive merriment. Lynn held out the candle to catch the flame, and said wrathfully:

"Now perhaps you'll explain why you told me that fool story about not coming down here after dark, and why you lied to me at all. Come on. Out with it."

Somehow Peewee contrived to look abashed. His light eyelashes hid his merry eyes and he said in an abject voice:

"I'm sorry, sir. Honestly, I'm that sorry. I hardly know how to tell you, but I couldn't sleep for want of a—a toddy, sir, and I came down to the cellar."

"You did, did you! You thieving rascal! After what Miss Valentine told you this afternoon. I've a mind to dismiss you on the spot. What would you say to that?"

"I can only say I'm sorry about my lapse," said Peewee primly. "I promise you it won't happen again."

Confound the beggar! thought Lynn. You can't help liking his saucy face. At least he's honest anyway. And I can't begin by dismissing servants. Besides

Felicity—oh, the devil take Felicity's soft heart.

"It's disgraceful," he said sternly. "I hope you realize that. Taking advantage of me, too, because I don't know my way about here. It's not good enough. Well, I'm giving you one more chance. Just one. If I catch you at this game again, out you go. Understand?"

"Yes, sir, thanking you, sir. It's very generous of you. I promise you—"

"No. I don't want to hear any more of your promises, Peewee. I don't believe in them. Confound you, you're a scoundrel. By the way, if you came down to the wine cellar how did you happen to be down that passage?"

"That leads to the sea, sir. I wanted to get a breath of fresh air."

Yes, and you're a plausible rogue, thought Lynn, watching the man's guileless face keenly. But all he said was, "All right. Now get away to bed."

"Excuse me, sir," Peewee said. "But was there something I could do for you here, sir? You wouldn't have been disturbed by something you thought was the ghost?"

Now he's curious as to why I'm down here, thought Lynn. Wants to know if I'm going to make a habit of it so that his own prowls will be disturbed.

"My dog was howling," he said shortly. "I came down to him."

"Oh, quite, sir. Nice little dog. Or it may have been an owl. There are a lot of owls around here. They sound peculiarly human at times. Especially waking one up out of a sleep. I wouldn't let the ghost worry you, sir."

"Confound you, Peewee, I'm not worrying about

the ghost! I'm not worrying about twenty ghosts! Get that into your head, and get to bed."

Half an hour later, in the soft moonlit darkness of his room, Lynn contemplated Buddy ensconced with great content in a hollow at the foot of the bed. There was a mystery at Carstairs, he was convinced. Whether the ghost was legitimate or faked, the mystery surrounding it was intriguing. But strangely enough, Lynn was not at the moment at all concerned with it. A sleepy and deplorably in-attentive dog had to listen to a soliloquy on the charms of Felicity Valentine, and the possible chances of Lynn and her becoming joint owners of Carstairs and of Buddy himself.

"I wonder what she's doing at this moment, Buddy. I couldn't expect her to be lying awake thinking of me. But at least the same moon is shining on us both. Do you think that's any consolation? No, I don't exactly, either. Oh, well. My God, Buddy, you're a shabby object on that quilt!"

Felicity applied rouge carefully, then rubbed it off again. Lynn, she imagined, would have simple but decided tastes. A too vivid application of rouge would not be one of them. Besides, with her bright hair and lips her skin really looked better as it was, extremely pure and with a faint wild-rose flush. "I'm glad I've got delicately shaped bones," she thought. "and my eyes really aren't too wide apart. Or are they? Anyway, they're a good color. I won-der if Lynn has noticed yet that I'm rather like poor Lynette Carstairs. Or perhaps he isn't interested anyway."

There was no need, Felicity decided, rubbing the

rouge off her cheeks and the color into them, to be so particular, as she probably wouldn't even see Lynn. She wouldn't ask for him, anyhow. She would just slip up to her room and get her navy and white suit, the only thing in her wardrobe that seemed at all suitable in which to become a music mistress. She wasn't going to let it seem that having the majority of her wardrobe at Carstairs was an excuse for popping in at all times. But perhaps Lynn might be about somewhere. He might look different in daylight, less attractive.

There was also that advertisement to put in the local newspaper. "Miss Felicity Valentine wishes to announce that she is taking pupils for the piano . . ." Really, it was rather humorous. Uncle's bad joke wasn't such a tragedy after all. She might even turn out successful. At least it would develop her resources, and goodness knows, they needed developing badly enough. No one should live all one's life in luxury. It was degenerating.

There wasn't going to be much space for a grand piano in this room, but it would have to go in somehow. It should arrive this morning if the men had remembered their instructions. The dusky little Canaletto, her own possession that she was bringing from Carstairs, could hang over the fireplace, where the light, fortunately, was excellent. For the rest the furnishings were quite good, deep brown rugs, chintz curtains with a pattern of tulips, and two low armchairs. The ceiling was raftered, and a gnarled old pear tree grew outside the window. In the bedroom there was the same cheerful chintz pattern, but the rugs were blue. For a couple of rooms in an inn, they were charming. As her home for a year—well, they were still charming, Felicity reflected doggedly. One couldn't expect always to live in the spaciousness and beauty of Carstairs. Everything was going to be wonderful—provided the pupils came along.

Yet all the time she dressed and reflected there was one thought in her mind dominating all others—a peculiar knowledge that all her life had been leading up to that moment last night when Lynn had walked into the music room and startled her at the piano. All her fears, her sorrows, her wonder, her joy, her high-spirited escapades, the unsatisfied and inevitable longings of her heart, her turmoil of mind, had had the startling happiness of that moment as their goal.

The knowledge was at once unreasonable and impressive. It made her feel sober and a little awed, and brought an unusual gravity to her face as she went down the stairs and into the street.

But her gravity was soon dispelled, for bowling down the street at a fine spanking pace came an old-fashioned red-wheeled carriage drawn by her uncle's pair of grays. Felicity stood stock still. For a moment her mind was whirled back to childhood and the memory of Uncle Lynnford, masterfully handling the horses, hooves clattering, red wheels shining, dashing down the avenue into Carstairs.

Then she realized that the equipage had come to a standstill a few yards farther on, and Lynn, on the driver's seat, was turning around yelling to her:

"Close your mouth! You look like the village idiot!"

Felicity flushed and closed her lips hastily, before

she realized that she had obeyed his impudent order. She went running up to the carriage, oblivious of the small crowd of people that had collected, and said indignantly:

"Lynn, if this isn't beyond all reason! If you want to go out, why don't you take one of the cars?"

Lynn, leaning over the side of the carriage, said with immense solemnity:

"All my life I've wanted to drive in a carriage. It's a marvelous thing to be able to realize a life-long ambition." His gaze roved fondly over the spick-and-span vehicle. "I had Williams polish her up for me. She's a beauty, isn't she? I'm going shopping. Can I give you a lift?"

In spite of herself, Felicity smiled.

"Lynn, you're absurd. Everybody's staring."

Lynn looked around in surprise.

"So they are. I feel a feudal lord. What should I do? Bow?"

"Just wave your hand. Sort of negligently."

"Oh, I see. Like Queen Victoria. You'd better get in and look after me. You know the ropes. Besides we've got to show the villagers we're not enemies. You know, the usurper and the usurped. Where are you going?"

"To Carstairs," said Felicity, climbing in somewhat precariously, for the horses were growing restive. "To change my frock."

"Good! Then we'll just call in and do my shopping on the way. I want an electric torch and a half a dozen batteries."

"What, are you going to light up the dungeons?"

"Yes, and search for that damn ghost."

Felicity seemed divided between amusement and gravity.

"You didn't hear it last night?"

"No, but I found that rascal Peewee snooping around in the cellars. That man's up to no good. I've given him one more chance. If I catch him again, out he goes."

"Oh, no!" said Felicity involuntarily.

"I mean it," said Lynn firmly. "Even if he is a special pet of yours. I really don't see why you should be so concerned about him either. Now, if you'll hold the horses for a minute I'll dive in here and get those torches."

Felicity watched his tall form disappear into the ship. She felt both happy and alarmed. Peewee, the careless fool! She would have to speak to him privately. How idiotic it was to sit perched up here, holding a pair of restive grays. What an idiot Lynn was—but what a charming idiot!

In a moment Lynn was out of the shop and had clambered up into the driver's seat.

"Now we're off. I really think my little morning airing has done me a world of good. How about you, my dear? You're still looking a trifle pale."

Felicity giggled at his mincing tones.

"I left my rouge off," she admitted candidly.

"Rouge!" shouted Lynn. "Do you use that vile stuff? Look, when you've got skin like a morning rose do you think it's sane, do you think it's even on the border-line of sanity, to plaster it over with some horrible chemical concoction?"

"My heavens!" murmured Felicity. "How you get worked up over a small thing. Well, to be candid I hardly ever use it. But Henry rather likes it."

"Henry! Who the devil's Henry? Not the gentleman you nearly killed the other day?"

"The same," Felicity said meekly.

"My God, you don't take orders from Henry!"

Felicity said aloofly, "What can that matter to you?"

"No two people," said Lynn, in parrot-like tones, "can use aloof answers and be aloof when traveling in such close proximity and publicity as the outside seat of a carriage."

Felicity looked at him with gravity.

"We're fencing," she said. "Why?"

For an answer she received a very straight gaze from those oddly blue eyes.

"God knows. Let's be honest. Have you ever been in love?"

"No," said Felicity, startled but truthful.

"Neither have I."

She knew he was speaking the truth also, and her heart gave a faint pleasurable throb. She felt absurdly light-hearted.

They had come to the entrance gates of Carstairs. The sun was making long lances of light between the trees, the leaves were polished and glittering.

"Go slowly here," Felicity said. "I always love it."

The sound of the horses' hooves slowed to a walk made an echoing clop-clopping. There was a moving pattern of shadow and sunlight over Felicity's green linen skirt and Lynn's hands holding the reins and the horses' backs.

"Sunshine through trees and a quiet day," said Lynn. "It's the most peaceful thing you'll ever know. We both like the same things."

"Yes," said Felicity, a little breathlessly.

"It's nice to know that. Don't you think so?"

"Well—yes, perhaps."

"No perhaps, Felicity."

Felicity found his eyes on her disconcerting. Again she was conscious of the throb of her heart.

"Where's Buddy?" she asked irrelevantly.

"In the stables with Williams. He didn't approve of the carriage. He has a distinct preference for cars—they having been conspicuous by their absence during most of his life. You're evading the subject, Felicity."

"What subject?"

"Another evasion. You know as well as I. Don't you think it's pleasant to like the same things?"

"There's a story," she said, "that Queen Victoria stayed here when she was a little girl. When she was the Princess Victoria and they didn't even know she would be queen one day."

"No!" breathed Lynn. "Not really! That's too good to be true."

"Why?" asked Felicity curiously.

"Because—my sacred aunt, this is marvelous! Because I'm writing a romance of the dear queen, and what could be better for atmosphere? She actually stayed here! Can you tell me which room she slept in? Can you?"

Felicity thought how his eager interest changed him, how wonderfully alive and alert his face had become. The face of Rupert Carstairs who had fallen on Marston Moor would have been like that when the bugles sounded and the king's standard fluttered at the head of a glittering column.

"The one that is mine, now, I think. Lynn, you didn't tell me about your book."

"Didn't I?" His smile had become young and shy. "I don't usually talk about it. Buddy's mostly my only confidante."

"Does he realize he's lucky?"

Lynn laughed.

"He sleeps through most of it. You would, too. Well, here we are." He jumped out of the carriage and handed the reins to the groom. "Fine horses, Williams. I've scarcely warmed 'em up. Do you hunt much, Felicity?" he asked, as he helped her down and they strolled up to the house.

"I ride a lot. No, I don't care a great deal for hunting. Uncle deplored that."

"Then you're still to ride. Whenever you like. I can't possibly stay here if I'm depriving you of things you're accustomed to. Felicity, tell me honestly, are you happy as things are now? Have you a grudge against me for stepping in like this? I don't mean against me personally, but me as a usurper."

"Why, no, of course not," Felicity said frankly. "I think the whole thing's an adventure. Honestly, I do. It's making me develop my resources, and they badly need developing."

"How old you are and how young you are. Felicity, the moment you want it, I'll go."

"But I don't want it. Truly."

"What about a reason or two. Just so I'll be sure."

"Well—because you like Carstairs in the way I do. Because it's making me self-reliant. Because you're writing a book. What is this, anyway? A questionnaire?"

"May I say something about your eyelashes?" asked Lynn irrelevantly.

"Gracious, you're making my heart flutter!"

"Mine's been fluttering all morning."

Suddenly they laughed together. Their laughter was gay and infectious. Felicity said:

"You're a conscientious young man. I like you for it."

"You're a resourceful young woman. But I like you better for your beauty."

Felicity ran from him, into the house and up the stairs.

"Come and see if you like the dress I'm going to be a music mistress in," she called breathlessly.

"I'm more interested," Lynn called, half way up the stairs, "in whether you are going to carry out the provisions of your uncle's will unreservedly."

Felicity laughed and flung open the door of her room and stopped dead. Lynn at her shoulder said, "What's up?" and gasped.

Polly's eyes were red from prolonged weeping. The tears had made havoc of her make-up, her wide scarlet mouth drooped, and she looked extremely forlorn. Yet she had contrived to make herself comfortable, taking off her shoes, wrapping the eiderdown around herself and curling up like a kitten on Felicity's bed.

When she saw Lynn, however, she leaped off the bed, flew toward him, flung her arms around his neck and burst out into loud sobbing.

"Oh, Lynn! Oh, darling! I thought you'd never come."

Lynn's mouth dropped. His eyebrows shot up. He tried to extricate himself from Polly's embrace.

"Listen, Polly! Felicity—Oh, hell!"

Afterward the only thing he could remember about Felicity was her bright contemptuous lips.

"Unreservedly, did you say?" she asked, in a proud scornful voice. "No, decidedly not!"

And she went out, banging the door.

Henry knocked tentatively at Felicity's door, called out who he was, and, reassured by the gentle tone of her voice bidding him enter, went in. He found Felicity sitting staring at the tremulous pattern of leaf shadows on the floor. For all that she appeared to notice his presence he might not have been there. Her grand piano, apparently just arrived, stood in the center of the room dwarfing everything else. One could scarcely move without knocking against a corner of it. But Felicity didn't appear to notice that either. It wasn't natural, thought Henry uneasily, forgetting for a moment his own troubles.

"Hello, Felicity."

"Hello, Henry. Sit down somewhere. Sorry I can't offer you a drink. I haven't got my cocktail cabinet installed yet."

Her voice was bitter. It was the first time, Henry reflected with surprise, that he had ever heard her speak bitterly about anything.

"Oh, that's all right, honey. I had one downstairs anyway. Say, that piano's taking up a lot of room, isn't it? Wouldn't it be better against the wall?"

"It would. The men just left it here. I'll get someone up later to shift it."

"I could give you a hand now."

"Oh, don't bother, Henry. Just sit down and stop fidgeting."

Henry dropped the ornament he had been fiddling with.

"Something biting you, honey?"

"Everything."

Henry felt dismayed.

"That's bad! Well, look, honey, if it's only money, we'll soon have some when we get things going at Carstairs."

"It's not money," said Felicity sharply. "And as for that business at Carstairs you don't even know if daddy will let you in on it. I'd say he wouldn't."

"But he's got to! Or else I'll spill the beans. He's got to."

Felicity eyed him wearily.

"Well, Henry, you can bluff pretty well, and you've probably got the whip hand over daddy, but I can't imagine you being mean enough to go to the police."

Henry's emotions were in a turmoil. Love for lovely unhappy Felicity, truculence about his intention of becoming a smuggler, dismay about his penniless state, and fear concerning what had happened last night struggled for the upper place in his mind. Eventually fear won.

"Felicity, I can't go to the police now because the most awful thing happened last night. A guy I've never seen before wants me to get a bit of jewelry out of England for him. Says it's worth a thousand and I'll get a hundred if I do the job all right."

Felicity didn't appear to be interested. She had moved across to the wall mirror and was doing something to her face.

"Well, you're rapidly embarking on your criminal career, Henry. Why did you say you'd do it?"

"Because this guy knows something about me. It

happened in Chicago. But it was all an accident. I swear it was. You know when a guy has a drink too many—well, you know how it is, Felicity. It wasn't my fault. I just didn't know what was happening. You wouldn't blame me for anything I did in a state like that, would you?"

But Felicity didn't answer. She was absorbed in the mirror. Presently she turned to show her lips crimson, her cheeks vivid with rouge. There was a queer defiance in her attitude.

"How's that, Henry?"

"That's swell, honey. You were too pale before."

Felicity seemed amused, with no pleasure in her amusement.

"You're not exactly a connoisseur in feminine beauty, Henry, I must admit. What were you saying before? I'm sorry I wasn't listening."

Secretly Henry was relieved Felicity hadn't heard his impetuous confession.

"Oh, that's all right. I'm just a good deal bothered about things. But you've got your own troubles. I hate to see you worried, honey. If pitching that guy out of Carstairs would do any good—"

"It wouldn't, Henry. Just forget about him. But it's nice of you to worry. Now if you wouldn't mind going, I've got ever so much to do. And I haven't even got a dress suitable to become a music mistress in. That's funny, isn't it?" Her voice was a little hysterical. "Imagine teaching the piano in the latest model from Chanel! Well, I daresay I can wear a pair of spectacles."

"Felicity, if I can do anything—"

"No, you can't, Henry. Just go."

Considerably perplexed, Henry turned to go, but at that moment there was a knock at the door and the large round face of Mr. Murphy, the landlord, peered in.

"Excusing me, Miss Valentine, there's a telephone call for you."

"Oh, who is it, Mr. Murphy?"

"The gentleman said it was Mr. Lynnford Carstairs speaking."

Felicity said sharply, "Tell him to leave a message. I'm busy."

Mr. Murphy departed. Henry stared.

"I thought you liked that cavalierly guy."

"Now, Henry if you start trying to be funny—"

"I'm not, honey. I'm not!" Henry assured her in injured tones. "I'm just relieved you're not going to run after the fellow. People would talk. They'd say you were after his money."

Felicity frowned, but what she was going to say was prevented by the return of Mr. Murphy.

"He says, Miss Valentine, will you tell him what dress it was you wanted and he'll bring it up."

"Oh, none. Tell him I don't want any. Tell him he can keep my whole wardrobe."

Again Mr. Murphy departed, muttering, "Much good it'd be to him." And Felicity said exasperatedly:

"Henry, are you still here?"

"Why, yes, Felicity! I was just going to ask you—I mean, I don't suppose you've changed your mind about marrying me. I forgot to ask you last night."

He was aware of Felicity's over-bright eyes on

him, of her mouth, with that weary scornful twist, saying:

"Why not? It does seem a pity to always disappoint you. Besides we're both practically destitute. Two destitute people would probably be happier than one. I wonder if that's true. We could probably try, anyway."

Henry gaped. He tried to speak and stuttered.

"Felicity! You don't mean it?"

"At the moment, Henry, I do."

"But, gosh, this is marvelous! You don't think there was something in that drink I had that's making me imagine things. Felicity, you really do mean it?"

"Oh, Henry, your head is thick! Yes, I do mean it." But the next moment she evaded his eager advance. "No, Henry. Don't kiss me now." She smiled with an effort. "You'll spoil my make-up."

Polly sipped her drink and sighed with pleasure.

"Gosh, Lynn, this is a marvelous place. You're someone of importance now."

"Huh! Yes, the villagers seem to think so."

Polly eyed his dark moody face.

"It doesn't seem to amuse you much."

"Well, it's not all amusement, Polly. There's a great deal of responsibility."

Polly put her glass down."

"I'm sorry if I barged in at the wrong moment this morning."

"Oh, that's all right, Polly. You're welcome at any time."

"But it was the wrong moment."

"Well, yes, it wasn't what one would call exactly opportune."

"Lynn, you don't have to be polite to me."

Lynn smiled wearily.

"Am I being too polite? Sorry. Have another drink? What do you think of my mansion?"

Polly refused the drink, sat up straight and said, without hedging:

"Look here, Lynn, I didn't want to come here. I didn't want to barge in on your private life. Honest I didn't. But Mrs. Miggs put my things out in the hall and locked my door and what was I to do? You were the only person I could come to. But if I'm in the way for God's sake say so, and I'll go jump in the sea. Honest, Lynn, I'll do it in any case if you don't tell me what was wrong about me being in that bedroom."

Lynn scowled, drawing his black brows together, then walked about the room and said over his shoulder:

"Polly, do you remember my telling you about a girl I had seen, a—a rather special sort of girl?"

Polly nodded sagely. "I remember."

"Well, she was the girl with me this morning."

Polly gasped.

"Gosh! Oh, gosh, Lynn, I was seven kinds of a fool to throw my arms around your neck."

"You were," Lynn agreed. "Fond as I am of you, Polly, I'd willingly have murdered you this morning."

"Why didn't you?" Polly wailed. "Oh hell! Now I've messed up your life as well as my own."

"And what's more," Lynn said grimly, "it was her room you chose to occupy."

"Her room?"

"She's Felicity Valentine, old Carstairs' niece. She's the girl I'm to marry if I want to stay here."

Polly twisted her hands in distress.

"Well, why don't you phone her, you goof? Phone her and explain."

"I did. This morning. She refused to come to the phone. I've been presented with a lady's wardrobe. A very expensive one, too, but a lot of good it is to me! Anyway, what could I explain? That I'm in the habit of keeping affectionate young ladies in bedrooms?"

"Oh, dear! Lynn, I'm sorry!"

Polly began to sniff, and Lynn said exaperatedly:

"For heaven's sake, don't cry about it! I just can't stand it if you begin to cry. Here, have another drink. I'll have up the Napoleon brandy if you like. No? Well, then, for goodness sake, cheer up. The mischief's done now. Truly, Polly, I'm glad to see you. Don't you worry about what's happened. We'll fix it some way. Now come and we'll see Mrs. Mell about your room."

Polly sniffed miserably.

"You fix it up about the room, Lynn. I think I'll go and have a look around in the garden and cheer myself up."

The garden, however, with its bright borders and shaggy old trees standing over their shadows didn't seem to help much. Polly wandered down a bypath, went through a lych gate and found herself in a narrow lane bordered with hedges of flowering sweet-briar. The scent of the blossoms had a penetrating sweetness. Bees tumbled in and out of them, the sun shone, swallows cut a swift circle against

124

the sky. But Polly noticed nothing. From time to time she sniffed forlornly. Her thoughts ran chiefly on how utterly vile life could be. Perhaps it would be a good idea to take that rash statement of hers seriously and end it all. Then she wouldn't be messing up Lynn's affairs as well as her own any longer. But a thing like that took a terrible lot of courage. Imagine feeling the cold waves crawling over you, seeping into your ears, your nostrils, your mouth, until you were sodden and drowned and dead.

So absorbed was she in that horrifying picture that Polly failed to notice the approach of an extremely large young man. She gave a final loud sob and the young man exclaimed:

"Gosh, you're crying!"

Polly jumped and hastily blew her nose, angry at being discovered.

"That I am," she said tartly. "It's fairly obvious."

But the large young man wasn't in the least rebuffed. He grinned in a friendly way and said:

"Okay, honey, you go right ahead and cry. Don't mind me."

"I will," Polly returned, sobbing into her handkerchief. "You just go and leave me."

"Oh, no, I can't do that. I can't leave you breaking your heart over something that maybe can be fixed up as easy as pie. Now you just tell me the trouble and trust me to find a way out. Say, do you know that last night I landed a big deal and this morning I got engaged to the sweetest kid this side of heaven. Sure, I can fix your trouble for you."

Polly, her sharp mind at work, was glancing

sideways at him out of the corners of her rapidly drying eyes. A Yankee, she reflected. That was as plain as the nose on his face. And what was more, he looked like a wealthy one. You could tell that by the cut and quality of his clothes. Maybe he was one of those millionaire playboys, maybe heaven had taken pity on her despair and had dropped a young and wealthy Yank right in the middle of her path. But wait a minute. He said he had just got engaged. That wasn't so good. Still, these wealthy Yankees didn't take engagements very seriously. He'd still be able to give a girl a good time. And Polly badly wanted a good time now that Lynn was mooning about over someone else. Maybe he'd even take her to Broadway if she was nice enough to him.

"You're quite a guy, aren't you?" she said admiringly. "Bet I can guess where you come from. The States."

"You're right first time. Say, you're cheering up fine, aren't you?"

Polly sniffed and thought it diplomatic to look lugubrious.

"I don't know that I am. I've been in an awful fix. But you wouldn't know what it was like to not own a dime."

"Wouldn't I," cried Henry excitedly. "That's just where you're wrong. That's just what happened to me yesterday. My father cabled to say he'd lost all his dough and would probably have to go on the breadline. But don't get downhearted about that. That's all okay now. I'm on top of the world today."

Polly, whose face had fallen, brightened up again.

"Didn't he lose it after all?"

"Sure he lost it. But you see, I put through a pretty slick deal last night and this morning Felicity said she'd marry me. Gosh, I've been asking her to marry me for weeks."

"Whom did you say?" Polly inquired sharply.

"Felicity. Felicity Valentine. Niece of old Lynn-ford Carstairs. She's lost Carstairs for a year—"

"Wait! Hold on! Is she the girl Lynn Carstairs is supposed to marry under the will?"

"Yes, but she doesn't want to marry him. People would think· she was doing it to get Carstairs, for one thing, and anyway she can't stand the sight of him."

Polly caught Henry's arm.

"Tell me, is that all absolutely true?"

"Sure, it's true. You don't think she'd be marrying me if she wanted this other guy?"

Polly breathed deeply.

"No, that wouldn't make sense. Gosh, you've taken a load off my mind. I'm sorry for Lynn, but it's not my fault after all. It would have happened this way in any case. So I don't need to jump in the sea."

Henry, looking bewildered but generally pleased with himself, said, "There, I said I'd fix it up, didn't I?"

"You did," said Polly, dimpling. Polly's features, after tears, were extremely attractive, and her dimples made Henry stare foolishly. "What's your name?"

"Henry B. Higginsbottom. I'd take it as a favor if you'd call me Henry."

"Mine's Polly Gay. Say, Henry, you've done me an awful lot of good this afternoon. If ever there's anything I can help you about—"

Henry was still staring at that delicious dimple in Polly's small round chin. Of course, her looks couldn't compare with Felicity's, but gosh, she was attractive. And now he came to think of it, she said gosh, too! In fact they got on fine together. Maybe they were twin souls. It would be nice to know somebody who would understand him.

"There's something you can help me with right now. I've got to celebrate my engagement and I can't celebrate by myself. I've been looking all morning for someone to have a drink with me."

"What about Felicity?"

"Oh, she doesn't feel quite up to celebrations. A bit worked up, you know. Girls are queer in some ways. She doesn't seem to think an engagement's worth a celebration, but when you've wanted one like I've wanted this one it's a different matter. Say, Polly, be a sport and come and have a drink with me."

Polly shut her eyes for an instant and had an entrancing imaginary vision of Broadway.

"Okay, Henry," she said airily.

CHAPTER SIX

THE Kitten was suffering from a cold in the head. His small bulbous nose was like a chilblain, his voice was thick and whispering, but sometimes it shot up startlingly into a thin squeak. It was a pity about his cold because it handicapped his eager explanation to Pope about the brilliant plans he had made for getting the diamonds out of England.

"Kiff," he said huskily, "you couldn't have done better yourself this time. I've got the whole thing cut and dried."

Kiffin Pope was in a weary cynical mood. He didn't care about the Kitten's cold. He rather wished he would die of it. The man offended him. His gross unhealthy bulk, his little avid eyes, his shiny nose, the thick peculiarly glutinous sound of his voice filled him with such a powerful disgust that it was only by steady concentration on the thought of the diamonds that he could suffer him in the room at all.

"Have you got the diamonds with you?" he asked.

The Kitten nodded, disappointed that his story was to be delayed, but gloating over the knowledge of all that blinding beauty hidden against his breast.

"Let's have a look at them. No, wait, I'll pull the blinds down and put on the light."

Pope moved softly about the room, drawing the blinds and pulling the heavy curtains across. Out of the corner of his eye he watched the Kitten fumbling inside his shirt and the look of absorbed anticipatory pleasure on his great heavy face. How blindly trusting the man was! Pope had only to take up his revolver and order the Kitten to hand over the jewels. Then the hundred thousand would be all his. The Kitten could go unharmed. He would be too scared to squeal. But no. That business could wait—meanwhile. The Kitten, in spite of his colossal stupidity, was useful. He could do all the work necessary to getting rid of the jewels first.

With the blinds drawn the room was in a soft unnatural gloom. Pope switched on an immensely powerful electric torch. The gleaming iridescent beauty of the diamonds lay in the hollow of the Kitten's two hands. They looked as fine, as pure, as brilliant as stars against the horny flesh of the palms holding them. The Kitten's mouth hung open with foolish reverence.

"Pretty little baubles, aren't they?" he whispered thickly. "Fit for the Queen of Sheba, eh?"

Pope put out his hand to take them. The Kitten's hands closed like a vise.

"No, you don't! No, you don't, Kiff! Hands off!"

Pope's lips were stretched back over his teeth. He was smiling.

"You're a possessive devil, Kit. Think I'm going to run off with them? You don't need to be scared. There's still honor among thieves."

He laughed softly, with some secret satirical mirth, watching the Kitten's face over the sharp incredible brilliance of the gems. Then he became impatient.

"Put them away, Kit, and let's hear your story."

The Kitten carefully replaced the necklace in a little leather bag that hung by a thin leather cord around his neck, and rebuttoned his shirt, patting it in place.

"It's a primitive method of hiding valuables," Pope commented. "One thing about it, a bulge would never be noticed on your figure. Tell me, have you discovered the Laughing Ghost?"

"How you will harp on that ghost business," the Kitten said plaintively. "No, I haven't discovered it. Haven't the faintest idea what is is. What's more, I don't want to know. It's got nothing whatever to do with the business."

Pope scowled.

"If Jensen said it has, it has, definitely. Well, what have you discovered that you're so damned pleased about?"

The Kitten's face worked. He grabbed his handkerchief and sneezed violently into it. His sneeze was a revelation. It shook his whole body. When he could speak his voice had gone up to its ridiculous thin squeak.

"Kiff, do you know what's going on at Carstairs? Smuggling! It's been going on for centuries. Sort of gentleman's game of getting good brandy cheap for adventure. Claus Jensen supplies the stuff. Lands it in the underground passages. There's a cargo-load coming in on the fifteenth. By the *Seagull*. The ship stands out to sea and they row a boat right into the caves. They're full of water when the tide's in."

Pope was listening intently. His eyes held a sparkle of light. "You surprise me, Kit. You've at last discovered something useful. Smuggling, eh? I suspected it. And Jensen will take the diamonds out that way. Well, now, you've got another job, Kit. You've got to find out how to deliver those diamonds."

"But I have, I have!" squeaked the Kitten triumphantly.

"That's where I've done my master stroke, Kiff. Everything's cut and dried."

"Let's hear about it."

The Kitten promptly embarked on an excited narrative of his meeting with Henry Higginsbottom.

"Dumb as they make 'em, Kiff. And I'd loaded him with drink and he was scared stiff. Besides, he badly needs money, and there's this scandal to hang over his head. He sure thinks a lot of that dame. And we're getting the job done dirt cheap. It's only costing a hundred pounds."

Pope was pondering. He said nothing. The Kitten watched him anxiously.

"I've done a good job, haven't I, Kiff?"

Pope passed his hands over his lean, pallid jaw.

"Maybe. Maybe. It might work. If this Yankee is as dumb as he sounds. The night of the fifteenth. I'll get in touch with Jensen and tell him to expect the jewels. Have a drink, Kit. I believe you've earned it this time."

"Sure, I will," the Kitten whispered fervently. "God, I've got a cold! Can't hardly speak. You and me are getting on pretty well together, ain't we, Kiff?"

"By the way, speaking of getting on, how is your friend, the St. Simon cop?"

The Kitten's face fell.

"Now you would mention him and spoil my pleasure. I don't like that guy. He stares at me like as if I'd murdered someone's baby. It's not as if he'd got the faintest reason to stare at me. I've never given him anything to suspect me about. But I'm not worried about him. He's dumber than the Yank." The Kitten's face crumpled up with irrepressible chuckles, tears squeezed out of his little eyes, his body shook with colossal mirth. "Why, do you know, Kiff, I told the Yank the jewels were only worth a thousand and he believed me. He believed me! What do you know about that?"

At six o'clock that evening Lynn strolled into the bar at the *Duck and Drake*. He thought that if he stood with his eye on the door he must see Felicity come down the stairs to dinner, and she surely couldn't refuse to speak to him if he accosted her, although three times she had refused to come to the telephone. But that gigantic young Yankee, more than three parts drunk, was at the counter, and he immediately hailed Lynn with surprising geniality.

"Hi! Come and have a drink with me. Got a li'l celebration." (Henry had already celebrated with Polly, three farmers, and a taxi driver, but he had discovered that unless he stayed drunk that business last night with the fat man, instead of being a slick deal, was an alarming catastrophe.)

"What's the celebration about?" Lynn asked,

his impatience mixed with tolerance. No one had any business to look like such a cheerful ass as this Henry Higginsbottom did. It was utterly ridiculous to be jealous of his friendship with Felicity. As if—

His thoughts were cut off.

"My engagement to Felicity," the young giant announced triumphantly. "Got engaged this morning. She's the sweetest kid—"

Lynn felt himself growing quite cold. He tried to think and couldn't. "My God!" he began violently. "Not Felicity!"

"Yesh. F'licity. I said F'licity, didn't I?"

Henry had difficulty in pronouncing the name now. He said it over two or three times to himself for practice, and Lynn, watching, said, "My God!" again, and just walked out.

At seven o'clock he had dinner with Polly in the lovely dim candlelit dining room. Polly's spirits, always elastic, had risen amazingly, and she chattered without cessation. "Lynn, this place sends shivers down my spine. It's spooky. I'll bet anything there's a ghost."

"Of course there isn't," Lynn said impatiently. "Ghosts went out with Queen Victoria. People are too hard-headed to make good ghosts nowadays." (I wonder what made Felicity do it. Surely she isn't in love with that fool. Surely it wasn't just because Polly was here.)

"That's too bad, Lynn. I'd just adore a real live ghost. Say, Lynn, I met a real Yankee today. Are you listening?"

"Yes." (Maybe she had intended marrying Henry all the time. He'd been hanging around here for long enough. But what girl in her senses, what girl as lovely and fastidious as Felicity—)

"Well, you looked miles away," Polly was saying accusingly. "This guy was pretty decent to me, Lynn. I liked him fine."

"Did you?" (Or was it for his money? He was supposed to have a millionaire father—most Yankees had or thought they had—and now Felicity was practically penniless.)

"Lynn."

"Yes, Polly."

"Did you know Felicity Valentine was engaged?"

"Yes."

"It's tough luck on you, Lynn."

"That's all right, Polly. Don't worry about me."

"I'm mighty glad it wasn't my fault, anyway. Henry told me he'd been asking her to marry him for weeks. Henry's a swell guy, Lynn. You'd like him."

"So you think," said Lynn grimly. "If you don't mind, Polly, I think we might talk about something else. I'm not frightfully interested in Henry Higginsbottom's past, present or future. I was going to the portrait gallery after dinner. Like to come and have a look at my ancestors?"

The lack of electricity was the trouble. Holding a wisp of a candle flame before a painted face that seemed amazingly alive in the wavering light was tiresome and a little eerie. Polly screamed when the bold, black-bearded swaggering, truculent face of Rollo Carstairs leaped out of the darkness, but she gave a little cry of admiration when they came upon the portrait of Lynette Carstairs, for Lynette was small and proud and lovely. Her gown was white and she had a Chinese red shawl draped over her shoulders and Chinese red earrings. The earrings and the shawl would be Rollo's gift to her, Lynn thought. He would want his wife to wear something brave and colorful. But the red suited her amazingly, and her lips, curved upward with an unquenchable gaiety, had the same color. Suddenly Lynn knew whom she was like. The grave dark eyes, the bright hair, the lovely gay lips, were Felicity's. Felicity was startlingly like this tragic lost lady.

"Look, Lynn," Polly was saying. "Here's someone with eyebrows like yours."

Lynn lifted the candle to look up into the lean, dark, youthful face of Rupert Carstairs, slain on Marston Moor. Why, the date of his death was almost identical with the date of Lynette's. Perhaps these two had loved each other. There was a reckless light in Rupert's blue eyes and Lynette was very lovely. But swashbuckling tyrannical Rollo had married Lynette—or perhaps he had been married to her before Rupert knew her—and Rupert had fallen with the King's men on Marston Moor. Poor unhappy children . . . . Were he and Felicity doomed to the same unhappiness? Or were they to break the spell?

It had grown so dark in the gallery that the still-eyed pale faces on the walls were like the bodiless faces of ghosts. In the dipping light they seemed to start and turn. Polly shivered.

"It's spooky here, Lynn. Let's go."

Lynn had turned for a final look at Lynette in her high-waisted gown and bold red shawl. Was it really true that her ghost haunted Carstairs?

"Lynn, listen! There's someone laughing."

Lynn started and listened intently. It was very quiet in the gallery. The stillness seemed to brood. He was just about to tell Polly that she was imagining things when, unmistakably, the sound of light, far-off laughter came to his ears.

Polly shivered again.

"Gosh, it sounds queer from in here. Almost like a ghost."

"Nonsense!" said Lynn sharply. "It's probably one of the maids."

"You don't need to snap at me like that," Polly complained. "I didn't say it was a ghost. Anyway, you told me Carstairs hasn't got a ghost. But all the same it did sound spooky. I don't see how you could hear one of the maids laughing in here, anyway. The kitchen's miles off and these walls are feet thick."

"They could have come to this end of the house. You don't hear laughter unless there's someone to laugh. Anyway, let's get out of here."

Polly agreed with alacrity. But at the door she turned to look back uneasily.

"It's just as if one of those guys in the pictures had laughed at us," she said.

Lynn tried to work at his book that night. He tried to conjure up the picture of a fat, plain little Princess Victoria playing sedately on the lawn outside his window. But the lawn, ashen with moonlight and splashed with alive black shadows, remained disappointingly empty. He couldn't get the memory of that light imagined laughter out of his mind. The gallery was so isolated from the rest of the house. It would have been practically impossible to hear one of the maids. And whatever one could blame Peewee for, he was out of this. Even he, with his versatility, could not laugh like a girl.

At last Lynn put his manuscript away and prepared for bed. It was half-past eleven and he was suddenly overwhelmingly sleepy. But on the verge of sleep he was startled into full consciousness by Polly's screams. In a moment he had leaped out of bed, grabbed his dressing gown and an electric torch, and was out in the passage just as Polly reached his door.

"Lynn!" she gasped in a breathless terrified voice. It's that laughing again! Just through the wall of my room. As loud as loud. God, I'm scared!"

Lynn gripped her arm.

"You're sure, Polly? You weren't having a nightmare?"

"Nightmare! My God, no! I've never heard anything clearer than I heard that noise. Come back to my room and listen. We might hear it again."

There was no doubting Polly's sincerity. Her eyes were wide and dilated, her breath came unevenly, the hand that held the candle trembled so much that fat streams of grease ran down the candlestick. It was obvious she was scared half to death.

Lynn picked up a coat and flung it over her shoulders.

"You might have got a wrap first. The ghost would have let you do that."

"The ghost!" Polly quavered.

"Whatever you heard," said Lynn impatiently, picking up his torch. "Come and let's see what this business is."

But back in Polly's room there was utter silence.

She pointed tremblingly to the wall with the fireplace. It was from there it came, she said. The sound seemed to come right down the chimney.

Lynn focused the light of his torch on the innocent-looking fireplace. The candle, quivering in Polly's hand, shook gigantic shadows about the walls. The foot of the bed, enormous and distorted, leaped across the ceiling. The room was alive with shadows, the silence complete.

Lynn shone his torch up the cavernous mouth of the chimney.

"It's large enough to harbor hobgoblins or several Father Christmases," he said. "But otherwise it's just a chimney."

"It's after one o'clock," Polly said. "So it couldn't have been one of the maids. Do you think there'd be a secret panel anywhere?"

"The house is probably full of them if it lives up to the reputation of old manor houses. But what in high heaven would anyone be doing laughing behind a secret panel? They'd be yelling for help. No, Polly, I think you'd better just forget it and go back to bed—"

The words were scarcely out of his mouth before a faint sound, startlingly near, broke into trills of laughter.

There was nothing startling about the laughter itself. It was high and sweet like that of a girl delightfully amused. The sinister quality was caused by the dead stillness of the house, the shadows in the high room, the fact that the sound came apparently from the depths of a thick wall.

Lynn could not control the shudder that went down his spine. Who had laughed? Someone in the passage? He knew, before he reached the door, that the passage would be empty.

Polly, spilling fat drops of candle grease, ran after him screaming.

"Don't leave me! Lynn, don't leave me!"

The sound of the laughter had gone. The passage, high and dark, was empty of all save shadows. Polly, clutching Lynn's arm, was sinking at the knees.

"Lynn, it's a ghost! I told you there'd be a ghost and you wouldn't believe me! Lynn, let's go back to London. I'd rather starve than be haunted."

"Go back to London, hell!" said Lynn impatiently. "I'm looking for this damn thing. It's not a ghost; somebody's doing it. Polly, you go back to bed and go to sleep. You'll be all right. I'm going to the cellars."

But the prospect of being left alone and of Lynn wandering about damp, haunted cellars was too much for Polly. She began to sob violently.

Lynn said, "Oh, Polly, for heaven's sake! I want to get at this mystery. I'll get Buddy to stay with you, or will you go to Mrs. Mell's room?"

"Is there something the matter?" came a bland deferential voice behind them.

Polly's sob ended abruptly in a shriek, and Lynn swung around to see Peewee, fully clothed, a lighted candle in his hand, his face as composed and guileless as ever, behind them.

For once Lynn was thoroughly glad to see him.

"Something wrong!" he exclaimed. "I'll say there is. If you can cure a woman of hysterics you shall have a bottle of the Napoleon."

"If we were to arrive at the cause of the hysterics, sir—"

Polly pointed a trembling finger at Lynn.

"He's going down to the cellars and there's a ghost!" she got out, between sobs.

Peewee's round face wrinkled earnestly.

"I wouldn't go down to the cellars now, sir. The tide's in and half the passages will be under water. Have you been hearing the ghost, sir?"

"Ghost be damned!" said Lynn angrily. "I'm going to get to the bottom of this even if I have to risk getting drowned in a couple of inches of sea-water. Give Polly some brandy or something. I'll take Buddy with me."

But Lynn, for all his determination, got no farther than the end of the passage, for at that moment shrieks filled the air, and Mrs. Mell, her voluminous night attire floating behind her, came flying toward him. One hand clutched her garments together, the other a bottle of smelling salts.

"It's the ghost!" she was shrieking. "Just through the wall of my room. I heard it! Help me, somebody, quick! I'm going to faint!"

"For heaven's sake, you can't faint now!" Lynn protested. "We've got to find this ghost."

Mrs. Mell rolled her eyes.

"But I always faint!" she stated plaintively, and collapsed into Lynn's arms.

Peewee and Polly came to his assistance at once. They lowered the prostrate woman to the floor and applied her own smelling salts. Peewee expertly felt her heart and said that she'd be better in a minute or two. She invariably had these turns if she heard the ghost. His expression was calm and benign, but

Lynn could have sworn he was laughing.

Polly, still sobbing in little hiccups, knelt over Mrs. Mell, who was beginning to stir. Presently her eyes opened and with Polly's assistance she struggled to a sitting position.

"I'm better now," she quavered. "I must have fainted. I always do when I hear the ghost."

"Yes," said Lynn grimly. "We've already heard that."

"Lynn, don't bully her!" Polly said indignantly. "She's scared. We're both scared to death."

"I should think, sir, it wouldn't be any use going down in the cellars now," came Peewee's deferential voice. "You never hear the ghost for more than a few minutes, and now that it's gone there'd be nothing to guide you."

Lynn looked from the two dishevelled women shaking in each other's arms to the round unperturbed face of Peewee. The silence in the house was intense. There was no hint that there had ever been eerie laughter from the walls.

"I suppose you're right," he said reluctantly. "But I'll search those passages tomorrow if the whole staff faints on my hands."

It wasn't until he got back to bed, with Buddy curled unadmonished on his feet, that he began to wonder how Peewee had arrived just at the critical moment. How the devil had he? His room was in the servants' wing. He couldn't possibly have heard any disturbance. Yet there he had been, fully dressed, undisturbed and deferential, but with that infernal twinkle in his eyes. The man was up to something.

Things were more composed in the morning. Polly

had decided not to rush wildly back to London. She had spent the remainder of the night in Mrs. Mell's room, during which time she had regaled that lady with a pathetic tale of her past vicissitudes until they were both so wrought up with the thought of Polly's unrecognized genius that they had forgotten the ghost. And then, just before Polly dropped asleep in the early dawn, the thought of Henry and the necessity for cultivating his acquaintance had come to her, and she had realized more fully what a fool she would be to rush away from Carstairs and all her wonderful opportunities simply because someone had laughed in the dead of night.

Mrs. Mell, too, though a little haggard, was her usual self, and Peewee, serving breakfast in the dining-room, was as bland as ever. It seemed as if Lynn were the only one who was taking the episodes of the night seriously. He was determined not to dismiss the affair as a nightmare, but to search the underground passages that morning, and discover the identity of the ghost.

Immediately after breakfast Felicity telephoned. Lynn knew, because he heard Mrs. Mell speaking to her. The conversation at first was unintelligible.

"No, we put her in the west wing. Oh, no, of course not in your room. Although she seems quite a nice young person. She was most kind to me last night when we heard the ghost. I fainted, of course. Yes . . . . Yes, I always do . . . . Which one did you say? The navy blue silk? With the white collar? Well, I wouldn't be sure. I'm never one at remembering clothes."

By this time Lynn, having gathered to whom Mrs. Mell was speaking, had rushed into the hall and unceremoniously taken the receiver out of her hand.

"Felicity!" he called wrathfully. "What the devil do you mean by getting engaged to that dumb Yankee?"

"Yes, I know, I'm an impertinent usurper without any morals," Lynn went on, defeating that chilling silence. "But that's no reason why you should rush off and get engaged to Higginsbottom. It doesn't make sense. I mean, apart from me, there are thousands of more intelligent men—"

He would hardly have recognized Felicity's voice, it was so cold, so much the great lady.

"You flatter yourself, Lynn. I didn't rush into this engagement. I've been thinking about it for weeks. Now if you'll let me speak to Mrs. Mell again—"

"Well, I'm going down in the dungeon to look for the ghost, today," Lynn shouted. "If I get lost you can have Carstairs. You can come and sing over my grave."

It was a foolish thing to say. It didn't even make sense, for it was obvious that if he did get lost he would have no visible grave to be sung over. But he had to say something violent to cool his temper. Felicity, lovely Felicity, has inherited a streak of her grandfather's eccentricity. Anyhow, he would solve the mystery about the Laughing Ghost and then simply walk out of Carstairs if he couldn't stand it. Felicity could have it as well as her dumb Yankee.

Peewee and Buddy went down to the cellars with Lynn. Peewee knew his way about the main passages, he said, but he strongly advised Lynn against exploring any of the smaller ones.

"The place is like a honeycomb, sir. You could get lost as quick as turn around. Besides, the tide comes up."

"How high does it come?" Lynn asked, flashing his torch on the rocky, perpetually damp walls.

"As high as a man's head in some of the caves," said Peewee, his voice sounding hollow and queerly eerie in the echoing passage. "Particularly in Rollo Carstairs' cave. I'll show you that one, sir. It's by way of being historic."

"Confound you, Peewee, don't develop into the perfect guide. You'll be showing me next where Lynette Carstairs scratched her last prayer."

"She probably did that, too, sir, but nobody's found it. I should say if you found it you'd find her bones."

Despite himself, Lynn experienced a cold sensation. The place was overwhelmingly gloomy, with the high jagged walls rising into darkness, the clammy sea wind coming from no recognizable quarter, the squeak and flutter of a disturbed bat, somewhere the drip of water. He felt glad for Peewee's solid little figure stepping delicately over the wet stones ahead of him, smug old hypocrite that the man was. He felt glad, too, that he hadn't come rushing down here in the dead of night with that sweet uncanny laughter still in his ears. The place would have been terrifying.

The faint little sea breeze was becoming stronger.

"Say, I'll bet they used this passage for smuggling once," Lynn exclaimed.

Peewee turned a gloomy face.

"I'm afraid, sir, it wouldn't do to inquire too

closely into the activities of your forebears."

"But, hang it, man, I don't think smuggling's a crime. It's a dashed good adventure."

For a moment it seemed, incredibly, that a flash of approval passed over Peewee's face, then it subsided into gloom.

"His Majesty's Government doesn't think that, sir. We're just coming to Rollo Carstairs' cave now. Mind that overhanging rock. You'll have to stoop. In here, sir."

Buddy dashed in ahead to sniff around the damp walls. In a way Lynn was glad of his lighthearted presence, for the place was morbid. Moisture, gleaming in the light of his torch, ran down the walls, there were seawater pools in the hollows of the floor, and a horrible clammy smell that seemed somehow to suggest death.

Peewee flashed his torch on the solid rafter across the roof.

"Look at the hooks, sir," he whispered. "Where Rollo Carstairs hanged three men at once."

Lynn gazed fascinated at the three blackened hooks embedded in the rafter. It almost seemed, as the shadows moved, that three shadowy figures swung lightly, as if they were made of paper or hollow clothes. It was indescribably horrifying. Even Buddy, sensing the atmosphere, began to whimper.

"We're just a few yards from the sea, sir," Peewee said. "You can get a breath of fresh air in a minute."

It was true, for through the opening of the cave, where the passage turned, there was a glimpse of white sunlit seashore. The air already was sweeter, and in a moment Buddy was racing on his stubby legs for the sea.

Lynn breathed deeply, getting the clammy air out of his lungs.

"I'll just go for a stroll along the beach, Peewee. You go up to the house again. I'll follow you presently."

"Yes, sir. But you won't get lost? You'll stick to the main passage?"

"Of course I'll stick to it. I've no desire to get lost in this foul place."

"Because if you were to get lost, sir, I couldn't guarantee anyone ever finding you, or even hearing you."

"Damn it, man!" Lynn exclaimed, impatient with Peewee's air of mystery. Was he really afraid of Lynn getting lost or was there something he didn't want discovered? "Don't you credit me with any sense of direction? I won't lose myself."

Buddy, ears askew, chased seagulls with more zeal than success while Lynn tried to scratch likenesses of Felicity in the sand, and imagined this peaceful curve of beach on a moonless night a century or so ago, when the smugglers, dark and furtive, bent over their oars as they guided their boat to the caves. It was difficult to imagine a scene like that out in the brilliant sunshine, but when he was back in the gloom of the caves again it might have been any period in the world's age. One might step out on to the beach, Lynn thought fantastically, and see Drake's galleons moored across the bay, or a fleet of Viking ships, highpowered and hostile. Or one might turn that rocky doorway into Rollo Carstairs' cave and see those dreadful light-as-paper men swinging from the three hooks. Here nothing marked the passing of the years. Time stood still. One might find Lynette Carstairs' lost bones, or herself in the flesh, lovely and lost and frightened.

But there Lynn had to take a pull on himself. It was foolish to let his imagination run away with him when he still had the return journey to make down a hundred yards or so of dark bat-haunted passage. If he wanted to solve the mystery of the ghost he would have to go at it in a cold practical manner, and not let his too elastic imagination see a form in every shadow or he would be in a state of neurosis in no time at all.

As Peewee had instructed him, he would stick to the main passage to prevent the possibility of getting lost, but he would examine the entrances to the several side passages he had noticed on his way down. The next time he came he would adopt the old method of a ball of string unravelled as he went so that he could search some of those mysterious byways without fear of getting lost.

This practical forethought was all very well, but Lynn hadn't anticipated Buddy's reactions. For half-way back, as he was in the act of focusing his torch on the entrance to a passage that ran at right angles to the main one, a disturbed bat fluttered in the darkness and Buddy went after it in pursuit.

Lynn didn't notice him go, and wasn't even aware of his absence until, in the distance, there came a short inquiring bark, followed by another, more imperative. Lynn started up in some dismay. Where had the dog gone?

"Buddy!" he yelled. "Buddy, come back!"

His voice echoed eerily through the caverns.

"Come back!" he heard the frail mocking answer. Buddy barked again, from farther away. Lynn put his fingers between his lips and whistled, but the whistle came back, too, on a ghostly note, and Buddy's answering bark ended in a whimper. The next time Lynn whistled, he howled. Lynn could picture the little beggar so well, with his drooping head and dark tearful eyes. He'd have to go after him. He couldn't be far and this passage seemed simple enough to follow. One couldn't get lost walking around a corner or two.

Lynn was convinced it was four corners he turned before an ecstatic small dog bounded out of the shadows at him. But when he retraced his steps, the four corners seemed to take him nowhere near the main passage. Indeed, he seemed to be farther away, he was forced to admit, for instead of being damp with sea-water, the walls were quite dry and his footsteps kicked up a little mist of dust. Where was he then? Lynn began to be conscious of panic. Surely he could not have lost himself as easily as that. He found himself mopping his brow, and desisted hastily. This wouldn't do. He mustn't get panicky. He would set out to retrace his steps with the utmost care, watching for any sign of growing dampness on the walls which would indicate that he was near the main passage.

An hour later, Buddy, covered from head to heels in the yellowish dust, crouched down on his forepaws and whimpered to be carried. Lynn looked down at him wrathfully.

"You got us into this mess," he said, "so I'm damned if I'll carry you!"

But nevertheless he tucked the dusty dejected animal under his arm and plodded on. The beam of his torch shone on cavern after cavern, dark and overwhelmingly silent. Lynn turned the forty-seventh corner and the only difference it had from the other forty-six was that he fancied he could hear the sound of the sea.

He had long since given up all hope of finding his way back to the main passage. The only thing to do now was to find some opening on to the beach. Otherwise . . . Lynn had been valiantly fighting off reflection of all those things "otherwise" might mean.

He was forcing himself to calculate, with exact accuracy, how many miles one could walk in a couple of hours and how far he must have walked already when the light of his torch shone on a massive oak studden door hung on rusty hinges in the roughly-hewn rock and standing slightly ajar.

What discovery was this? Exhausted and more desperate than he cared to think about, Lynn's heart beat so rapidly that he could scarcely breathe. With fantastic thoughts as to hidden smuggled hoards—it must be something valuable to require so stout a door—he tiptoed forward and entered the chamber.

Or was it a dungeon? That was what it appeared to be, for all it contained was a rough wooden chair and table, and a wooden plank that may have been a bed. Otherwise there was nothing at all save that clinging yellow dust his feet had stirred, and a couple of shiny black beetles scuttling down the table leg and across the floor.

Lynn could have wept with disappointment. To have expected a pirate hoard or at least a way of escape, and then to find nothing but an empty prison was too much to bear. Apparently one of the Carstairs had used this place for shutting his enemies out of sight and sound. Perhaps old Rollo—Simultaneously with that thought Lynn's torch flashed on a mark scraped in the wall, a rough cross, the horizontal bar too high up, almost obliterated, and beneath it some faint lines that might have been initials. Carefully he blew the dust out of the crevices and studied the marks. *"The Lord is my refuge and . . ."* His heart almost stood still for beneath the unfinished text was the name *Lynette Carstairs.*

Suddenly Lynn knew. This was her dungeon where old Rollo had imprisoned her. This was where she had endured solitary confinement for six long weeks, until at last she had escaped by means undiscovered to this day; where, in her loneliness and desperation, she had cut the rough cross in the wall, the gloom so intense that she could not see to shape it perfectly.

With the knowledge, horror swept over Lynn. He could almost see that despairing little figure, once as lovely and gay as Felicity, kneeling before the cross she could not even discern in the darkness.

"Oh, my God!" he whispered, then gripped Buddy tightly beneath his arm and said urgently, "We've got to get out of here, old man. And quickly. Or we're done for!"

Another hour passed, an hour of stumbling down the dark interminable passages, struggling against the horrors that beset him, particularly the one that Death, a bulky tremendous shadow with the bold tyrannical face of Rollo Carstairs, was just behind him. All one's life Death strolled behind one, but sometimes he grew impatient, took a long stride, and caught up . . . .

And then suddenly, haggard, dusty, dripping with sweat, Lynn came upon a passage that was damp and smelled of the sea. Its walls were not of rock but of stone, built by man, and immediately before him was a flight of steps such as ran down the cellars. At the top of the steps was a door with a catch that would surely slide the door open.

Lynn didn't dare to suppose that the catch wouldn't work. He wouldn't have had the strength with which to climb the stairs if he had. Clutching an impatient and whimpering Buddy beneath his arm, he struggled to the top and pulled the catch. The door slid back easily on oiled hinges. There was some tapestry to push aside and then Lynn, grimy, dishevelled, covered from head to foot with yellow dust, and with an even grimier dog in his arms, stumbled into one of the Carstairs' bedrooms.

And in the center of the room stood Peewee, with Felicity crying broken-heartedly in his arms!

They sprang apart at once, Peewee for once looking abashed, his stiff light hair seeming to stand more stiffly over his head; Felicity, her mouth open in an arrested sob, staring with lovely wet eyes.

Lynn dropped Buddy to the floor.

Felicity gave a little inarticulate cry, took a step toward him, then turned and ran out of the room. Lynn made to follow her, but suddenly the power seemed to melt out of his legs. He got only as far as stumbling to a chair where he collapsed, the brilliant daylight in the room blinding him.

"Where have you been, sir?" came Peewee's voice from a long way off. "We have been very anxious about you—very anxious indeed. As for that door you came through, sir, I had absolutely no idea of its existence. I can't imagine—"

"Why you forgot to lock it," Lynn finished wearily. "But never mind the door just now. Never mind me. What was the meaning of that perfectly disgraceful scene a minute ago?"

"Well, sir—" Lynn couldn't tell whether Peewee's hesitation and embarrassment were real or simulated. The fellow was such a guileless rouge you never could tell with him. "Miss Valentine was a little upset. A purely personal matter sir. I've known her since childhood. We're old friends separated in social standing, so to speak. Crying is a common occurrence among females, if I may say so, sir. Shall I get you a drink?"

Lynn signaled him back from the door.

"No, no!" he said irritably. "How often girls cry isn't the point. The point is, if she must cry in somebody's arms, hasn't Henry Higginsbottom got a prefectly good pair?"

CHAPTER SEVEN

A HOT BATH, a brandy and two hours' rest restored
Lynn to his normal health and composure after his
alarming experience. The same treatment, with the
exception of the brandy, did the same for Buddy,
although Buddy had not the agony of an unhappy
love affair on his mind, and was therefore more
exuberant.

As for the scene in the bedroom that Lynn had so
unexpectedly stumbled on, a further cross-examina-
tion of Peewee had elicited no more information
as the cause of Felicity's grief than that she was
fretting about being away from Carstairs. She loved
the place so deeply. "She's that sort of person, sir,"
Peewee had said. "Places mean more to her than
people, often." Like himself, Lynn thought. It was
hard to reflect that yesterday that knowledge would
have filled him with great delight. Now it only
accentuated his loss. It was harder still to realize
that he was responsible for keeping her from her
home. He almost felt like packing up and going
straight back to London. But there were too many
things here that had caught him.

For Polly's sake, Lynn assumed cheerfulness at dinner, and discussed with her what should be done about her future.

"Not that I'm anxious to get rid of you," he assured her. "I like having you about. But it's for your own good. The longer you're out of circulation, the quicker they're all going to forget you. Supposing I lend you twenty pounds—I've got a hundred ready cash to work on—and you go back to London and try your luck. Get a new hat or two. Look prosperous. It's surprising what an effect that has on the mass mind. If there's nothing doing you can come back."

Polly cupped her chin in her hands. Her round face behind the candle flames looked little and earnest.

"That's mighty good of you, Lynn. That's the sort of thing I'd have known you'd do. But if you wouldn't object to my company I'd like to stay here a few days longer. I feel as if I can't walk out on you now and leave you to the ghost and everything."

Lynn was surprised.

"But I thought last night when we heard the ghost you were ready to walk back to London."

"I was, too," Polly confessed. "But I'm not so scared about that now. Mrs. Mell's fixed a bed for me in the room next to hers—I'd hate to sleep in that great room you had me put in again—and I feel that if you can stick it, so can I. Besides—there's something else, Lynn."

"What's that?" Lynn encouraged, for suddenly Polly was looking unusually self-conscious.

"It's that Yankee guy I met. He said he was broke, but somehow I don't believe him. I mean, a Yankee can be broke one day and rolling the next. And anyway, if he can get engaged to an expensive-looking girl like Felicity Valentine—Sorry, Lynn, I didn't mean to tread on your toes."

"You didn't," said Lynn shortly. "And if you're interested, Henry Higginsbottom's got a millionaire father."

"I know. But he told me his father had lost all his money in some smash. But then last night he'd put through some slick deal—you know what Yankees are for slick deals. It's probably almost as slick as you inheriting an earldom. So I guess he's a millionaire again by now."

"I guess he is," Lynn said gloomily. "But what's all this got to do with what?"

"With me staying here," Polly explained, fidgeting with her dessert spoon. "Well, you see, I'd kind of like to get to know him better. A millionaire Yankee can get you on Broadway as quick as a wink. I mean, a girl would be a fool to turn down a good opportunity like this."

"She certainly would," Lynn agreed. "But I don't quite see where or how the opportunity comes in."

Polly's face fell.

"No. I'm not so sure either. I didn't see him all day today although I was down in the village twice. I only saw a fat guy with a ruby I'd give my eyes for on his finger. But you can do something about it, Lynn."

"I can?"

Polly leaned forward, her round little face alight with eagerness.

"I was talking to Mrs. Mell this morning, and she says the Carstairs always held a ball here once a year. A period ball that absolutely everyone came to. You know, in the big ballroom, with dozens of candles, and everybody in hoops and knee breeches and things."

"Well, what about it?"

"I thought you might do the same. I thought you might hold it right away, as a sort of welcome home stunt. Only you'd be doing the welcoming yourself. I'd be Nell Gwynne or somebody."

Lynn hesitated. His ready imagination showed him the gleam of the paneling, the sweep of stiffened skirts, the movement of a fan, the sweet sedate music, all in the dipping candlelight . . .

"Yes," he said slowly. "It might be an idea. But what's this got to do with Henry Higginsbottom?"

"Well, you see," said Polly eagerly, "you'd have to ask Felicity Valentine, and you couldn't ask her without her fianceé, and then, well, maybe I'd get to know him better. . . ."

After dinner Lynn lighted a cigarette and strolled out on the terrace. The moon had risen, and the shadows, even of the smallest shrubs, were long and narrow. A faint silvering of moonlight lay over the ornamental lake, the air was elusively scented. The quiet was bewildering. It was dreamlike and exquisite.

A background like this, that was both beautiful and secure, behind one, thought Lynn, was the first step toward heaven. Or perhaps the second. The first was even more important. (*Felicity*, his heart ached.) But it was strange that the serene graciousness of this old house and the moon-drenched garden hid all the dark terror and despair of those underground passages. If ever he came to possess Carstairs completely he would have all those tortuous passages blocked up. No one should ever risk losing his life there again. And perhaps no one would ever hear the ghost again.

But there Lynn sighed. It was no use planning things like that, for unless Felicity came to love him he would never own Carstairs. He would never marry her except with her full love. For himself, the first ecstatic love had changed. It had grown deep and desperate and enduring. He had too much imagination for self-conceit or false heroics, but he knew the way he loved Felicity was the way men loved women they died for.

Still, there it was. Felicity, with her inheritance of Carstairs' recklessness, had got herself engaged to Henry Higginsbottom and he, like a fool, could not control his wayward temper when he spoke to her, so that the breach had widened. Supposing it widened too much to cross! There was a good deal of foolish pride as well as recklessness in a Carstairs . . . .

Lynn sighed again and thought of Polly's suggestion to hold a ball. That was certainly a good idea. Mrs. Mell would be able to tell him all of the people he should invite, and Felicity would be bound to come. She couldn't refuse . . . .

Here Lynn's reflections broke off abruptly, for suddenly, across the garden, through the oaks that bordered the drive, he saw someone moving. Someone in white. A girl. Going toward the stables.

Felicity! In the white dress she had worn to dinner last night, and then down to the *Duck and Drake.* Lynn could have bet the last penny of his hundred pounds on that. He whistled soundlessly, crushed out his cigarette butt, and ran down the steps and across the garden.

From the gate leading to the drive he could see the glimmer of her white dress, her hair as black as night in the moonlight. She carried a cloak over her arm and she was hurrying. Lynn followed her to the end of the drive and then stood beneath the shadow of a tree watching her cross the yard. She went straight for the garage where the Packard was housed, opened the doors and disappeared inside. Presently there was the sound of an engine starting. A few moments later the garage was illumined with the car's headlights, and the car itself slid quietly out into the yard, turned beneath Felicity's expert manipulation, and headed for the drive.

Where was she going? Lynn waited until the car had passed him, then tore for the other garage. If he was not mistaken, Henry's Bentley, repaired after the accident, would be there. It was. Lynn jumped in, started the engine, switched on the lights, backed out, and turned in pursuit of Felicity before her car's headlights had vanished.

Lynn knew his capabilities as a driver. They were what had got him his job with Joe Rogers. But he had seldom driven down a main highway for fifty miles with the speedometer needle flickering between seventy and eighty all the way. How that girl could drive! By the time she finally slowed down and pulled the Packard into the side of the road, Lynn was in a state divided between admiration for her skill and fury at her recklessness. He pulled the Bentley up behind her car and got out to go to the driver's seat where she sat waiting for him.

Her hair was tossed all over her head. It made her face look small and irresponsible and rather deliciously young. But she wasn't smiling. Neither was Lynn.

"What in heaven's name are you up to?" he demanded agitatedly. "Driving at that breakneck speed?"

"It's a way I have of calming my nerves," Felicity told him gravely.

Lynn stared.

"Do you mean to say you drive in that suicidal way just when it suits your mood?"

She nodded.

"Always. When things are"—she hesitated—"trying. Like the day Henry and I had the race."

"Were things trying then?" Lynn couldn't refrain from asking.

"Well—perhaps boring is a better word."

"What were they tonight?"

She looked at him with her ironic eyes.

"Boring—just the same as then. By the way, where are you going—at that suicidal pace?"

"Following you," said Lynn bluntly.

She didn't look in the least disconcerted, not even angry. Lynn felt baffled. He thought he would have preferred her anger to this studied irony. Yet she was so achingly lovely. She was so reckless and mad-headed he could throttle her, yet she was so sweet.

"You drive well, Lynn. No wonder you were a success as a motor mechanic. Well, I've had my airing so I'll be getting along home. Good night."

Lynn matched her coolness with his own, and

opening the door of the Packard climbed in beside her.

"Henry can collect his bus in the morning," he said. "I'll come with you."

Felicity released the clutch. Lynn thought he detected a controlled agitation in her movement.

"I didn't hear me asking you," she observed.

"No, actually you didn't ask me. But after all, since this is virtually my car . . . Well, for this year, anyway. I mean, I wouldn't like you to smash it up."

"I'm more likely to smash it up with you beside me."

Lynn grinned. Now she was losing her temper and becoming human.

"Things I want to talk to you about, Felicity," he said quietly. "You will answer, won't you?"

He saw her bite her lip, but something of the stubbornness went out of her face.

"I don't see why you must chase me fifty miles to ask me questions."

"Well, hang it all, I can't get hold of you any other way."

"I'm busy," Felicity murmured. "I've got two pupils already. Their names are Judith and Emily and they're the only daughters of Mrs. Briggs, the dressmaker. They're sweet, but their ear for music is deplorable."

Suddenly Lynn could see her guiding the fat unskillful little fingers over the piano keys, her face sweet, patient, absorbed as the children's. The vision was unwanted and disturbing. It made it difficult to keep that aloofness in his voice.

"I'm glad about that," he said sincerely. "But

it makes me feel rotten idling in luxury while you slave."

"I'm not slaving. I'm having fun. And exploring the passages under Carstairs isn't exactly idling. Nor fun—when you get lost."

"That's what I wanted to ask you about," Lynn began eagerly. "Were you crying today because you were generally unhappy about things—or because I was lost?"

It was a conceited assumption, of course, to suppose she would cry because he was lost. But Lynn had had it all afternoon, and had been rather desperately anxious to know. He watched her, waiting for her answer.

"Actually," she said in her little bright voice, "it was about something purely personal. Do I disillusion you?"

She was deliberately mocking him. Lynn felt his temper rising.

"Well, the next time you want to cry about something purely personal don't choose my butler's arms to do it in. Hasn't Henry got a good strong pair?"

"They're strong enough, certainly. They're suitable for quite a lot of purposes. But honestly, Lynn, they're not the sort of arms a girl would want to cry in. Not like yours."

Lynn flushed and scowled.

"You don't need to be subtle. I was coming to the explanation about Polly."

Felicity said nothing. Lynn noticed that her foot had gone down on the accelerator and that the hedges were slipping past faster and faster.

"Polly's a nice kid," said Lynn. "She's been my best friend for a year. She's stood by me when I've been out of a job and I'm standing by her now when she's out of one. That's absolutely the only obligation I have to her. Hell!" he said impatiently. "I don't see why I should have to make all this explanation to you."

"I don't either," said Felicity calmly. "There's really no necessity. Particularly since I'm marrying Henry, anyway."

"Why?" asked Lynn bluntly. "For his money?"

"Aren't you being rather personal?"

"Yes," said Lynn gloomily. "I suppose I am. But there's a dickens of a lot I've got to find out. What the ghost is, where it is, how I can be reconciled to it, how much Peewee knows and what he's up to. What Henry's slick deal that he told Polly about is, why you're marrying him, why you chose my butler's arms to cry in. It's a wonder I know who I am myself."

Felicity chuckled faintly to herself and slowing down swung the car off the main road onto a little grassy track that ran down to the cliff's edge. There she stopped and the ocean, brilliant, colorless, curved like a bowl against the sky, lay before them. A little wind, light as naked feet, ran through the grass, the low crash and drag of waves on shingle came up from the beach.

"We're just beyond Carstairs," Felicity said. "How high the stars are tonight. Sometimes when I've been on the beach they've been so low you'd think you could just climb to the top of the cliffs and reach them."

Lynn gazed moodily at her. What a complex piece of mechanism a human being was. Here was Felicity, twenty minutes ago so hot and restless she had to risk her life to calm her nerves, and now she was in that mood of dreamy philosophy necessary to meditation on the stars. She had thrust her untidy hair behind her ears so that her profile had a clear sharp look. There was a shadow in the little hollow at ˉher throat. She was sitting very still. Lynn wanted so much to kiss her that his body ached. Of course that would be the end of everything, but—

His thoughts broke off as she began to say softly:

> ". . . The world which seems
> To lie before us like a land of dreams,
> So various, so beautiful, so new . . ."

She paused. Lynn finished in a quiet, certain voice,

> "Hath really neither joy, nor love, nor light,
> Nor certitude, nor peace, nor help for pain . . . ."

"Uncle's favorite poem," said Felicity. "We said it the night he died. I think of it when I come here."

She started the engine and shifted over from the driver's seat.

"Drop me at the *Duck and Drake*, would you, Lynn, and then take the car home."

The moment for kissing her had gone. And she had gone so far away, too. As far as death. It was as if old Lynnford Carstairs, who had brought them together, yet sat between them.

Lynn drove in silence through the sleepy village.

The houses had soft humpy shadows, here and there a lighted window gleamed, yellow and comfortable. The chimneys and rooftops made angular crooked outlines against the sky. The street was white with moonlight. It was like a village in a fairy tale, Lynn thought. Everything since he had come here had been like a fairy tale, with macabre parts to accentuate the lovely peaceful ones—dining with Felicity in the candlelit drawing room, walking with her on the terrace while darkness settled over the garden, driving down the sun-spattered drive with Felicity beside him in the carriage, with her tonight in this village grown quaint and old in the moonlight . . . .

"Why did you take me to your favorite place tonight?" he asked.

Lynn stopped the car before the *Duck and Drake* and went around to open the door for Felicity.

There was a sudden look of pleasure, lovely as a flash of sunlight, on her face. Then it had gone, and, gathering up her skirts to step out of the car, she said in a self-possessed voice:

"I thought you'd know it was my favorite place. I just wondered if you were the sort of person one could sit and look at the sea with."

"Was I?" Lynn asked eagerly.

She stepped out of the car, saying in a low voice:

"It doesn't really matter. Good night, Lynn."

"Then can we go again?"

She had opened the door and stood in the light streaming out across the pathway. The brightness gave her eyes and her blown hair and her long white dress a kind of luminous glow. It was true, she was the lovely lady out of an old lost tale.

"I'm afraid not, Lynn. The next time I'll probably be going with Henry."

The anti-climax was so great that Lynn could have wept. He could think of a dozen things to say, but the only one that came to his tongue was the childish retort:

"I'll bet he doesn't know *Dover Beach*."

But at that precise moment Henry, very large and red, also a little drunk, appeared in the hall.

"Hello, Felicity. I've been looking for you. Want you to meet a pal of mine. He's arrived here unexpectedly. Knew me when I was in—huh, when I was a kid." He stared hazily at Lynn. "That your chauffeur? Well, tell the fellow to go!"

It was only two weeks until the date the *Seagull* called, and the Kitten decided there was no better place in which to spend it than St. Simon. It was a peaceable little village. No one would dream of looking for the thief of the Windermere necklace in a one-eyed town where doves and church bells made more noise than the traffic. The sea air would be good for his cold, and he would be out of reach of Kiffin Pope. Pope was a clever guy, but he sent shivers down the Kitten's spine. Sort of devilish, he was. Probably more than a little crazy. The Kitten was determined that after this business was over he would never give Pope another opening to blackmail him.

So the Kitten took a room at the *Duck and Drake* and settled in. At first everything promised well. The room was comfortable, the liquor good, his cold improved and he had the satisfaction of seeing that big Yankee, Henry Higginsbottom, wince every time they encountered one another. Just as he did when Pope fixed his fish-like gray stare on him. Maybe there was someone of even lesser importance who winced when Henry appeared, but short of a worm it would be hard to imagine who that would be.

But the Kitten's dream of peace at St. Simon was short-lived. He knew he was a pretty large person, but he didn't take up so much of the village when he went out that he couldn't get out of sight of that flat-faced St. Simon cop. It didn't take him long to discover that wherever he went Constable Diver, with painstaking unobtrusiveness, appeared on the horizon. His gentle little ambles in the copse by the river, his strolls through the village on such errands as buying tobacco and the daily newspaper, his basks in the sun outside the *Duck and Drake*, were all disturbed and ruined by the proximity of that fool cop. If it wasn't that the fellow looked so dumb the Kitten would have imagined he was being shadowed. The whole thing worried him, and he finally decided that the best way was to take the bold course and make friends.

So the next time he sat on his favorite seat outside the *Duck and Drake* he watched, through half-closed eyelids, the wary approach of Constable Diver. The man had his eyes glued on the Kitten's chest, and there was that familiar suspicious look in them, as if the Kitten had murdered someone's child, and around his neck hung the fatal dagger.

Despite his efforts to remain undisturbed, the Kitten felt a cold sweat breaking out on his forehead. He was convinced the little bag containing the diamonds was making a bulge as large as an ostrich's egg through his shirt and massive tweed jacket. Supposing the fellow produced a warrant to search his person. . . . Involuntarily his hand went to his chest, and he sat up in haste, coughing, explosively.

"Oh, good day, good day!" he said genially, as if had just become aware of the cop's presence. "Nice day."

Constable Diver grunted. His eyes were fixed so absorbedly on the Kitten's chest that it seemed he couldn't distract his attention even by so simple an act as uttering a word.

"Got a terrible cold," the Kitten said wheezily. "Thought a spot of sunshine might help it. Wrapped up in red flannel," he said, rubbing his hand over his chest. "Makes me seem a mite bulky."

That was a master stroke, he reflected, exuding self admiration. Cop looking for fatal knife, or maybe—yes, just fantastically maybe a hundred thousand pound string of diamonds, and all he found was a strip of red flannel. That cold of his was proving a godsend, damned if it wasn't.

"Have a drink with me," he invited cordially. "Liquor's not bad for a country pub. My name's Jenkins. Ernest Jenkins." (Incredibly enough that was the Kitten's name, but very few people, with the exception of Scotland Yard and the officials at Dartmoor, knew it. Yet, also incredibly, it suited him. If he hadn't been cursed with those amazingly slick fingers he could have been the average man's dream of the perfect publican.)

The Constable shook his head and said coldly:

"Can't drink on duty, Mr. Jenkins."

In spite of the fictitional red flannel his eyes remained fastened on the Kitten's chest. The Kitten grew restive, then impatient. Finally he lost his temper.

"Well, is there anything wrong with me?" he demanded. "Anything to stop me sitting here? Anything you don't like about my clothes? If there isn't would you mind hopping it. You keep me awake!"

He jerked his hat down over his eyes to indicate the end of the conversation, folded his hands on his chest, and prepared to sleep.

"Sorry, Mr. Jenkins," came the cop's voice. "I was just interested in something."

"In what?" demanded the Kitten irritably.

"In why some people think around their neck is the safest place to hide valuables."

The Kitten shot up in deadly alarm. But Constable Diver had turned already and was marching with slow dignity down the village street.

The Kitten mopped his brow and tried to compose himself. The fellow was evidently guessing, for if he had had even the faintest suspicion it was diamonds the Kitten was cherishing he'd have arrested him there and then. But he knew something. And the thing to do now was to plant the necklace before things became too hot.

But where was he to plant it? He hadn't the faintest idea, unless it was in the dungeons of Carstairs.

The dungeons of Carstairs! The Kitten sat upright again, as his inspiration came. Of course! Where else but the dungeons of Carstairs?

The Kitten invited Henry Higginsbottom to his table at dinner that night. Henry came reluctantly.

"Say," he said crossly, "don't you think it would be kind of wiser if we weren't seen together? I mean, we're pretty conspicuous, and until this business is over—"

"You're quite right," said Kitten magnanimously. "But I want to talk to you tonight. Ain't you eating anything?"

Henry scowled at his soup.

"Don't know that I'm very hungry. You've spoiled my appetite. Why don't you stay in London? It would be a whole heap safer for everybody."

The Kitten quivered with laughter. It was amazing how this young Higginsbottom restored his good temper.

"I kind of like this little village. I'm just recuperating from a nasty cold. Climate's good. Only one thing that worries me." He glanced warily around, saw that nobody was within hearing distance, and leaned across the table whispering, "Henry, I want your help tonight. I'm going to plant the goods."

Henry's eyes popped.

"The diamonds? How?"

"Wait and I'll tell you. And don't say diamonds out loud like that! That village cop's taken a dislike to me. He's snooping around too much."

"But what can I do? I can't put him off the scent."

"Do you know the layout of the cellars under Carstairs?"

"Some of them," said Henry guardedly. "The main ones. It'd take a hundred years to know them all."

"Can we get in without going through the house?"

"Sure, there's an outside door in the south wall. It's scarcely ever used, but it leads down to the main passage."

"Good!" said the Kitten, with intense satisfaction. "We're going there tonight."

Henry, in alarm, spilled his soup.

"We! Tonight! But that's not fair! You can't spring this on me tonight. I just got engaged and Felicity will be expecting me to take her out tonight."

The Kitten calmly took a large mouthful of soup.

"Do you want me to break up that nice little engagement of yours?"

Henry's face crumpled.

"But you can't do that now. Not after me promising to deliver the di—the goods for you. You can't double-cross me like that!"

"I'm not double-crossing anyone. I'm only asking you to show me the dungeons tonight. After all, I'll have to know my way about them—to see if you deliver the goods safely, for one thing."

"You mean—you'll be watching me!"

"Sure, I'll be watching you," said the Kitten genially. "After all, you're practically a stranger to me. I mean, a guy who could get into a mess like that in Chicago mightn't be exactly trustworthy."

"Okay, I'll come!" Henry said hurriedly. "So long as you lay off that Chicago business. But what am I going to tell Felicity?"

The Kitten leisurely cleaned up his soup plate and beckoned to the waiter.

"Tell her your past's caught up on you," he advised affably.

It was midnight before the two finally set out for Carstairs as the Kitten wanted to make quite sure Constable Diver had gone home to bed, and that there was no one else hanging around to watch them creeping up the lane behind Carstairs and across the south garden.

There were thick fast-moving clouds in the sky, so that one moment the garden was sharply brilliant with moonlight, and the next eerie in the gloom. The house, high and solid, looked like a battlemented castle beneath the flying clouds. Not a light showed. The stillness was intense.

The Kitten moved with his accustomed noiselessness, but Henry crashed through the shrubbery and across to the house like a young elephant.

"I've never been this way in the dark before," he muttered. "When can we use that torch?"

"Not until we're out of sight of the windows, fool! Thank God, I don't have to make a burglar out of you!"

"I shouldn't want to be a burglar," Henry said huffily. "I think it's a lousy profession. The door's hidden in this ivy. We'll have to use the torch now."

The Kitten loomed up behind him and flashed the torch.

"Make it snappy, then. Wait a minute, you'd better show me how the door's opened. I might be coming this way myself some time."

Henry obediently demonstrated how the large rosette in the middle of the door turned and swung the door open on a pivot, disclosing a flight of stairs and a pitch black passage.

"Nifty, eh!" muttered the Kitten. "These old guys knew all there was about hiding their tracks. Well, ain't you going down?"

Henry hesitated, glancing regretfully at the moonlit garden. An owl called on a long-drawn note. The wind stirred and a faint hollow chilling sigh came out of the caverns.

"It's damn dark," he muttered. "You might take a header."

"*You* might," said the Kitten impatiently. "I can look after myself. Get along now. What you scared of? The ghost?"

Henry gasped and went down the flight of steps precipitatedly.

"Gosh!" he breathed. "How'd you know?"

"How'd I know what?" the Kitten demanded irritably. To tell the truth, he hated the look of the place himself. It was uncomfortably dark and damp, and it smelled horrible. He wasn't an over-fastidious person, he'd been in some pretty queer places at times, but this haunted-looking darkness gave him the jitters. There'd be bats, for sure, and bats drove him crazy.

"That there was a ghost," said Henry, watching the Kitten's careful progress down the stairs. "There is one, too. Servants at Carstairs are scared stiff."

The Kitten reached the bottom of the steps and trod unexpectedly in a pool of water. He gave a yelp as the cold water shot up his leg, and his cry disturbed a bat, which fluttered clumsily about him. What with trying to hide his fear and loathing it all, the Kitten lost his temper and his discretion with it.

"For God's sake!" he shouted angrily, "don't stand there talking about damn fool ghosts! Show me where the smuggling goes on and then let's get out of here."

"I was only warning you—" Henry began mildly, but the Kitten cut him short.

"Get going, you hear me!"

Since Henry was leading the way, he had to carry the torch, which meant that the Kitten had to follow behind in semi-darkness, stumbling over holes and grazing his shins on rocks. By the time they had reached Rollo Carstairs' cave he was bathed in perspiration and completely out of breath.

"Let's stop a minute," he panted, "while I get my breath. You didn't need to go so damn fast."

"I want to get out of here," Henry said uneasily. "Place gives you the creeps. Look at those hooks where old Rollo Carstairs hung three men in a row. Almost think you can see 'em hanging there, if you look long enough."

The Kitten stared fascinated at the blackened hooks. That was some way to bump off your enemies. He'd like Pope to have a look at those hooks. They'd give him a start. This would be a good place to have Pope alone some day, when he knew too much . . . .

"They land the stuff in the next cave," Henry said. "Row in to the entrance when the tide's full. Where are you going to plant the diamonds?"

The Kitten's gaze traveled speculatively over the walls. "Don't hurry me. We'll just take a look around. We've got to be careful—"

But he never finished what he was saying, for at that moment, apparently close at hand, came the sound of laughter. A girl's laughter, light and fresh and delightful. It was so unexpected and so strange in that dark foul spot that the Kitten jumped convulsively.

"Say, where's that dame?" he demanded angrily.

Henry tried to speak, but couldn't. His eyes bulged, his large face was ashen. The light of the torch described crazy circles as his hand shook.

Silence, deep and uncanny, descended.

The Kitten made for the door.

"If there's anyone spying on us—"

Henry grabbed his arm.

"Don't go out there!" he whispered desperately. "There's no one out there. You won't see a thing!"

"Why won't I?" demanded the Kitten impatiently. "If someone laughed—" Then suddenly he stopped short and fear began to creep over him. What was it Pope had said? *Find out about the Laughing Ghost!*

"What's it mean?" he asked in a whisper as fearful as Henry's own.

But, before Henry could answer the laughter came again, sweet, mocking, utterly terrifying in that horrible darkness. By the time it had ceased, Henry and the Kitten were practically in each other's arms. Henry was shaking violently, and for the Kitten's part, he would have preferred the day of judgment.

"It just laughs," Henry was trying to say audibly. "You never find anything. Some Carstairs dame got lost down here once and went crazy. They call it—"

The Kitten grabbed the torch from Henry's trembling hand, interrupting him urgently.

"We've got to get out of here. And quick! It's the supernatural. I know that sort of thing when I come across it. I'm sensitive to it. Inherited. I'd a great-grandmother who had a curse on her. Used to go paralyzed for a couple of days every time it worked. Honest to God! We've got to get out of here."

The Kitten was already out of Rollo Carstairs'

cave and making off down the passage the way they had come.

"Paralyzed!" exclaimed Henry between chattering teeth, as he blundered after him. "That's awful!" His own legs seemed suddenly to have developed a peculiar stiffness. He could hardly keep up with the Kitten. It was amazing how quickly so large a person could move.

The way back seemed endless. The Kitten's breath deserted him again and he breathed in great gasps, the sensation that wraith fingers were clutching at his hair, at his fat neck, at his coattails, growing on him, until, when at last he reached the flight of steps leading to the garden, he collapsed in a heap.

"Gosh!" Henry panted, almost tumbling over him. "You haven't got paralyzed, have you?"

The Kitten rose slowly.

"Of course I haven't! But God help me if I ever come down here again! Give me a hoist up these steps, will you?"

It was not until the ivy-covered door closed behind them and they were half way across the lawn, the moon clouded, the bushes dark and friendly, that the Kitten remembered the diamonds still around his neck.

" 'Struth!" he ejaculated, stopping dead. "Am I a fool or am I? Blamed if I haven't forgotten what we went down for."

"The diamonds!" Henry ejaculated in his turn. "We forgot to plant 'em!"

"I'll say we did," said the Kitten, sitting down behind a rhododendron and pulling the leather bag from around his neck. The calmness of the garden and the cool air were restoring his equilibrium, and he was beginning to feel extremely ashamed of his recent conduct. "You with your damn fool talk of ghosts. Scaring me stiff. Now I've got the jewels around me neck still, and that cop knows it."

"Knows it!" gasped Henry.

"Well, he as good as told me. So there's only one thing for it. You'll have to take them."

"Me!" Henry was horrified. "But you wouldn't trust me with valuables like that!"

"I wouldn't want to," the Kitten corrected. "But I've got to. You'll have to keep them till the fifteenth. Hang them around your neck same as I do."

The Kitten undid his collar, fished deeply in his flesh, found the cord and unfastening it drew out the bag containing the diamonds.

"There they are," he said in a reverent voice, fingering the knobby bag.

Henry squinted sideways at the bag. It might have contained a scorpion for all the favor with which he viewed it.

"But I don't want 'em," he protested weakly. "I hate to have 'em. You'd much better plant 'em somewhere. How do you know I won't skip out?"

" 'Cause you won't. 'Cause I'll be watching you, sticking closer to you than your shadow. 'Cause, since the time I was copped in thirty-one I never go out without this friend in my pocket." He patted an ominous bulge in his hip pocket, and, squeezing up his little eyes into thoughtful slits, grew lyrical. "Have you ever seen a dead man, Henry? I have. Once. He'd been dead quite a while. His face was black and he hadn't any eyes, just holes that you could see the skull-bones through. He wasn't a man at all, he was just a Thing. Wise men don't die, Henry. Leastways not until they've got their family weeping around them and know they'll be decently decked up with satin and fal-lals so no one will ever see their black faces."

Henry's petrified silence indicated to the Kitten that his point was driven home effectively. It was just as well, because his own flesh was beginning to creep a little at his loquacity. He smiled paternally.

"So it'll be quite safe to give the diamonds to you, Henry. Because if they aren't delivered safely on the night of the fifteenth, well, I hate to think what'll happen to you." He sighed deeply and looked at the moon. "I know you'll take as good care of them as I would myself. Like to have a look at them?"

Henry shook his head dumbly, but the Kitten, ignoring him, slid the diamonds out into the hollow of his hand. Gosh, he'd hate to part with them. How beautiful they were, icy, brilliant, brighter than a woman's eyes. A handful of moonlight . . . .

"Pretty little sparklers, eh?" he said lovingly, replacing them in the bag, and leaning forward to hang the bag around Henry's neck. His face was gentle and critically admiring, as if he were decorating Henry with a daisy chain.

"I hate to do this, but it's the only way."

Henry jerked uneasily beneath his fingers.

"But supposing," he said piteously, full realization of the situation dawning on him, "the cop takes a dislike to me."

The Kitten chuckled gently and comfortably.

"He won't. Not with your face. I'd hate to think

what the profession was coming to if you were mistaken for a crook."

Henry muddled about Felicity's room that morning, picking up things and putting them down, striking a loud random note on the piano, drumming on the window pane, until Felicity could have screamed.

"Oh, for heaven's sake, Henry! Can't you go for a walk or something?"

Henry stared at her moodily, his lower lip hanging. He didn't want to go for a walk. He hated going out alone now. If it wasn't the Kitten lurking around corners, appearing unexpectedly in his path, smiling that horrible fat wicked smile, it was that flat-faced earnest-looking cop staring at him suspiciously. The funny thing was that almost always when Henry saw the Kitten, the cop was there, too, as if the two of them were shadowing him. Those cursed diamonds around his neck weighed about half a ton and he felt like a criminal. If the fifteenth didn't come soon so that he could get rid of the jewels he wouldn't be able to stand it.

"I walk all day," he said petulantly. "I do nothing but go for walks. There's nothing else to do in this lousy place. Let's go and find some golf links or something."

"I've told you I can't, darling. I'm busy. I've got to get this theory marked before Josie comes for her lesson. I'm trying to earn my living honestly, if you'd only realize it."

But Henry hadn't finished complaining.

"Here we've been engaged for nearly a week," he said, "and you've scarcely been out with me.

Anyone'd think you were ashamed of me."

"Well, whose fault is that?" Felicity retorted heatedly. "Last night when I was going out with you, you vanished with that fat horrible-looking man—"

"Oh, Mr. Jenkins," Henry said, too hastily. "He's a nice guy, Felicity. I like being nice to him. Well, what about the night before that when you went out driving?"

"I've got to go for a drive sometimes, Henry. It's only reasonable."

"Sure," Henry grumbled. "And you've got to go with that guy with the funny eyebrows."

"I've explained about that. I didn't *go* with him. I only came home with him. But you'd never understand if I explained a hundred times."

"I guess I wouldn't," said Henry. "But anyway—" He drummed fretfully on the window pane. "Say, honey, it's a lovely day. Let's go out somewhere. Do your music teaching this afternoon."

"No, Henry. I've told you I can't. I'm busy and anyway I'm expecting father."

"Is your father coming here this morning?"

"Yes. Why?"

"Nothing." Henry looked uncomfortable. His hand strayed to his chest. "He's not so pleased about what I know."

"No. I shouldn't think he would be."

"But he's letting me come in. I'm to be there on the fifteenth. I've got to be, as a matter of fact. Say, Felicity!" Suddenly his face had become alarmed. "We're not likely to hear the ghost, are we?"

"I should say it's extrememly likely we will."

"But, Felicity—do you really think that?"

He was so obviously scared that Felicity grew suspicious.

"Henry, have you been down in the cellars at night?"

Henry looked guilty.

"Well, yes, I did go just for a look around. Thought I'd better be familiar with the place. And I heard the ghost while I was down there. It was ghastly!" He mopped his brow agitatedly at the memory.

In spite of herself, Felicity laughed.

"Then you wouldn't be frightfully keen about spending the rest of your life at Carstairs?"

"Oh, no! We won't have to do that!"

"You will if you marry me. Lynn will be going at the end of the year and I'll be going back."

"But, Felicity, I thought some nice place in Chic—well, say Boston or somewhere, you know, with central heating and so on."

"Listen, Henry," said Felicity seriously, "I'm not interested in some nice place in Chicago or Boston, centrally heated or otherwise. Carstairs is my home, and that's where I'll live no matter whom I marry. I expect the man I marry to realize that."

"But, honey, with ghosts and things scaring you crazy all the time it's not reasonable. You couldn't expect me to stand for that."

Felicity looked at him with her clear eyes.

"Then perhaps you'd better find some nice girl to marry you, one that isn't encumbered with a family mansion and ghost. Because my mind's made up and if you honestly can't stand the ghost—"

"Hell, Felicity, I'm in love with you."

"But more with your bodily comfort, Henry. And you've got such a large body you need a large amount of comfort. You think it over because I'm going back to Carstairs. And the ghost's been there for three hundred years, so it's not likely to move out for you."

After Henry had gone, small Judith and Emily Briggs arrived for their lesson, and after that Mrs. Menzies, the verger's wife, arrived to discuss whether Felicity would give music lessons to her five-year-old-son. And when they had gone her father arrived. So Felicity, to her relief, had no time at all for reflection. Her reflections all went in one direction nowadays. Why had she lost her temper because that girl Polly had thrown her arms around Lynn's neck so possessively? And why, in her anger, had she allowed herself to get engaged to Henry? Uncle Lynnford hadn't wasted a great deal of time over copybook morals, but one thing he had always been more rigid about than an untruth was that she must never break a promise. A Carstairs might burn and plunder, but he must keep his word. So Felicity spent a good many anguished moments imagining herself standing at the altar (more probably in a Registry office, she told herself cynically) beside Henry, and with a lean dark graceful ghost between them.

Guy Valentine stretched himself out in the lowest armchair as if it were a relief to relax, and lit a cigar. His eyes, like clear water, rested on Felicity humorously.

"Well, my dear, how's the pin money lasting?"

Felicity, ignoring his question, handed him a folded invitation form.

"Look at that, daddy. What are we going to do?"

Guy unfolded the form and glanced at it composedly.

"Oh, the ball," he said. "I know about that. You didn't send me that life-and-death message simply because young Lynn Carstairs is holding a period ball? He's only living up to tradition."

"Yes, I know, daddy, but don't you realize what night he's fixed? It's the fifteenth!"

"The night the *Seagull* arrives," Guy said, his composure unchanged. "Yes, my dear, I haven't forgotten. I should think the ball might help rather than hinder matters."

"Help! With all those people about!"

"*And* young Lynn entertaining them. Remember that. It's keeping him safely above ground. He's got a most infernal habit of poking into things."

Felicity looked alarmed.

"Isn't he afraid of the ghost?"

"It disturbs him, but he isn't afraid. He's not the sort of person who gets a shivery spine. To be quite honest, Felicity, in other circumstances he's the sort of person I'd be glad to be with in a tight spot in the jungle."

Felicity tried not to show her instantaneous pleasure. On second thoughts she tried not to feel pleased. Why should she, because daddy had approved of Lynn, and, indeed, had given him the highest form of praise he knew.

"Then you think one day he ought to know about things?"

"Yes. But not just yet. We don't want to do anything rash. We'll carry on for a while."

Felicity looked thoughtfully out of the window. In the distance, beyond the church, she could see the trees of Carstairs, and, smudgy against the sky, one corner of the roof and a chimney. It was strange how like an exile she felt.

"How's Peewee?" she asked.

Guy's merry eyes twinkled. He looked hugely amused.

"He's incorrigible, Felicity. There's no subduing the beggar."

"Daddy!"

"Oh, it's all right. Young Lynn rather likes him. He'll let him go a long way before he actually does lose his temper. You know, Felicity, I like young Lynn. You might do a great deal worse—"

But Felicity, swinging around, interrupted hotly,

"Daddy, if you start talking to me like a wise father, I won't listen!"

Guy Valentine looked faintly wistful.

"No, I suppose I haven't earned that privilege. But I've got a dashed fine collection of skins to bequeath to you. Anyway, chicken, why be upset because I suggest you might be wise to marry young Lynn?"

"Because," said Felicity, in her distress very near to tears, "if you'd only come to see me sooner you'd have known. I've been waiting to tell you I'm engaged to Henry."

"What!" exploded her father. "That brainless giant."

"He asked me so often," Felicity said defensively. "And I said 'no' about nine hundred times. And one day he got me off my guard. I couldn't help it, daddy, if Lynn had a girl there who's apparently madly in love with him. It wouldn't have been so bad, even, if he hadn't given her my bedroom!" she added bitterly.

"There's one thing in being jealous, my dear,

and another in doing a fool thing like promising to marry Henry Higginsbottom. Well, it's obvious now that we've got to keep Lynn from finding out about the smuggling. If he's going to break one of the terms of the will by not marrying you, there's no need to risk his approval or disapproval of our means of income. We'll have to play a deep game, my dear. But as for your marrying young Henry—"

"He's really very nice, daddy. He's got the kindest heart."

Guy looked thunderous.

"Don't you start defending that blackmailer to me," he said violently. "He's wormed himself into our secrets and now he's going to marry you. Don't ask me for my consent because I'll never give it. What that young man needs is to be bumped off on a nice dark night!"

CHAPTER EIGHT

NEVER HAVING given a ball before, Lynn was immersed in the activity that preceded it. With Mrs. Mell's assistance he sent out invitations to everybody whom Mrs. Mell said should be acquainted with a Carstairs, then felt distinctly like the lord of the manor as the answers began to arrive. There was only one acceptance in which he was really interested, and that was Felicity's. She did accept, by a polite gracious little note—like the lady of the manor, Lynn thought. But of course she would have to come, for appearances' sake. Nevertheless, it was going to be wonderful dancing with Felicity in the great candlelit ballroom.

Polly did a neat little cut and shuffle of delight when the large black scrawl of Henry Higginsbottom indicated his acceptance ("Lynn, if he doesn't fall for me as Nell Gwynne I'll go right back to London tomorrow!") and Mrs. Mell sniffed and jingled happily as everybody who was anybody politely accepted the invitation to dance at Carstairs.

Then there was the decorating and the music and the catering and his own costume to arrange about—

and a couple of explorations, armed with a large-sized ball of string, in the cellars for some clue regarding the ghost. The searches were fruitless, and after each one Peewee wore an annoying I-told-you-so expression for a couple of days. Indeed, Lynn was beginning to wonder himself whether that laughter were an hallucination, for nothing had been heard of it since. The nights were quiet and undisturbed. Or perhaps he slept too well.

Then, on the morning of the night of the ball, Lynn suddenly grew completely tired of it all. He was seized by the sudden frenzy that comes to a writer who has allowed day after day to drift by with no work done. Here he had been at Carstairs nearly three weeks and had allowed himself to become so completely absorbed by the preparations for the ball, and the ghost and the general air of mystery that hung over the place, that little Queen Victoria was still where he had left her, receiving her colorful Indian subjects. The spell of words on paper had caught him again. He must work or go crazy.

So he shut himself in the library and spread out his manuscript. Buddy, under the table, breathed heavily in sleep; a little of the sunshine from the garden came in through the tall windows, it was very warm and quiet. None of the sounds of the bustle and confusion in the ballroom came through the closed door. Presently, even the disturbing image of Felicity faded from Lynn's mind and he began to work. Soon he was completely absorbed.

Lynn wrote almost without pause for two hours. When he did stop he was conscious of that familiar dazed feeling of unreality. The people in his mind were more real than his surroundings. He strolled through the long windows into the garden, but even there the sensation of unreality persisted. The day was extraordinarily hot and clear. The lily pond was a shimmer of blue silk, the shrubs had circled themselves with narrow black pools of shadow. The sky quivered. It was going to be hot for the ball. All at once, it was as hot as midsummer. It would be a clear night with a new moon rising early. Perhaps Felicity would walk with him in the garden. Perhaps he would talk about what he had written this morning. It was extraordinary with what fluency and ease he could write here. There seemed to be something thoughtful and quiet about the atmosphere. But the house had grown very quiet. There was only a far-off hammering in the ballroom, and someone singing in the kitchen garden. And Buddy growling in the library. . . .

It wasn't at first that Lynn realized Buddy was growling. He was only half-conscious, his head still peopled with imaginary figures, and Buddy's low grumble had risen to a bark before he reentered the library. Then he was just in time to see a flash of white and Chinese red vanish through a long open doorway in the paneling. A wisk of skirt, a little red heel as the paneling slid shut. . . .

In an instant Lynn was there and fumbling for the catch. In five minutes he had found it, and the opening was revealed again. Buddy hung back, whimpering at the sight of the dark narrow passage, but Lynn was too excited for caution. He didn't even stop to get a torch, so afraid was he that the mysterious visitant would have vanished. He ran recklessly down the passage and then came to an abrupt stop as it ended in a small room, so dark that he had stumbled against a table invisible in the gloom before he could steady himself. Something slithered off the table into his arms. It was a round hard flat object. Lynn had just time to be aware of that before a blow struck his head and the darkness became complete.

Hours later, it seemed, he struggled through a mist of pain and darkness to become aware that someone holding a lighted candle was kneeling beside him. Someone in white. Lynn opened his eyes wider. The pain in his head was intolerable. It must have been making him delirious, for there, kneeling over him, was a lady he already knew. The face floated before him, vague and pale, the only color in it the vivid lips. She had escaped from her dungeon, or she had walked out of her picture, for here, in her long white dress and Chinese red shawl, with her Chinese red earrings and vivid lips, was Lynette Carstairs. The Laughing Ghost!

By midday it was so hot that Polly put on a silk blouse and blue linen shorts to walk down to the village. She wanted some cherry colored ribbons for her hat. Her Nell Gwynne costume had arrived with Lynn's from London an hour ago, but the ribbons of the hat, in spite of her express instructions, were blue. You'd have thought a firm like Wilson's would take more notice of a customer's instructions, Polly reflected, but it didn't matter, as long as she could get cherry ribbons in St. Simon. It gave her an excuse to walk into the village. Especially in her blue linen shorts. Nobody could wear shorts better than Polly, and she knew it. If legs as nice as hers didn't twinkle on Broadway before she was much older it would be just too bad for the American nation. And the only person who could tell them that was Henry Higgins-bottom.

But Henry, since his engagement to Felicity Valentine, seemed to be living the life of a recluse. The first real live American playboy Polly had met, and as soon as she met him he went into retirement. What luck! Still, he would be at the ball tonight, so that was something. If she couldn't interest him in her Nell Gwynne costume and all, she would give up her ambitions and get a job in Woolworth's.

Thus reflecting, Polly strolled down the winding drive into the village. It was so quiet that the doves from the church roof pecked in the square. The shadow of the spire lay straight as a sword across the street. In the distance children played, gesticulating with spidery arms. It was so hot that the stones burned through the soles of Polly's sneakers. Lord, what a dead place this was! And Lynn liked it, ghost and all (Polly shuddered at the recollection of the ghost), he actually liked it!

Polly went into a tiny old-fashioned embroidery shop for her cherry ribbons. The shop was dark with age. It looked older than Carstairs. It was funny to think that perhaps some other girl had come here to buy a ribbon for the ball at Carstairs on a day when Nell Gwynne still lived. Then, what with the heat and her unusual reflections and the desire for someone to admire her shorts—was there no one alive in this place?—Polly discovered that a large ice cream was a distinct necessity.

So she ordered one in the nearest shop, took it across to a table to eat it, and found herself sitting face to face with Henry Higginsbottom absorbed over an even larger ice cream.

"Well, I never!" exclaimed Polly. "I thought you must have gone back to the States."

"Hi-ya, Polly!" Henry's face had lighted up with a gratifying amount of pleasure, and his eyes ran with satisfactory dilatoriness over Polly's attire. She swung a slim brown leg ostentatiously.

"Hot, today."

"It's hot, all right. Almost as hot as Chicago in summer."

Henry took a large mouthful of ice cream and mopped his brow. He had changed, Polly thought. There was a funny scared look in his eyes. His fresh chubbiness seemed to have wilted. He had the look of a kid expecting to be detected at any moment with forbidden cake. Polly felt puzzled and curious and at the same time something unexpected came into her attitude toward him. You would hardly expect to feel sympathy for so fortunate a person as a millionaire's son, but that was just what Polly began to feel for Henry. It was rather sweet. It made her feel kind of trembly. She had been terribly fond of Lynn, but she had never felt anything like this for him, nor for anyone else.

"Things all right?" she asked companionably.

"Uh-huh."

"You don't sound so sure about it?"

"Uh?" Henry looked startled. "Yes, I'm okay."

He ate diligently. He didn't seem to want to talk. Polly was puzzled and intrigued. There was enough mystery at Carstairs without anyone so simple and honest as Henry getting mixed up in it. Anyway, one thing was certain, and that was that he needed cheering up.

"I've been getting some ribbons to put on my hat

for tonight," she said. "It's going to be a nice night."

"Hot," said Henry.

"Yes, but fine. Gosh, I'm excited about tonight. What are you going as?"

"George Washington," said Henry gloomily.

"My goodness!" Polly exclaimed mildly. "Why?"

"Well, he was an important guy in America. I got to be patriotic. I wouldn't want to go as some Englishman."

"I'm going as Nell Gwynne," said Polly.

Henry looked unenlightened.

"Who was she?"

Polly looked at him pityingly.

"No, I suppose you wouldn't know. Listen, and I'll tell you who she was. She was a poor but beautiful girl who sold oranges and acted on the stage, and the King of England fell in love with her. I think it was all most frightfully romantic. Kings can't do that now. I mean, if they do they've more or less got to abdicate."

"Yeah, I know. They've got things tied up nowadays. You can't have much fun." Henry's eyes rested on Polly speculatively. They brightened and he said, "I guess it's a pity I'm not going as the King of England."

Polly giggled happily, and neatly licked the remaining drop of ice cream off her spoon.

"Never mind. Probably George Washington had fun sometimes, too. What's Felicity going as?"

But Henry, at the mention of Felicity, sighed profoundly and slumped back in his chair.

"I don't know. She won't tell me. She's keeping it a secret." He looked infinitely depressed. "You know, Polly, Felicity's changed since that guy came to Carstairs. She's not the same girl."

Polly leaned her elbows on the table, cupped her chin in her hands, and put all the sympathy she could into her round blue eyes.

"Spot of trouble, Henry?"

Henry glanced around the shop warily.

"You've said it," he whispered darkly.

The air of mystery surrounding him grew.

"Well," said Polly in a bright voice (she would die of curiosity if she didn't find out now what was the matter), "you cheered me up that first day I was at Carstairs, so maybe now I could cheer you up if you'd let me."

A look of gratitude spread over Henry's large face. He suddenly looked eager and relieved.

"That's swell of you, Polly. You're a nice kid. I'd like to talk to you, but—"

He glanced around again. The shop was almost empty, the proprietor dozing in the seat behind the counter. But Henry still seemed uneasy, as if he thought the walls might be listening.

Polly jumped up.

"Let's go some place where we can talk. What about the lane behind Carstairs where I met you that day?"

Henry followed her out. As they stepped into the hot dusty sunlight Polly noticed he pulled his hat well over his eyes and looked around with the same peculiar wariness, as if he were expecting a bogeyman or something to grab him. When they had gone a little way he said out of the corner of his mouth:

"Take a glance around, Polly. See if there's anyone following us."

Polly did as she was bid. (A little shiver of excitement had gone down her spine. Maybe he was a gangster, or maybe gangsters were after him for his money!) But there was no one in sight, only the yellow sunlight and the black shadows, and the doves walking about with a tiny brittle sound.

"There's nobody," she said.

"Not a fat man?" Henry asked anxiously. "A very fat man, fatter than me?"

"You mean that fellow with the ruby ring?" Polly asked excitedly. "I've seen him. Is he following you about?"

"Well, not exactly following me," Henry said guardedly. Just kind of keeping an eye on me. Friend of the family, so to speak. Knew me in Chicago."

"Then he'll be pleased about the nice girl you're marrying," Polly said maternally.

But that was the signal for an unexpectedly violent outburst from Henry.

"Polly, Felicity's the sweetest kid and I love her like hell, but she's just plain unreasonable. Do you know what she wants me to do? She wants me to live at Carstairs!"

"After Lynn goes? Well, you'd expect that, wouldn't you? It's her family mansion. After all, it's a nice place, Henry. Not that it's the sort that appeals to me. I mean, no electricity and rooms the size of the Albert Hall nearly, and the ghost—"

"Yes," said Henry gloomily. "The ghost."

"Have you heard it?" Polly asked interestedly. Henry nodded.

"It's pretty terrifying, isn't it? I nearly died of fright. I'd never have believed in ghosts before, but you've only got to spend one night at Carstairs and even the shadows make you jump. I've slept next to

Mrs. Mell ever since we heard it."

Henry said nothing. He seemed sunk in gloom.

"Mrs. Mell says she wouldn't be surprised if we heard it tonight," Polly went on. "She says you almost always hear it when there's a new moon. Wouldn't it be a thrill at the ball?"

But Polly's light-hearted chatter ceased when she saw Henry's obvious terror.

"Tonight, did you say?" he whispered. "Oh, my God!"

They were in the lane now. There was a deep warm scent of clover and the grass was cool. It seemed incredible to Polly that anyone could look so afraid of a ghost in such brilliant sunlight. She herself felt brave enough to search all the cellars at Carstairs alone.

"You are scared, aren't you?" she said sympathetically. "I'm not this time. After all, there'll be crowds of people and lights. It'll be rather a thrill."

"Yes, where there are people and lights." Henry swallowed convulsively. "Let's sit down on this tile a minute."

He was quite white, Polly noticed. She touched his hand and found that it was trembling. He looked so young and unhappy. It was too bad that he should have all this worry. Visions of Broadway had vanished. Henry was no longer a magician who could open closed doors, but a small boy in trouble. She patted his hand and smiled brightly.

"Never mind, Henry. It'll all come right."

"Think so, honey?"

Polly's heart jumped. She felt queer and trembly again when he called her honey.

"I guess so. I don't know what's worrying you, but

I'm your friend anyway. You can count on me."

Henry looked grateful and admiring, and then suddenly happy.

"You're a wonderful kid, Polly. I like you. We speak the same sort of language, too. Felicity hates me to say gosh."

"You don't say!" said Polly indignantly. "Well, that's mean."

Henry's arm slid around her waist. His big fingers touched her breast. She could feel them through the thin silk of her clothing.

"You're kind of soft," he muttered foolishly.

Polly slid around in his arms and lifted her face. She was trembling with delight.

"You can kiss me if you like," she whispered.

Henry gaped down at her. His eyes wandered over her round flushed face to the soft line of her throat and breast. Suddenly his arms tightened around her, but his lips never touched hers, for Polly had to cry out.

"Ouch!" she exclaimed. "What's that hard thing you've got there? You nearly broke my bones."

Henry's hand wandered nervously over his shirt front.

"It's my chest," he said uneasily.

"Chest nothing!" Polly retorted. "You're not pigeon-chested, are you? You've got something hidden in there.

"No. Honest, Polly—"

"You can't tell me! You've got something there you're scared about."

"Well, yes," Henry confessed. "Yes, I have. But it's nothing much. And I'm not scared. Honest!"

"Then if it's nothing much and you're not scared

you can tell me what it is."

"I couldn't do that, Polly. I mean, it's private property. I'm looking after it for somebody."

"Funny place to put it, around your neck," Polly said suspiciously.

"Well, you see, it's a safe place. I mean, it isn't the sort of thing you leave lying around. It's—" Henry lowered his voice. "It's diamonds."

"Diamonds!" Polly went pale with excitement. "Show them to me."

"I can't Polly!"

"*Please!*"

Polly wasn't an actress for nothing. She knew how to put all the beguilement in the world into her voice. Henry couldn't resist it. He fumbled at his shirt buttons.

"All right, honey. Just a glimpse, though."

He found the little leather bag, damp with his perspiration, undid the fastening, and tipped the diamonds out. They flashed with a thousand colors in the sunlight. They were so brilliant that Polly blinked and gasped.

"Gosh!" she breathed, and could say no more.

Henry's confidence was returning.

"Pretty little sparklers, eh? I don't mind saying I'm a bit nervous looking after them."

"Gosh!" said Polly again. "They'd be as good as the Crown jewels, wouldn't they?"

"As good as anything anyone ever had," Henry said loyally.

"But what are you doing with them?"

"I told you," Henry said defiantly. "I'm looking after them for a friend. Until tonight."

"Did you say—" Polly was trembling with excitement. "Henry, did you say until tonight?"

"Yes."

"Will your friend be at the ball?"

"No. My God, I hope not!"

Polly didn't have time to wonder at his fervency. She was completely obsessed with a wild glorious hope.

"Henry, you like me, don't you? You trust me?"

"Why, sure, yes, honey. I like you a lot. Trust you, too."

"Then would you let me wear those tonight?" She pointed to the glittering stones in Henry's hand.

Henry looked horrified. "Absolutely not!"

"Please, Henry! Please, darling!" Tears of anxiety and pleading stood in Polly's eyes. "Listen, all my life I've wanted to wear real diamonds. I've even dreamed about it. I mightn't ever have the chance again. Henry, you wouldn't want me to be an old woman and never have worn diamonds. Maybe to die and not have worn them."

"I know, honey, but—"

"They're so beautiful, Henry. They'd look good on me when you see my dress."

"But I thought Nell Gwynne was a poor orange girl," Henry protested feebly.

"She was, too. But I told you the King loved her, didn't I? He'd have given her things like diamonds. It'll sort of show that you think a bit of me, too."

"Sure I do, honey, but—"

"Then let me wear the diamonds. *Please*, Henry!"

Polly had flung her arms around Henry's neck. Her face with its bright excited eyes and parted lips, was close to his. He couldn't resist it. He shrugged his large shoulders fatalistically.

"Okay," he said. "Okay, honey. You can wear 'em. And if we die for it, we die for it, that's all I can say."

When Lynn came completely back to consciousness he was lying on the leather couch in the library with crowds of people standing around him. Or at first, to his dazed eyes, it looked like crowds. There was Peewee, with a look of concern sitting strangely on his merry face, Mrs. Mell, every now and again giving a sharp little jingle as she moved agitatedly, Polly openly crying and Felicity. Of them all, Felicity was the only one who showed no expression. She simply looked far-away.

Lynn's eyes had opened so slightly—his head ached violently and the slightest movement of his eyelids hurt—that none of them had noticed his return to consciousness. There was a cold pack on his head, which he disliked, and they hadn't let Buddy in. He was whimpering at the door.

Lynn pushed the cold pack on to the floor, and said irritably:

"What is this, anyway? A deathbed scene or a wake?"

"Oh, darling!" Polly cried. "We thought you were dead."

"Well, just remember in the future I like to do my dying in private," Lynn said, glaring as hard as possible with his half-open eyes at Mrs. Mell and Peewee.

They both ignored the hint to go. Mrs. Mell wrung her hands.

"It was *dreadful*," she said agitatedly. "Was it the ghost?" Her big black eyes peered fearfully at Lynn.

Lynn had an uncomfortable remembrance of that vision he had seen or dreamed of, Lynette Carstairs,

misty and vague and lovely in the circle of candlelight, her gay shawl and earrings, her vivid red
mouth that once someone had loved to kiss. Would
a ghost have bright warm lips? His head hammered
with trying to think.

"What happened?" he asked Peewee briefly.

"Peewee found you unconscious," Polly put in excitedly. "You'd knocked your head on a piece of jutt-
ing rock or something. Gosh, you scared us all."

"You really shouldn't wander about those passages,
sir," Peewee put in disapprovingly. "I've told you so
before. If I hadn't found you—"

"How did you know where to find me?"

"I found that sliding door open, sir. I naturally investigated. It was a shock to me to find you unconscious, sir. You had apparently fallen down a step in
the dark and knocked your head.

Lynn felt his head gingerly. He didn't believe the
story, because one didn't fall and strike one's head
on the *top*. Peewee was telling another of his special
brand of fairy stories, as usual. But what the devil
had happened?

"I say it was the ghost," Mrs. Mell interposed,
jingling all over. "I always knew it would do bodily
violence one day. Why, I've got a cousin who knows
the cook at Black Friars, and she said—"

"Never mind now," said Lynn impatiently. "We've
enough to do managing our own ghost without
someone else's as well." He turned his head to the
sliding door which was still partly open. "I suppose
you will say, Peewee, that you didn't know that door
was there, either."

Peewee simply looked smug.

"No, sir. That's true, I didn't. But Miss Valentine

says her uncle used it sometimes. The small room where you fell was a sort of secret hiding chamber. It had been used by refugees during the Middle Ages. If you noticed before you fell, there's still a little furniture in it. A table and a chair."

Lynn turned to Felicity.

"Is that true?"

She looked at him with her grave dark eyes.

"Yes. They even say Lynette Carstairs was imprisoned there for a short time, but the servants could hear her calling so she was shifted further away, to the cellars."

The room was bright with sunlight. The windows were open, and the heat outdoors came in like a warm breath. But it seemed, after Felicity's words, that a cold shiver went through the room.

Mrs. Mell sighed deeply and whispered, "Oh, the poor thing!" And Polly, a shiver running from her scalp to her warm brown legs, said: "Gosh, Lynn, I wish you'd keep out of those cellars. They give me the jim-jams."

"Miss Gay is right, sir," said Peewee. "It isn't wise to pry into the past."

Felicity had walked over to the window, and stood with her back to them. Her head had a curious disconsolate little droop.

"Yes," said Lynn. "That's all very well, all that ghost stuff, but I went down there because the door was open. If it is a secret door that nobody knows about, *who opened it?*"

His words left a startled hush in the room. Mrs. Mell gave a faint little scream.

"Oh, dear! In a minute I'll faint!"

Polly breathed, "I'm glad it's daylight."

Felicity, at the window, said nothing.

"There are some curious mysteries about Carstairs," Peewee began blandly. If I may say so, sir, no one has ever done himself any good by trying to solve them. Perhaps one of the servants knew about the door, or perhaps, as a fantastic supposition, it was the ghost. In any case, you'd be as well not to worry about it any more today. I'd advise you, if your going to be fit for the ball tonight, to have a little lunch and then rest all the afternoon."

It was a sensible suggestion, and Lynn could do nothing but agree to it. Besides, his head was aching too much to think. There was nothing in his mind but a confused blur of that whisk of red heels through the open door, and then the vision that had bent over him in the candlelight. Tomorrow he would try to straighten it out. Today it didn't matter. And Felicity was here. It was funny how once she had been in a room one always associated the room with her. It was going to be like that all his life, even after she had become as much a ghost to him as was Lynette Carstairs.

"All right," he said wearily. "Have lunch served in the dining room. Felicity, you'll stay, won't you?"

Felicity turned. Her gaze was not hostile, only far-off.

"I really oughtn't to. I've a pupil this afternoon."

"What time?" Lynn asked.

"Three o'clock," Felicity admitted reluctantly.

"And it's one, now. You've got a couple of hours."

"I know, but—"

"It's charming of you to visit me while I'm unconscious," Lynn said, with irony. "Is it really necessary to run away the minute I show signs of returning intelligence?"

Felicity flushed.

"I only came up to get some things for the ball," she said defensively. "But if you put it that way, I guess I can stay."

All the same, lunch was a dreary affair. It was so hot. Lynn felt dizzy, and found he could scarcely eat. Unless he focused his eyes intently, things swam vaguely in a blur of shadow and sunlight. Felicity sipped iced water and looked cool and delicious in a white frock. Only Polly, still in her shorts and with her brown legs twisted around the legs of her chair, did justice to the cold chicken and salad. It took a long time for her to be affected by the atmosphere in the room. Her own naturally high spirits seemed to surround her so effectually that any pervading atmosphere was shut out.

"Say, Lynn, I've had a lovely morning. I've been down to the village and I came home with—er—down the lane. It's going to be a gorgeous night for the ball."

"Hot," said Lynn.

"Gosh, isn't anyone interested enough in this ball not to care if it is a bit hot?" She turned to Felicity. "Lynn's going as a cavalier, and I'm Nell Gwynne. What are you going as, Miss Valentine?"

"Oh, just in an old costume I've got," said Felicity vaguely.

"Oh," said Polly. But in another moment she had turned exuberantly to Lynn. "Say, Lynn, you can't guess what I'm going to wear to the ball tonight. You'll get the surprise of your life."

"Oh!" said Lynn, in his turn. "What is it?"

"I'm not going to tell you. You'll see tonight."

"Well, I hope it's not something stolen."

Polly giggled happily.

"Oh, no. Hen— I mean, it's just being lent to me."

Felicity said nothing. Polly, on the point of chattering on, was suddenly aware at last of the atmosphere. Lynn was looking like a ghost, and Felicity as if she were not there. So she subsided and the rest of the meal was completed to the accompaniment of polite remarks from Lynn and polite answers from Felicity. Polly swallowed the last of her dessert and dabbed her mouth with her napkin.

"Will you folks excuse me? I've got an awful lot to do this afternoon. Ribbons to sew on and things."

She got out of the room hastily, and Lynn found himself alone with Felicity.

"More dessert?" he asked politely.

"No thank you."

"Another peach?"

"No, thank you."

"One doesn't feel very hungry in this sort of weather."

"No."

"Come out in the garden for a little while. It will be cooler."

Felicity pushed back her chair.

"I ought to go. And oughtn't you to lie down?"

"No," said Lynn irritably. "Everyone in this house seems to have one idea, and that is to make me lie down. What's wrong? Do you want me out of the way?"

"Lynn, don't be silly."

He followed her to the window.

"Felicity, what is wrong between us? Polly? Or

Henry? Or what? The other night when we drove together I thought we were friends again, but now you're further off than ever."

Felicity looked at him with her clear far-off eyes.

"We are friends," she said. "And Lynn, in spite of what you say, you ought to lie down. You're looking rotten."

Lynn ignored her advice, and said impatiently.

"Felicity, what is wrong between us? You're unhappy, aren't you?"

"No." She shook her head reflectively. "I'm not unhappy. Just in a sort of negative state. It's rather pleasant."

"Is it because you've got to be away from Carstairs?"

Felicity pressed her head against the window pane.

"I didn't say I was unhappy," she said defiantly.

Lynn stood behind her, looking at the way her curls rested on her neck. Lightly, as if they were light as thistledown.

"If we were married," he said, "this is where I'd kiss you." He touched the nape of her neck with his fingers. "When you were dressing or when you stood like this. I think things like that would be very precious."

Felicity moved away. Her eyes were dark and stormy. Strangely enough, Lynn had the impression that if she did not become angry she would cry.

"Well, we're not married."

"No, but I'm in love with you."

Felicity turned a startled face to him. Suddenly all the brilliant life was back in it. She looked so lovely and distressed that Lynn almost took her in his arms then and there.

"It's not because of Carstairs," he said. "I love it,

but I loved you before I knew it existed."

"When?" asked Felicity, on a swift little breath.

"The day you had the smash with Henry and came into the garage. The first time I saw you. We dreamed about you after that, Buddy and I. You were so blown-about and dusty and gay. As if everything were a jest."

"Sometimes one *has* to think that," Felicity murmured involuntarily.

"Sometimes one can. But not always. You can't just now, can you?"

All the lovely light went out of Felicity's face.

"Things are so complicated," she said, in apology.

"Yes. That's why I'm leaving Carstairs. It will remove at least one complication, won't it?"

"Leaving!" Felicity's eyes had widened to startled incredulity. "When did you decide that?"

"This afternoon. Ten minutes ago."

"But, Lynn! That means you'll lose your legacy and everything."

"I know. But after all, it's really yours, isn't it? I'm a—"

"You've overworked that word usurper," Felicity put in.

"But it's true. I am one. This is your home. You love it. You're unhappy away from it. You're going to marry Henry Higginsbottom, so since there's no possibility of us fulfilling that term in the will, I'll lose Carstairs anyway. The only decent thing is to hand it back to you right away."

"That's nonsense!" said Felicity heatedly.

"It's not nonsense. It's such a thing as gentlemanly honor. You know, it's a funny thing, my mother gave me the sort of education I'd need to be a Carstairs, and instead it's taught me how to be honorable enough to renounce being one."

Felicity said nothing for a moment. She watched a bumble bee backing cautiously out of a foxglove outside the window. She traced a line down the pane with her fingernail and said in a very small voice:

"Lynn, don't go."

"It's for you, dear."

"You know what everybody will think—that you're running away."

"From the ghost?"

Felicity nodded.

"Especially after today."

"Especially after today I find it harder to go. There's a lot to be explained here, Felicity. I've never been so intrigued by anything. But after all, no matter what the mystery is, it isn't my business. That's the crux of the whole matter. I hate to pry. If I'm not going to own Carstairs by marrying you, there's no point in my becoming reconciled to the ghost."

"No," said Felicity inaudibly.

"But don't worry about it now. Buddy'll miss his silk eiderdowns, no doubt, but it'll do the little beggar good. Felicity, promise to enjoy the ball tonight. It's the one and only party I'll give as lord of the manor."

Felicity nodded.

"All right, Lynn."

"We're not quarreling any more, are we? Hatchet's buried?"

She nodded again, and said:

"I daresay we're both too hot-tempered ever to agree."

"Yes. That's probably true, too. But don't let's

sound like an obituary notice."

"No." Felicity was smiling. She was quite composed and it wasn't for a minute that Lynn could tell what was different about her. Then he realized that all the lovely gaiety had gone out of her face.

Felicity was driving all the way to London to buy a fan for the ball. Henry thought she was crazy. But he went with her when she invited him. He was extremely uneasy about that promise to little Polly Gay (there was a sweet kid, if ever there was one!) that she could wear the diamonds to the ball, and he was afraid if he stayed around the *Duck and Drake* too long that fat Jenkins would notice his uneasiness. There was not much his sharp, bright little eyes missed. Besides, he was glad for the chance of a private talk to Felicity. He had tried not to notice lately that she was avoiding him, but it certainly seemed like it.

Although it was late afternoon, with lengthening shadows, the heat persisted. The sunlight was yellow as candlelight over the fields. There was no wind, save the warm rush of air made by the speed of the car.

Felicity had taken her hat off, and her hair was flying back from her ears. She had that lovely blown look that always sent a flutter through Henry's pulses, but her delicate little chin was in the air, and she was driving very fast, a sure sign of her perturbation. Somehow Henry found himself thinking of Polly. Certainly Polly hadn't the distinction of Felicity. Felicity had all the qualities of a great lady while Polly was just kind of homey and sweet. But there was something in Henry that responded to that sort of girl. After all, his father had been a clerk in a dry-goods store until he had discovered the best way of canning food, and although one could acquire wealth, one could not acquire breeding all at once. Probably not for a generation or two, Henry thought. As a matter of fact, if Pop remained broke and the bottom fell out of his smuggling business—it was bound to before long, with that Lynn Carstairs poking his well-bred inquisitive nose into everything —he wouldn't so much mind dropping the middle "B" out of his name and starting life afresh as plain Henry Higginsbottom. A while ago he wouldn't have believed himself capable of such an ambition, but what with all the worry he had been having and meeting little Polly Gay who hadn't any money either . . .

The silence was becoming oppressive.

"Hot for the ball," he commented. "You're going some pace, Felicity."

"Yes," Felicity answered. Henry wasn't sure which comment she was answering, but she didn't seem interested in either.

He began again.

"My costume looks swell."

"Does it?"

"Say, honey, I wish you wouldn't be so secret about what your wearing. You're not aiming to go as the ghost or anything, are you?"

"It's not important what I'm wearing," Felicity said impatiently.

"Now there's a feminine contradiction," Henry burst out. "It's not important what you're wearing, yet you drive all the way to London to get a fan to go with it."

"I couldn't get one in St. Simon. And I'm not going right into London. I'm only going as far as Jedwill's.

They have some lovely antiques. Besides, I wanted to drive."

"Well, so did I," said Henry, "provided it's sociable. Gosh, I wish that other business was over tonight. I'd enjoy the ball a million times more."

"Whose fault is it?" said Felicity unsympathetically. "You weren't asked to join in."

"Sure, I know that, but with my father broke, what could I do?"

"Get a job as I advised you at the beginning. You don't know, Henry darling, what a shopkeeper is lost in you."

A shopkeeper! Henry felt a spark of definite interest. If Pop could make a million out of canned goods, couldn't he do the same in his own line? And it was so safe. Safety had suddenly become the loveliest thing in the world. Henry sighed. He could never feel safe for two minutes on end while those damn diamonds hung around his neck. Heaven knew what would happen tonight.

"Say, Felicity! Does the ghost ever do anything? Except laugh, I mean."

"Lynn went down in the cellars today," Felicity said slowly, "and Peewee found him unconscious."

Henry's eyes bulged.

"My God, Felicity! Is that true? But how did he know it was the ghost? Did he see it?"

At the sight of fear, Felicity relented.

"Well," she said, "we told him he'd fallen down a step, which he didn't believe. Actually daddy probably had something to do with it. Between daddy and the ghost—" she broke off, frowning. The speedometer needle had slid around to sixty.

"Say, not so fast," Henry remonstrated. "We're

getting too near London." His relief that Lynn's injury was explainable was so great that he could afford to be generous. "You don't like that guy to be knocked about, do you?"

Felicity's lips were set.

"I was furious with daddy. One way or another he'll have Lynn killed yet. After all, he'd only found—" She stopped abruptly.

"What?" asked Henry.

"Oh, nothing much. Something we needed tonight."

"That guy pries too much. He's got Carstairs. Why doesn't he keep his nose out of this?"

"The same," commented Felicity quietly, "could be said about someone else I know."

Henry flushed.

"But that's different. I'm the man you're engaged to."

It was funny how a simple statement like that should send the speedometer needle sliding around to sixty again.

London, noisily alive, stained with a thousand years of smoke, carrying the sunset like a luminous cloak over its grime, clamored around them. Henry watched the houses slip by.

"Say, Felicity, what's Claus Jensen like?"

Felicity looked at him sharply.

"Why do you want to know that?"

"Well, I have to. For tonight."

"You don't have to see Claus tonight."

"But I do. You don't understand. There's—" Henry stopped. He'd nearly let it slip about the diamonds. "I'd kind of like to have a look at him," he finished lamely.

Felicity had slowed down to a crawl. Horns were honking impatiently behind her.

"Henry, are you double-crossing us?"

"Why, no! Honest, Felicity! I'm not doing anything of the kind."

"Well, it sounds like it."

"You don't trust me."

"No. I'm afraid I don't."

"That's a nice sort of thing to be told," Henry said in an aggrieved voice. "The girl you're going to marry doesn't trust you."

Felicity ran the car alongside the curb, stopped it and got out.

"I'm not sure she is the girl you're going to marry. I'm going in here. I'll only be five minutes." There was no change in her tone between the first and second statements.

Henry clambered out after her and followed her into the shop. He was extremely agitated.

"Felicity, what did you say? Did you say you're not going to marry me?"

"We've absolutely nothing in common," Felicity said over her shoulder, winding her way through the shop. "What floor do you suppose I'll get a fan on?"

"Ask a floorwalker," said Henry. "And that's not true. We have got things in common. We both like motoring and—and hamburgers, and—"

"The second floor," said Felicity to the floorwalker. "Thanks, I'll walk up. Henry, don't be idiotic. We can't get much happiness out of smashing up cars and getting indigestion. Besides, well, Lynn—"

Henry panted up the stairs after her.

"Yes, I know it's that guy," he burst out angrily.

"You've thought of nothing but him since he came to Carstairs."

"Actually it was slightly before that," Felicity corrected. "One day when we saw the facsimile of Rupert Carstairs in a garage." She had stopped before the counter and spoke to the assistant. "I want a fan, please. One suitable to wear with seventeenth century dress."

Henry stood beside her, absurdly large and hot and angry.

"Felicity, do you mean to say you're jilting me here, in a shop!"

"I'm only telling you, Henry, we've so little in common. I mean, a husband and wife—" The girl had come back with the fans and Felicity stopped what she was saying to look at them carefully, one by one. She was completely absorbed over the delicate fragments. You'd never know, Henry thought in bewildered anger, that she was just jilting her fiancé.

"These are very nice," she said courteously. "But I wonder if you have something in ivory and red. It's for a rather special occasion. I don't mind if it's expensive."

"Yes, madam. I'll see." The assistant went away again.

"Lot of fuss over a fan," Henry grumbled. "You'd think it was more important than a husband."

"You see," said Felicity, going on with what she had begun to say, as if there had been no interruption. "A husband and wife should be in sympathy over almost everything. And we're not. Why, we even look at a little thing like a fan in different ways."

"It's that guy with the funny eyebrows," Henry exploded angrily.

A lovely flush spread over Felicity's face.

"Yes, it is," she said softly. "I'm sorry, Henry. I'm afraid it is. You see, I don't love you. I get bad-tempered with you and I'm not a bad-tempered person, really. And Lynn told me something today that's rather changed things for me. Tomorrow he was going to leave Carstairs, but of course I can't let him."

The shopgirl laid another fan on the counter. It was of ivory and lace, and there was a knot of crimson ribbon tied to it.

"This, madam?" she asked. "It's the only thing we have. I'm afraid it is rather expensive."

"Oh, it's delightful," Felicity breathed. "It's almost identical with the one I'm copying. How much is it?"

"Fifteen guineas, madam. It's an antique."

"Good. I'll take it."

Henry gasped.

"Felicity! You said your costume wasn't important, and now you pay all that for a fan."

Felicity laid her hand on his arm. Her eyes were so wide and bright and gentle that suddenly he was emptied of all anger.

"Henry, do you mind terribly? About us, I mean? You see, it wouldn't work out. I know it wouldn't. You'll find a nice girl who'll speak your language, who'll like hamburgers and football matches, and perhaps a very kind person like Henry B. Higginsbottom—"

Henry shook her hand off.

"Drop the 'B,'" he said gulping. "I've a notion after tonight I won't be using it. Okay, Felicity, I guess you're right. We weren't getting along well. Polly—I mean—well, what about that damn fan!"

Felicity took the parcel from the girl, and handed her the money.

"I'm afraid Uncle Lynn's first lesson is lost," she said turning to Henry. "I've spent my year's allowance in exactly three weeks."

But Henry was scarcely aware of what she said. He was marveling at how completely she had changed, at how glowingly exquisitely alive her face had become.

Dart in hand, the Kitten tensed his monstrous body for the throw. The whole room waited. Forgotten pipes, trailing spirals of blue smoke, lay in wrinkled hands, half-empty mugs of ale stood on the tables or supported on bony knees, the silence was so great that you could almost have heard a fly walk across the ceiling.

It was the finals of the St. Simon Darts Championships, and the Kitten, with one more throw to go, was running neck to neck with Ned Higgins, five times the village champion. It was so tense a climax that everyone had forgotten to breathe. The Kitten himself was more excited and on edge than he had been even at the moment that he had extracted the diamonds from Lady Windermere's safe, with the lady herself sleeping quietly in bed a couple of yards away.

One more throw. . . . He leaned forward, holding the dart lightly between his pudgy sensitive fingers. Someone stood at his shoulder. He frowned, putting out his left hand to wave whoever it was away, and a soft scornful voice said in his ear:

"Easy does it, Kit."

The Kitten jumped convulsively, at the same time

throwing the dart. It was a badly calculated throw, the worst he had made the whole evening, and the championship that had been practically his was lost to Ned Higgins.

The room was in an uproar, everyone congratulating the stoical Ned and commiserating with the Kitten. But the Kitten could see only one person, the thin, slight, elegantly dressed, cold-eyed man with the skeleton's grin who was standing at his side.

"What are you doing here, Kiff?" he whispered thickly.

"You'd better be polite to me," Kiffin Pope said, in a low voice, "or I'll be telling them where you learned to play darts. Ah well, it's a harmless little pastime, even for prisoners."

"Shut up!" growled the Kitten, glancing around nervously. "What do you want here?"

Pope moved around the room easily, his gaunt face grotesquely genial.

"A very pleasant exhibition, gentleman. What about drinks all around? Then you'll forgive me if I rob you of your budding champion. We have a little business."

Good humor ran riot. The Kitten, glancing around the smoke-filled noisy room as he reluctantly followed Pope out, thought it was the loveliest place on earth. What the hell did Pope want now, coming down from London and robbing him of his innocent triumph at darts. (They had all been eating out of his hand, those good simple villagers.)

"Where's your room?" Pope asked over his shoulder. "Take me to it."

"It's up here," said the Kitten weakly. "Nice room. Gets the morning sun." (Supposing Pope wanted to see the diamonds! He'd just about kill him if he knew he'd handed them over to Henry.)

"Yes. Never mind the atmosphere," said Pope, following the Kitten into the room and locking the door. "What about these walls? How thick are they?"

"Gosh, Kiff, you're a suspicious devil. No one will be trying to listen to us. They're as innocent as the day down here. No one's got a thing on me. They think I'm a pretty good sort of fellow."

"H'm," said Pope, staring at the crimson jacket, voluminous white breeches and cockaded hat that lay on the bed. "What's all this? Are you quite sane, Kit, or is the village atmosphere going to your head? Simple festivities, no doubt."

"Sure, I'm sane enough, Kiff. That junk's for the Carstairs' ball tonight. Big turn-out. I've got to keep an eye on the Yank."

"A ball at the Carstairs! Tonight!"

The Kitten winced at the sharp encounter of Pope's eyes.

"Yes. The new owner's giving it. Fancy dress. I was a bit windy about it at first, but I think maybe it's a good thing. It'll keep 'em from listening to what's going on underground."

"Nice sense of the appropriate you have, Kit," commented Pope, turning the triangular hat in his hand. "A pirate, eh? You'll be staggering! Colossal! I like to see you with the right party spirit."

"Cut that stuff!" said the Kitten curtly. "Tell me what you're here for. Don't you trust me to deliver the diamonds?"

"During a lifetime of experience, Kit," said the Pope in his soft scornful voice, "I've found it never pays to trust anyone. Not even you. Although quite frankly, Kit, of all the crooks I've dealt with you're the one I'd trust most. That's not because of your shining character. It's because I know you're too scared to try double-crossing me."

"Honest, Kiff!" protested the Kitten, mopping his brow.

Pope crossed over to the window to draw the blinds. In the subsequent gloom he looked bloodless and macabre, like an elegantly-dressed ghost. If you got your fingers around his neck, thought the Kitten fantastically, there'd be nothing there.

"Well," said Pope, "what's the Laughing Ghost?"

The Kitten quivered with the recollection of that night in the cellars below Carstairs.

"It is a ghost! Same as it's called!"

Pope stared with his weary hooded eyes.

"Is that all you've found out?" he asked contemptuously.

"But Kiff, what else could I find out? It's a real ghost! You don't see nothing. You just hear it."

"I never was the kind of person who believed fairy tales," Pope commented ironically.

"But, Kiff, I'm telling you! It's the ghost of some dame who got bumped off a couple of centuries ago. It laughs in the cellars at night. I know, 'cause I've heard it. Ask Henry Higginsbottom if you don't believe me. He'll tell you. It's a ghost, all right, Kiff. I know. I'm psychic to 'em. They can't fool me!"

Pope laughed his dreadful soundless laugh.

"All right, Kit. I still don't believe you, but maybe you'll have the chance to prove it to me tonight."

The Kitten felt a creeping down his spine. He had known the moment he saw Pope that something unpleasant was going to happen, but anything quite as unpleasant as this he had not imagined.

"Tonight? How do you make that out, Kiff?"

"You know your way through the cellars, I presume?"

"Oh, yes, sure, sure!" the Kitten hastened to answer. "I thought it wise to know the layout of the place. Got young Henry to show me."

"H'm. I'm glad one wise thought at least got into your thick head. Can you get down to them from the outside of the house?"

The Kitten nodded.

"There's a door in the south wall."

"What time is it safe to go there?"

"Well, not until practically dark," the Kitten said uneasily.

"All right. I've my car outside. I'm leaving now, ostensibly for London. I'll meet you up the road from Carstairs at dusk and you can take me down to the cellars."

"But, Kiff!" The Kitten was coming out in large drops of perspiration. "Honest, it's not necessary for you to see the cellars. Henry and me'll do the job—"

"Henry and you will probably bungle the job so badly that there'll be nothing in it for anybody. What are you aiming to do as your share?"

The Kitten pointed reproachfully at the finery laid across the bed.

"Haven't I told you I'm going to the ball? Gate crashing at that, to keep an eye on Henry. I'll see he's off down to the cellars with the diamonds before midnight. I'll stake my life on that."

"You've worked that out well," Pope said reflectively. "So you plan to stay nice and safe aboveground while Henry does all the dirty work."

"But hang it all, Kiff, he's getting a hundred for it! Just for handing a string of diamonds to another guy."

"And you're getting fifty thousand for holding a candle lighting him to the cellar door. Equality of.distribution, eh, Kit?"

"Well, how are you going to earn your fifty thousand?" The Kitten burst out angrily. "You sit tight in London and don't do a damn thing!"

"On the contrary," Pope put in softly, "I'm going to be down in the cellars tonight, also. We both are."

The Kitten's burst of anger died. His balloon-like face went pulpy.

"Both!" he echoed foolishly.

"Yes, both of us. You're going to be there to see Henry does his job, and I'm going to be there to see you do yours. This is too big a thing to slip on, Kit." His hand strayed carelessly to the slight bulge in his coat pocket.

The Kitten, watching him, was mesmerized into docility.

"Yes. Yes, I guess you're right, Kiff. What do you want me to do?"

Pope, with a touch of macabre humor, removed his hat and put on the cockaded tricorne at a jaunty angle. His face, beneath the triangular brim, was cadaverous and dreadfully amused. Even without the jacket and sword he looked the part excellently, cruel as a hawk, a pirate who neither gave nor asked for quarter.

"What you are to do, Kitten," he said gently, "is to take me down to the cellars at dusk and leave me where I'll be able to see what's going on without being seen myself. You are to watch the Yank all evening, give him the diamonds at midnight, and follow him down. Is he scared of you?"

"Scared!" said the Kitten in a satisfied voice. "I'll say."

Pope looked faintly incredulous.

"Good. If that's true, there'll be no harm in letting him know you're following him. He'll be anxious enough to hand the goods over to Jensen. And remember, I'll be watching the two of you. I don't miss much when I watch."

"I could believe that," the Kitten muttered. "But honest, Kiff, if you spend the whole evening in those cellars—it's dark as hell, and any minute you might hear a dame begin to laugh, sort of high and sweet."

For a minute vicious anger looked out of Pope's eyes. Then he controlled himself and said in his soft contemptuous voice.

"Don't criticize my plans, Kit. It's not wise. You'll do exactly as I say, and if you slip me up you'll have more to worry you than a ghost that laughs." He stood up to go. "All right, Kit, now you can go back to your darts."

"Darts!" thought the Kitten, watching the spare gray figure go down the stairs. When he had already ruined the championships for him, and left him with the anticipation of going down into those horrible haunted cellars at midnight. His face puckered up, like a monstrous child's on the verge of tears.

"What's the *use!*" he said despairingly.

CHAPTER NINE

Eight o'clock. The chimes of the church clock died away. The doves fluttered out and settled back on their perches, gray and brown and smoky blue ghosts. The sky was tawny with sunset, the shadows fading. The shimmer of heat had gone, but the air lay still and warm and close as it had all day. It was so quiet that the drowsy sea shed a faint autumnal brilliance on the oak and cedar leaves. As it faded they grew black as shadows. The road running up to Carstairs was the last thing from which the light died. . . .

The chimes of the clock echoed in Felicity's room. Felicity laid down her comb and picked up a hand mirror to look at the back of her hair. It was piled high in glossy curls. The top of her ears showed and her slender neck. Turning, she saw her face, a delicate oval, with full bright lips and brighter eyes. Even in her petticoat she looked strange and old-fashioned, as if she had really stepped out of the past. The hairdresser had just gone, and Mrs. Briggs was coming in a minute to put on her gown. The gown lay on the bed, its ivory satin as smooth as the inner side of a seashell. The red shoes were on the floor and the Chinese red shawl hung across the foot of the bed. Felicity was so happy she could have died.

Mrs. Briggs, every square inch of her quivering, came up the stairs and knocked on the door. Felicity went to open it. She was so happy that even with those few steps, in her petticoat, she looked as if she were dancing.

"Well, dear, everything all right?" Mrs. Briggs panted. "Did you get your fan?"

"Oh, yes," Felicity said eagerly. "It's a beauty. Look!" She displayed the fragile affectation. "Wasn't it funny that a fan should be the only thing we forgot? If I hadn't gone up to Carstairs this morning to look at the portrait I wouldn't have thought of it."

"Well, that's very nice, dear. Now shall we get you into your dress?"

Felicity obediently held up her arms for the gown to slide over her head.

"Mrs. Briggs!" she said in a muffled voice from the depths of it.

"Yes, dear."

"Isn't it a lovely night! It's so warm and still. You can hear the sea."

"You're very excited, aren't you, dear?"

Felicity's head, her glossy curls undamaged, emerged from the low neck of the gown.

"I'm happy," she said simply.

"Because you're going to a ball?"

"Mostly because Henry and I have decided not to get married. Mrs. Briggs, you were very clever to copy this dress from a portrait."

"Yes. I don't mind admitting I surprised myself.

Now, hold your breath a minute, dear. It's lucky you've got such a small waist. I won't have to lace you very tight."

Felicity held her breath for a second. But she was too excited to stay quiet for long.

"Mrs. Briggs, it's possible I'll be going back to Carstairs soon."

"What! Is that nice young man leaving?"

"He says so, but he's not, really. That's why I broke my engagement with Henry. You see—"

"You're in love," Mrs. Briggs said, in her warm comfortable voice.

"Well—maybe," Felicity admitted, looking at her alight face in the mirror. "But it's not going to make any difference. I'll still teach Emily and Judith. After all, they were my first pupils. And you'll still make things for me. Now I wonder, should I have the shawl pinned to stop it from slipping?"

There was a tap at the door.

"Telephone, Miss Valentine," called Mr. Murphy.

"Oh!" breathed Felicity. "It might be Lynn."

She cast one glance over her shoulder at the image of Lynette Carstairs in the mirror, and picking up her hooped skirts, ran downstairs.

As Lynn went down the stairs the tall old clock at the top chimed eight. The tiny delicate chimes echoed even more delicately through the high hall. The clock was like a large, very solid, dignified old woman with a very small sweet voice. Lynn had not realized how much a part of Carstairs it had become to him. When he awoke in the night in London he would be listening for the exquisite stillness that per-

vaded Carstairs, and for the delicate little voice of
the clock speaking out of the darkness.

But the clock, like the sturdy little heart of the
house, was only one of many things. It was strange
how he had slipped into life here as if he had been
here always. For all the rest of his life this was going
to be the place that was home.

But he had to be unselfish and quixotic and honorable, thought Lynn, prowling about the house like
a nervous ghost. He was dressed already for the ball
in his cavalier costume, and looked slim and elegant and foreign in the dark green silk and lace. He
went down to the ballroom, lit for the ball. The floor
shone as brilliantly as the paneled walls, and the
candle flames were reflected everywhere. One could
almost see the ghostly whirling of skirts in the long
walls too. His own reflection looked more as if it
belonged to those intangible whirling ghosts than
to the present.

Well, perhaps tomorrow there would be a faint
dark slender shadow in the walls to show he had been
here. There would be no other trace left. His
clothes were packed in the shabby bags he had arrived
with, his manuscript, increased by a paltry two thousand words since he had been at Carstairs, was neatly
tied up. Buddy slept in blissful glory on the silk eiderdown for the last time. Tomorrow it would be exit
imposter, and no one would have any regrets over
his going, nor realize the immense sacrifice he was
making. It was true what Felicity had said. People
would think he had run away from the ghosts, as the
servants had at various times. They wouldn't know
that he had become so absorbed and fascinated by

the mystery that he would do anything in the world, save the one thing that was making him go—the possibility of destroying Felicity's happiness—to stay and solve it. He was sure it could be solved. The happenings of today proved it. One did not come out of an encounter with a ghost with a very painful swelling on one's head. There was something tangible there, and he'd have found it out if it hadn't been for Felicity and the feeling he had that she didn't want him prying into her mystery. Or was it a mystery to her? Was it a mystery to any of them, Mrs. Mell, Peewee, Henry?

Lynn stopped thinking. Thinking made his mind go around in circles. He strolled into the hall and up the stairs again. The strange thing was that although he was going tomorrow he was conscious of an elusive happiness. Something sweet was in the air. . . .

Polly, her stiff petticoats rustling, came running down the stairs.

"Lynn, have you been in the garden? Have you seen anyone? Say, Lynn! You look the image of Rupert Carstairs in the gallery. Sort of dark and thin and brilliant."

She ran on, a rosy ghost herself. Lynn was left on the turn of the stair. Rupert Carstairs! And Felicity like Lynnette! It was strange. On an impulse he thought he would go to the gallery and look at the pictures. To cut through the servants' hall and the small side door was the quickest way. But at the entrance to the servants' hall he paused. Peewee was speaking on the telephone. And his voice was so unlike Peewee's usual bland tones that Lynn stopped involutarily to listen.

"You'll have to do it, Felicity," said the crisp well-bred authoritative voice. "You'll have to be there at midnight. There's no other way."

Already the grass was wet with dew. Polly hesitated, wondering if she should run back and change her slippers, but it wasn't far enough to the shrubbery for them to get very damp, and she wanted Henry to see her in full costume. She held up her skirts as she ran, her bonnet, tied with the cherry ribbons, fell back on her neck. Moths rose on powdery wings from the grass. The garden was full of perfume. It had grown so dark now that the infant moon, slipping down behind the yews, was a bright curved thread in the sky.

Henry was waiting behind the big rhododendron. Polly wanted to hug him, it was so sweet of him to remember to be there.

"Oh, darling!" she cried. "Did you bring the diamonds?"

Henry silently handed the jewels to her. They were warm from his hands, and shone with a sharp brilliance.

"For God's sake, be careful of them!" he begged. "If you knew the risk I'm running! Not that it matters much," he finished, shrugging his shoulders fatalistically.

"Why doesn't it matter?" Polly asked.

"Things have been happening to me," Henry said gloomily. "The sort of things that make you think life isn't worth a damn."

At another time Polly would have been as curious as her curious little mind knew how, but now she could think of nothing but the diamonds.

"Fasten them around my neck, Henry?" she begged eagerly, holding up the diamonds and turning around.

Henry obeyed, his fingers clumsy with the fastening, his warm breath going down Polly's neck.

"There you are," he said. "Now for God's sake, be careful whom you show them to. And it's only till twelve o'clock, mind. You've got to give them back to me at twelve sharp."

Polly fingered the diamonds reverently. Her eyes were large with awe.

"All right. Tell me how I look, Henry. Am I nice?"

Henry's gaze went over from her tumbled bonnet to the tip of her blue silk slippers. His face cleared a little, a brightness came into his eyes.

"Gosh, Polly, you're cute."

Polly nodded in satisfaction.

"You won't forget to dance with me, Henry?"

"Oh, no! I'll be dancing with you. Now I've got to go and get ready. You'll recognize me as George Washington. And do be careful of that necklace. It's mighty valuable."

Polly stretched out her arms. She looked entrancing in the dusky light.

"Wait, Henry! I've got to kiss you for them."

The sudden shy pleasure on Henry's face was very sweet to her. For a moment she even forgot the diamonds.

"Well, there you are, Kiff," said the Kitten. "This is what they call Rollo Carstairs' cave. It's right next door to where they bring the stuff up, Henry says. I hope you'll be all right. If you hear the ghost don't go looking for anything 'cause you won't find nothing! Now I gotta go."

He went with undisguised haste, his torch flickering against the black walls and then vanishing. Darkness, as thick and impenetrable as a wall, came down. There was a clammy wet sea-smell that was melancholy and unpleasant. It was strange how it could be so cold down here after the heat of the day. There was an ancient foul chill that had remained unstirred in the air for centuries.

Kiffin Pope flashed on his torch to look at his watch. It was just after eight. There were four hours to wait. Well, that wasn't long. Once he had waited fifteen years to breathe free air again. That had seemed a long time. Four hours in comparison with that was less than nothing. And the reward was worth it. A hundred thousand pounds for spending a four hour vigil in a damp dark spot! It meant he could take a long rest from this sort of thing. With the Kitten out of the way—Pope patted his bulging coat pocket and smiled in the darkness. God, what a trusting fool the Kitten was! Guiding his own murderer to the spot where the murder could best be committed. It was the most staggeringly ironical thing Pope had ever come across. It was colossal. Of all his varied career, this would be the peak of his achievements. It would be the perfect murder. No one knew he was associated with the Kitten. Tomorrow or at some future time the body of an unknown man would be found in the underground passages at Carstairs. Probably it would be identified eventually, probably murder would be suspected, but there would be no clues and the motive would be missing. Poor old Kitten! Pope thought musingly. No one would regret his death. He would have been a dangerous man had he had any brains. As it was, he had put Pope in the way of a good thing, and it was just his bad luck that he hadn't known it was against Pope's principles to share spoils with anybody. Now he would never know because he would too soon be dead.

Poor old Kitten, probably now getting vaingloriously into his absurd pirate's disguise. He'd be a gaily-colored corpse. Perhaps he'd light up these damned passages a bit. It wasn't pleasant sitting in the dark, but it would be unwise to keep a torch alight. Someone might come down. The silence, apart from the melancholy rise and fall of waves on shingle, was deadly. Sometimes a bat fluttered eerily. Any living person seemed continents away. The place was like an enormous vault. It would certainly be easy enough to imagine a ghost. There was no doubt a gullible person like the Kitten would be half-crazy with terror. Pope wasn't afraid of any thing like that. He wasn't afraid of the Laughing Ghost or the rising tide or the silence or any number of smugglers. But already within twenty minutes, he was beginning to hate the dark. It took all his self-will to keep himself from flashing on his torch and leaving it burning. For presently, if he knew anything about this particular form of hell. . . .

Someone was speaking to him over his shoulder. Pope shuddered violently. For four hours he would have to go through this hell. He, who was going to shoot the Kitten without drawing a longer breath, could not have looked over his shoulder for all the riches in the world. For already someone was there, that familiar shadowy form.

"Kiffin Pope . . . is afraid of the rope . . ." a voice was saying in a low mocking chant.

Katie Diver put down her knitting and got up with deliberate care. Her kindly placid face remained undisturbed.

"Tom," she said quitely, "there's no hurry, but I think you had better ring the nurse."

Constable Diver clattered to his feet in complete consternation.

"What! Katie, you don't mean tonight!"

Katie smiled gently at him. Her smile was as maternal as if her husband were no older nor wiser than the child not yet born.

"It's got to be some time soon, Tom. It'll be nice to get it over."

"Katie, are you feeling very bad?"

"Just a little, dear. We'll get the nurse around. There'll be no hurry for the doctor for hours, probably."

"It's eight o'clock," said Constable Diver agonizedly. "I've got to go on duty in half an hour. I'll ring the chief and get special leave."

His wife laid her hand on his arm.

"Tom, don't be a fool! You'll do nothing of the kind. You'll go on duty as usual. Honestly, dear, there's nothing you can do here. I've got to do this job myself."

Constable Diver stared at her foolishly.

"Yes, I guess you do, Katie. You know I wish I could help."

"Yes, I know you do, Tom. But you mustn't be silly and worry a lot. I'll be as right as rain. Go and have a look at the ball at Carstairs. It'll take your mind off things."

"Oh, Katie!" Constable Diver burst out. "I wish I could bring off something good tonight. Something that would be of help to you and the youngster. I'd like that youngster to be proud of his old man. There's a chap down here I've been shadowing, but I guess I'm on a false trail. Thought he'd stolen something, but probably it's just a cheap ring. You couldn't expect anything like the Windermere necklace here."

"Of course not, Tom. If that were here half of Scotland Yard would be, too."

"Yes, I guess so," Thomas said gloomily. "Not much chance of promotion here. But I'll certainly keep an eye on Carstairs."

"Yes, dear," said Katie faintly, clinging to the arm of the chair. "And now, please ring the nurse."

CHAPTER TEN

THERE WAS a mad and brilliant scene in the ballroom at Carstairs. Knight and lady, jester and buc-
caneer, troubadour and Spanish dancer rubbed shoulders, all in the candleshine. The orchestras played
waltzes and minuets, Peewee was kept busy trimming
candles, Lynn, his easy lord-of-the-manor smile growing strained, was rapidly growing bored with being
polite to a lot of strangers for whom he cared less
than two hoots. Polly was in her element showing
everyone how to dance the minuet. She was doing it
extraordinarily well, too, her gay petticoats swinging,
her eyes as bright as the beads around her neck.
(Good lord, what were those beads, Lynn wondered.
They looked incredibly like diamonds, but it would
be as likely for Polly to have a necklace of diamonds
that size as for her to have a necklace of stars.)

Lynn was trying to listen to what Lady Maplethorpe, whom Mrs. Mell had informed him was his
nearest neighbor of importance, was saying.

"You're a Carstairs, young man," she was telling
him, with evident relief, her bright curious old eyes
looking him up and down. "Good and straight as

they make 'em. I'm glad about that. Dreadful to have an outsider at Carstairs. I've known your family all my life. Been visiting here since I was wheeled in a perambulator. Good show, this. It does you credit. Equal to anything they had in my young days. Where's Felicity?"

That was precisely what Lynn had been wondering ever since the ball had started. He had seen her as she had come in. She had given him her hand and smiled up at him, her small bright face looking out of the hood of the long cloak she was wearing. Then she had gone on upstairs to the bedrooms, and hadn't appeared since.

"I can't imagine," he said uneasily. "No doubt she'll be down in a minute. It's so difficult to recognize people in this sort of costume."

Peewee slipped quietly behind them, snuffing a candle. Lady Maplethorpe peered after him through her lorgnette.

"Do you know, that butler of yours seems familiar to me. I feel I've seen him somewhere. Where did you get him from?"

"I'm afraid I don't know his credentials, Lady Maplethorpe. Felicity engaged him."

"Ah! Probably I've seen him in somebody's home. He seems familiar. So strange! Tell me, how do you like the ghost?"

"Very well," said Lynn absentmindedly, thinking of Peewee and the unexpectedly cultured voice with which he had spoken over the telephone.

Lady Maplethorpe's laughter had attracted other people. They were clustering around Lynn with well-bred curiosity.

"Listen to this!" the old lady was saying mischievously. "Mr. Carstairs likes the ghost very well. What'd old Lynnford say to that?"

Lynn laughed with them all. His face, thin and dark above his unaccustomed finery, was suddenly young and gay as he laughed.

"Well, no," he said. "I don't exactly like it. I'm afraid I didn't mean that. But it interests me enormously. Tell me, wouldn't old Mr. Carstairs approve of my liking it?"

"No. He liked people to be afraid. Liked the servants to be scared stiff. Took a sort of proprietary interest in the ghost. I mean, if he couldn't have one that sent a chill down your spine he wouldn't have one at all. Only failing of dear Lynnford's. Perhaps only an eccentricity at that. We all have 'em."

"Mr. Carstairs, do you think we'll hear the ghost tonight?" This is an awed voice from a pretty Victorian miss.

"My housekeeper," Lynn replied gravely, "assures me it's always heard when there's a new moon. I doubt if we'd hear it here, though. Up in the bedrooms—"

"Gad, Carstairs!" interrupted Dick Neville, "my wife envies you. She's always complaining that we haven't a ghost to entertain our guests with."

"Yes, but only if we could see it," little Ann Neville said, with a pleasurable shiver. "It would be so much more thrilling. It's supposed to be Lynette Carstairs, isn't—"

Her words broke off with a startled gasp. Her eyes widened. Everyone turned to look where she was looking. There was a stir at the door, the dancers stopped, and the guests drew back to allow Lynette Carstairs, in her trailing white dress, to enter!

She stood a moment at the door, as lovely and in
substantial as the candlelight, then walked daintil
down the room. The little red heels of her shoes click
ed with a brittle sound as she walked on the polishe
floor, the silk of her gown shirred, her earrings flash
ed. She slid the Chinese red shawl off her shoulder
and turned with her gay friendly smile.

"Hello, everybody! Have I made a sensation?"

"*Felicity*!" gasped Ann Neville.

Lady Maplethorpe turned to Lynn accusingly.

"This won't do, young man. Your uncle wouldn'
have stood for it. When he had a ghost, he had one
No fakes for him."

Lynn rubbed the tender spot on his head reminis
cently. He was bewildered. Had it been Felicity i
this costume whom he had seen?

"No. So I believe. But I assure you, Lady Maple
thorpe, I knew nothing of Miss Valentine's plan."

Felicity, breaking away from the crowd that ha
gathered around her, came over.

"No, he didn't, honestly, Lady Maplethorpe. And
didn't plan to be a sensation. I just thought I'd copy
the costume from the picture in the gallery. Not tha
I haven't helped make Lynn's ball a success for him,"
she added laughingly.

Lynn looked from the laughing interested guests t
Felicity. She was so exquisite in that long white
dress. All the lovely alive look had come back to he
face, her lips were red as her shawl, her eyes bright
er than anything he had ever seen.

Lady Maplethorpe shrugged her shoulders.

"Well, no doubt Mr. Carstairs will find you're a
wicked minx soon enough. Run along and dance, the
pair of you."

Felicity laughed that low delicious gurgle which Lynn hadn't heard since the night he had first come to Carstairs.

"She seems to have sorted us out already, Lynn. Let's dance."

Lynn took her in his arms. She was smiling with her bright lips. She was frighteningly beautiful. They waltzed around the room, and everyone looked at them.

"Do you think they're admiring us," Felicity surmised interestedly. "Or are we like a pair of ghosts? You're astonishingly like Rupert Carstairs. Do you suppose he was in love with Lynette?"

"He is, tonight."

Felicity laughed.

"Don't be serious tonight, Lynn. I'm happy."

Her gaiety was so lovely that it was almost infectious. But now at last the unreasonable sensation of happiness that had been with Lynn all evening left him. His heart was sinking into his buckled shoes.

"Are you happy because you're coming back to Carstairs tomorrow—when I'm gone?"

"As a matter of fact," said Felicity, looking at him with guileless eyes, "I've unpacked your bags. Buddy simply hated keeping guard over them. I left him asleep on the eiderdown."

"The devil you did!" Lynn exploded, swinging her around agitatedly. "What did you do that for?"

"Oh, just—Lynn, you're dancing too fast. I'm out of breath."

Lynn slowed his steps. His head was bent over hers. He could smell the fragrance of her hair. She had unpacked his bags. She wanted him to stay. Oh glory!

"Come out in the garden," he said sternly, "and

kindly explain your high-handed actions."

"Oh, I couldn't let you run away from the ghos and have you called a coward," Felicity said lightly. Her eyes were bright and tender. "How's your head?"

"Better. Come out in the garden, Felicity. It's coo and there's a new moon. And I'd like a lot of thing explained—particularly how that door in the librar came to be left open, and why I thought I saw a ghos in red shoes."

Felicity drew away from him, laughing.

"Do I have to teach you etiquette? You can't leave your guests until midnight at least. There are respon sibilities in owning Carstairs. And there are hundred of people you ought to be dancing with instead of me I'll come with you after midnight. I'll know all the answers then."

Lynn, longing to have her alone (Why was she sud denly so beautifully alive and gay?) was forced to agree.

"You'll have invented them, no doubt. All right then. After midnight. If you don't spend all the inter vening time dancing with Henry Higginsbottom."

Felicity laughed over her shoulder. Her voice came back lightly.

"I shan't be dancing with him at all."

Peewee was watching her as she walked across the room. Lynn was suddenly aware of the odd narrowed look in his eyes. They were not Peewee's bland merry eyes at all. He forgot his overwhelming delight at Felicity's answer about Henry (they must have quarreled and it had made Felicity as gay as a crick et), in his rememberance of that strange telephone conversation he had overheard. *You'll have to do it Felicity. You'll have to be there at midnight!*

Midnight! So that was why she couldn't meet him until afterwards. But what assignation had she?

Polly, tugging at Lynn's arm, interrupted his thoughts.

"Lynn, have you seen Henry?" she was asking anxiously. "It's ten o'clock and he hasn't arrived yet."

"No, I haven't," Lynn said vaguely. Polly's problems had become of very little interest to him. "I think he and Felicity have quarreled. Probably he won't come."

"Not come!" Polly echoed, her eyes wide with alarm. But he's got to!"

"Perhaps if you went and fetched him," Lynn suggested teasingly. "By the way, Polly, where did you get those diamonds? I hope they're not real."

Polly fingered the necklace stabbing her round young throat with brilliant prismatic rays of light.

"Why do you hope they're not real?"

"Because I'd have to have the house full of private detectives if they were."

Polly giggled triumphantly.

"Well, I'll tell you something, Lynn. They are real. They're enormously valuable. Henry lent them to me to wear tonight. Everybody's just *staring* at them. I feel like the Queen of Sheba."

Lynn was staring at her in genuine alarm.

"If I were you I'd feel an escaped thief. Where the devil did Henry get them?"

"He said he was looking after them. That's why I'm worried about him not being here, because he said he had to have them back by midnight. If you see him come, tell me. He's George Washington."

She drifted away disconsolately. Lynn, with a vague

sense of horror, was beginning to piece things together. Felicity had a mysterious assignation at midnight. Henry had a necklace of diamonds worth several fortunes that must be in his possession by midnight. Of course, Henry's father being a millionaire, the diamonds may have genuinely been his, but if so, why that talk to Polly about a slick deal, why the anxiety about midnight? What did it all mean? As Lynn stood pondering he was suddenly conscious of Peewee watching him with his mirthful inscrutable gaze.

At half-past eleven Polly suddenly saw the figure of a very large and anxious George Washington come into the ballroom. With a little cry of relief she broke away from her surprised partner and threaded her way through the dancers toward Henry.

"My goodness!" she cried, shaking his arm. "Where have you been?"

Henry's George Washington costume was exactly correct in every detail. But anything less like the small, cool, composed figure of Washington would have been difficult to imagine. He was so overwhelmingly large and so far from composure. His triangular hat was tipped slightly over one eye, giving him an agitated rather than a rakish look, his face was crimson, his large mouth hanging loosely and moist and his eyes full of a queer troubled look of fear.

"I've got here at last," he said breathlessly, and his eyes fell on the diamonds around Polly's neck.

"I should just think it's time," Polly said indignantly. "I've been worried stiff. Especially since you'd quarreled with Felicity. I thought you might be doing something silly."

"Who said I'd quarreled with Felicity?"

"Lynn did," said Polly, wondering at his agitated voice. "Why, Henry, you're shaking. Has something scared you? Have you seen the ghost?"

Henry mopped his brow with a ridiculous lacy handkerchief. His hat slid a trifle over his eye.

"No. But I was followed. Thought it was a ghost at first. But it was a pirate. Cutlass and everything. Was I scared! Wasn't at first I realized it was Mr. Jenkins. My friend," he added belatedly.

"Why, you silly goat!" Polly exclaimed gaily. "He's probably dressed in fancy dress. He's probably coming to the ball."

"Yes," Henry muttered. "That's what I'm scared of. And you with those diamonds. I think I shook him off, but he'll probably be here any minute. Gosh, it's hot! And there's lightning outside. Polly, you've got to give me the diamonds."

Polly put her hand to her neck defensively.

"Not yet, Henry. Please! I haven't enjoyed them a bit, yet, worrying about you. But now you're here I can have a good time. Let's dance."

Henry looked down at his close-fitting nankeen trousers.

"If I dance in these duds," he said darkly, "they'll split. They're scarcely made to be walked in, even. And I can't dance those fool dances." He looked around uneasily. "Give me those diamonds, honey, there's a good girl."

"No," said Polly obstinately. "And I can teach you to dance. I've been teaching everybody."

Henry looked at his watch. It was twenty minutes to twelve.

"I'll dance with you when you've given me the diamonds. Come into an alcove."

"But I can't, Henry. What'll everybody think? They've all been simply green with envy, and now if I suddenly appear without the diamonds—"

"You promised, honey. You should have thought of that before."

"I didn't promise till twelve o'clock. There's still another twenty minutes."

It was too bad, she thought. Here she was looking absolutely ravishing—everyone said so—and all Henry could do was fuss about the diamonds. He was looking around again now, his big face hot with worry and perplexity.

"But I can't wait that long, honey. It's dangerous. I've got to—"

"Henry! What's the matter?" Polly exclaimed anxiously, seeing no one enter but a colossally large pirate in a scarlet coat who was edging around the room with a sliding stealthy movement, as if he wished to escape detection.

"Is that your friend, Mr. Jenkins?" Polly asked innocently.

"Yes," Henry muttered, suddenly seizing her arm so violently that she gave a stifled "Ouch!" of pain. "We've got to get out of here. Quick! Before he notices us. And for God's sake don't let him see those diamonds."

"But, Henry!" Polly protested as she was propelled helplessly to the garden door. "Have you gone nuts?"

"No, but I will," said Henry between his teeth. "Sure as fate if I don't get those diamonds out of sight this minute."

A peculiar little feeling of fear slid over Polly. All

at once she remembered the slick deal Henry had boasted about. Was it anything to do with the diamonds? Were they stolen?

It was very dark in the garden. Big soft clouds were moving across the sky, and as Henry pushed Polly out of the light from the ballroom windows a flash of summer lightning lit the garden. A warm gust of wind sent her petticoats billowing. It pushed the bushes and they moved forward. Suddenly she was so afraid she was trembling.

"Henry!" Her voice shook with fear, but suddenly she knew she had to be firm. It was desperately necessary, if she were going to save Henry from this thing that was happening to him—if she were going to find out whether he were worth saving. "You've got to tell me something before I give you these diamonds."

"I'll tell you anything," Henry promised nervously, "so long as I get them."

"All right." Polly stepped back a pace. She unfastened the necklace and slid it into her hand. The dim light showed it glinting faintly, and her own pale face above it. "Are they stolen?"

"Why—why, I wouldn't know," Henry said agitatedly "How would I know, honey?"

So it was true. Polly's little bright figure wilted. A vast depression settled over her. She had liked this big Yankee so much, first because he was the son of a millionaire, and then, quite honestly, just for himself. He was so big and simple and sweet. And now —now he was just a plain crook. Well, the time had come for her to do something about it.

"You'd know all right," she said grimly. "You can stand there dressed as George Washington and tell me a downright lie. Well, I'll tell you what I think, Henry Higginsbottom. I think you're just lousy letting me wear something stolen and risk getting arrested."

"But, honey you insisted."

"Yes, but I didn't know you'd stolen them."

"But I didn't!" Henry protested. "I didn't steal them at all. I just got dragged into this."

Polly seized on the glimmer of hope.

"Didn't you want to come into it?"

"No, I didn't. I hated it like hell. But what could I do? Mr. Jenkins knew something about me he was going to tell Felicity, and anyway I needed the money badly enough."

"Mr. Jenkins," said Polly slowly. "But I thought he was your friend."

"Friend! Listen, this is how much he's my friend," Henry said earnestly. "If he was drowning and I just had to reach out my hand to save him, I wouldn't do it."

"You mean he blackmailed you to look after the diamonds for him after *he* had stolen them!"

"That's it exactly," Henry said gloomily. "Now I've got to get them back or he'll kill me. He's the sort of guy that doesn't stop at killing."

"Gangster type!" said Polly, nodding. "And what are you going to do with the diamonds when I give them back to you? Play hide-and-seek with Mr. Jenkins the rest of your life?"

"No." Henry took her arm and led her across the lawn toward the big rhododendrom. "Come over here, honey. I guess I'd better tell you everything."

The story horrified and thrilled Polly. It was an exhilarating feeling tumbling right into the middle of a drama like this. Smuggling at Carstairs, and Lynn knowing nothing about it! Henry hearing the ghost down in those dark passages at night! The diamonds that had to be got out of England by midnight! It sounded like something out of the Arabian nights. But her chief feeling was one of the most intense relief that after all Henry was no more a crook than she herself. It was simply bad luck that had got him mixed up in this. He was so dumb he just couldn't look after himself. So it was quite obvious she would have to do it for him.

There was nothing indecisive about Polly. She had made up her mind instantly what should be done.

"First thing," she said determinedly, "is to get rid of the diamonds."

"Well, that's what I've been telling you all along," Henry protested. "We've got to hand them over to Claus Jensen."

"Not that way, you goof!" Polly said impatiently. "They're stolen goods, don't you understand? If you hand them over you're liable to be arrested as an accomplice. We've got to get rid of them some other way."

"You mean, hand them to the police?"

"Nope. We can't do that, either. You've had them too long. No, there's only one way. We're going for a little walk down to the river."

Henry just stared.

"You mean—those jewels—" The idea was too much for him. He could only say feebly, "Polly, the river's half a mile away."

"What if it is. We've got legs. And you might at least be grateful. I'm ruining my shoes for you."

"But, Polly—"

"Don't stand wasting time talking. Come on!"

Henry tried to tell her on the way about the certainty that Mr. Jenkins would kill him, but Polly wouldn't be convinced. She said the thing to do was to get rid of the diamonds first, and be scared afterwards. This resolution stayed firmly with her until they stood on the river bank above the dark slow water.

"For God's sake, Polly, do you realize what you're doing?" Henry said piteously.

The diamonds hung in Polly's hands. They were so luminous in the darkness that they seemed alive. She was trembling all over.

"Of course I do!" she sobbed, letting the diamonds slide from her fingers and fall with an almost inaudible splash into the river. The dark stream swallowed their brilliance. It flowed on as if nothing more precious than a handful of pebbles had been commited to its keeping.

"Why, Polly! Why, honey, you're crying!"

Polly turned angrily to Henry.

"Of course I am. Those lovely, lovely diamonds that I've wanted all my life just thrown away!"

Henry slid his arm around her quivering shoulders.

"Never mind, honey, I'll buy you some more some day."

"Yes! If you live long enough."

Henry shivered violently.

"I told you the risk—"

Polly sniffed, recovered from her momentary agitation, and once more capably took the situation in hand.

"You'll have to go right back to the States to Chicago or wherever you came from," she said decisively. "Don't go back to the *Duck and Drake* tonight. I'll ask Lynn to let you stay at Carstairs. And tomorrow you'll have to go."

"Gosh, honey, just as I'm getting to know you!" Henry said dolefully.

"Yes," said Polly coldly. "And now you'll tell me just what happened in Chicago that you didn't want Felicity to know."

At the moment that Lynn missed Felicity from the ballroom the laughter sounded. Perhaps if at that moment the music hadn't been stopped no one would have heard or noticed it particularly. At the same moment the warm gusty wind that had arisen half an hour since battered against the house, and whether from accident or design, Lynn could not have told. The big French windows at the end of the ballroom burst open and half the candles blew out. Immediately all the chatter and laughing ceased. A little audible gasp went around the room. Someone gave a scream, instantly suppressed. The blown candlelight showed the company in their motley dress like dim and brilliant phantoms.

For thirty seconds that almost bewitched immobility held the room. Then Dick Neville said in a falsely boisterous voice:

"Well, there you are, Ann, there's your ghost!" and at the moment the words left his lips the high, clear laughter came again. It seemed to come through the walls or the ceiling. It was impossible to tell where it came from, but in the half-lit ballroom with the warm gusty wind flickering the candles madly, it was indescribably eerie.

In a split second thoughts ran through Lynn's head.

The other night when he heard the laughter it had been as still as death, the vast shadowy house might have been a tomb; tonight there was the summer lightning splintering the darkness, half the candles were out and a wind was breathing deep gusty breaths against the windows. This ghost had a fine sense of the dramatic. Therefore—was it a ghost?

The laughter had died away again, and a confused babble of voices broke out. Little Ann Neville was on the verge of hysterics, Lady Maplethorpe's dry, humorous voice was saying in Lynn's ear:

"Congratulations on the stage management, Mr. Carstairs!"

Lynn turned to protest vehemently.

"But I had nothing whatever to do with it. The thing's a complete mystery to me. Can you see Felicity anywhere?"

"Well, whether it's a mystery or not, you've made your ball a success. It'll be the sensation of the year. No, I haven't seen Felicity for half an hour."

Lynn looked around. People were recovering and beginning to move about. A monstrously fat person in a pirate's costume whom Lynn couldn't remember having seen before slipped unobtrusively out of the door. Someone was striking matches and lighting the blown-out candles. The scene was so rapidly becoming normal that Lynn couldn't explain the sensation of horror and fear that remained with him. Where was Felicity?

"Lady Maplethorpe," he said urgently, "look after things for me for five minutes. I'm going to look for Felicity. I'm afraid—"

But he hadn't moved a couple of steps before shrieks sounded in the hall without, and the next moment Mrs. Mell flung herself into the room and collapsed on the floor. At the same moment the laughter came again, further off, and with a strangely human tremble of fear at the end of it.

Felicity's voice! By that tremor at the end, Lynn recognized it, and in a flash he saw it all: Felicity's midnight assignation, Mrs. Mell's timely fainting fit, too much of a coincidence the second time for it to be genuine (it was a dupe to lend color to the ghost theory and hinder him from immediate investigation), and cursed himself for the fool he was not to have seen all this before. Ignoring the prostrate figure of his housekeeper and the pandemonium among his guests, he dashed out of the ballroom and along the hall toward the library. Felicity was down in the cellars laughing. But she was frightened. Something had frightened her. The quiver at the end of her laughter had been unmistakable.

As he entered the library the clock on the stairs spoke midnight in its tremulous old lady voice. The secret panel was closed, but as Lynn reached it he gave an exclamation, for there was a fragment of white silk caught in it. A fragment of Felicity's gown! So she had come this way.

Retaining enough sense this time to equip himself with a torch, and also, from some blind instinct, seizing a candle out of the sconce above the mantelpiece (one may get lost and one's torch battery burn out) Lynn opened the panel and peered into the darkness.

On second thoughts he refrained from going into that dark narrow passage. This morning he had rushed blindly into it, and had come off second best. He could be of no use to Felicity unconscious. Nor could he be of any use to her lost in a maze of unknown passages. This time he must keep his head and act sanely. He would go down into the cellars and take the main path through the passages, the way that ran to the sea.

In less than five minutes he was down the cellar stairs and smelling the cold damp salt tang that came up the black passage from the sea. Suddenly, as his torch lit the dark way down to the caves, he thought of Peewee. Peewee had been in the ballroom when the candles blew out. There was a small clear picture in his mind of someone else, one of his guests, in Elizabethan ruff and balloon sleeves, thoughtfully lighting more candles. Then was Peewee down here too? But he wasn't afraid of Peewee. It was time that engaging rascal was dealt with.

Something above the murmur of the sea was in the darkness. Voices. Far off, but unmistakable in the echoing caves. Caution stayed Lynn's hurrying footsteps. He went carefully, keeping the light of his torch focused on the ground. Something was happening down here—something that would probably lead him to discover his unknown assailent of the morning. It would give him advantage to see before he was seen.

On tiptoe he passed Rollo Carstairs' cave. A little ahead a faint yellow light glimmered on the wet walls of the passage. There were small dark pools of water on the ground where the tide was creeping in. A mutter of voices came out of the cave from which the light shone. With extreme wariness Lynn moved toward the entrance. At the last moment he fanicied he heard almost soundless footsteps behind him, and someone breathing. But he was too absorbed to look around.

Within the cave an amazing scene met his eyes. He might have been conveyed suddenly back to the middle ages, or it might have been an old colorful painting come to life. Even he, in his dark gallant dress, might have been part of it. The only incongruous figure was Peewee's.

A smokey ship's lantern set in the middle of the floor lighted the scene. A couple of sailors in blue jerseys were bending over a pile of cases. A tall fellow with a magnificent head of blond hair and heavy blond eyebrows stood over them, in the background. Peewee in his absurdly respectable butler's suit watched with his unfamiliar keen narrowed eyes, and in the center, deliciously young and virginal and lovely in her long white dress, stood Felicity.

"All right, Claus," she was saying in her clear authoritative voice. "That's the lot, I think. You've done remarkably well. The next time you come I might be introducing you to the new master of Carstairs."

"Felicity, don't be a fool!" ejaculated Peewee sharply, in his unexpectedly well-bred voice.

Felicity took no notice of him.

"I will be, Claus, or else we won't be wanting you to call again."

The big man called Claus smiled a slow deep attractive smile.

"I've been coming a long time, Miss Felicity. Ever since you were no bigger than my little Anna at home."

Felicity smiled.

"How is Anna, Claus?"

"Sweet. Sweet as honey, Miss Felicity." A deep light shone in the man's peculiarly golden eyes. "I am taking her home an English doll. She will laugh, I think. Then is the new master to know about all this?"

"No!" said Peewee sharply. "Felicity's losing her head."

"On the contrary," Felicity returned, "I'm keeping it."

Lynn stepped laconically into the room.

"Yes," he said composedly. "I'm inclined to agree with Felicity."

No doubt his own figure in the dark graceful costume looked as strange to them as theirs did to him. Their faces in the lantern light looked ludicrously startled. The big, blond, golden-eyed man gaped, Peewee started forward, the two sailors stared with eyes that saw not another human being but a ghost with an alien grace. Felicity's face, after its first surprise, changed to a brightness that rivalled the lantern light.

"Lynn!" she cried.

"What the hell are you doing here?" demanded Peewee. "Claus, cover him, you fool!"

The big sailor glanced quickly at Felicity for confirmation, and in that split second another voice, thick and excited, broke in:

"It's never wise to hesitate. Cover your man first and think afterward. Don't move anybody. It won't be safe."

It only needed this fantastically colossal figure in the pirate's dress to complete the strangeness of the scene. Lynn stared in bewilderment at the big figure with the little, bright frightened eyes standing in the opening of the cave covering them with a very serviceable-looking revolver. For a moment his quick brain failed to see how to act. Besides, he fancied he saw something move behind the big brilliant figure in the doorway. A bat, no doubt, but it may have been more men. This was like a scene out of a comic opera.

Peewee was the first to find his voice.

"What's the game?" he asked sharply.

"Don't talk," commanded the big man in his thick eager voice that trembled slightly. It may have been from anger, but it seemed more like fright. The man's face was curiously puffy and damp with sweat. "Which is Claus Jensen?"

The blond man made a movement.

"I am."

"Have you got the diamonds?"

One of the sailors, who apparently understood nothing that was going on, began to talk excitedly in French. Lynn distinctly saw someone move behind the big pirate, and as the pirate involuntarily looked over his shoulder, with a nervous movement, Lynn acted. He lunged forward, knocking the light out, and as the inevitable pandemonium arose he grabbed for Felicity in the darkness, found first a little jabbering sailor, impatiently pushed him aside and encountered the heavy silk of Felicity's dress, then her hand.

The thick, excited, terrified voice of the big man was screaming:

"I'll shoot! Anyone who moves I'll shoot!"

"Keep your head, Kit!" came another voice, clear and cold. Suddenly a torch light shone in the doorway and Lynn, his arm around Felicity's waist, took two strides to the opening of the cave, half pushing, half-carrying her with him, and was out in the passage.

The explosion of a revolver sounded behind them. Lynn was scarcely aware of the flash of pain that went through his shoulder. He had acted on the instant, knowing it was the only thing to do. God knew how that light-hearted smuggling scene he had broken in upon had turned to this desperate pass, but he had only one idea in his head, and that was to get Felicity safely out of what looked like what was developing into an ugly brawl.

It was utterly dark. Or not quite. Sudden stabs of light from the torch of their pursuer lit momentarily the black way. Lynn, with Felicity's hand in his, tripping and stumbling, felt his way along the passage, trying to elude that following light. His own torch had been lost in the struggle in the cave. He was running blindly in the dark, taking no heed of where he was going. Once Felicity panted:

"Lynn, be careful! If we're — lost — it might — be worse!"

"Do you know the caves?" he whispered back.

"Pretty well."

"Then we'll risk it."

He thought for a moment that he had eluded that searching light, but the next moment it was on them again, close and brilliant. Felicity blundered into the rocky wall and gave a suppressed cry of pain. Lynn guided her around a corner that the ray of light had lit. Vaguely he realized that the floor was no longer damp, but covered with that fine yellowish dust he had been aware of the other day when he had been lost. The light vanished a moment, the

/

darkness was complete, then its long brilliant shaft lit up the cave they were in and a slight dark figure, indistinct in the shadows, but giving a curious impression of fleshlessness stood in the doorway leveling a revolver at them.

Too late Lynn realized that the only outlet to the cave was the doorway through which they had come, and which that indistinct, oddly menacing figure was barring.

"It was thoughtful of your ancestors, Miss Felicity," the stranger was saying in a dry precise voice, "to fit out some of these caves with such stout doors. No doubt they had as good a reason as I have for using them. I'll just bar this door, if you've no objections. You'll be quite safe here until I come back. Perhaps in the meantime you could be persuading your friend to hand the diamonds to me when I come for them. It would save time later. I'm sure you've no wish to stay here longer than necessary."

He stepped back to swing the massive door on its rusty hinges forward. Lynn caught a glimpse, in the gloom of a peculiarly pallid face, with lips drawn back in a skeleton-like grin, before he sprang forward. But it was too late. The door swung shut in his face and the heavy bolts dropped. A fine cloud of dust descended from the ceiling of the cave. The darkness was complete.

CHAPTER ELEVEN

THE KITTEN hardly knew what had happened to him after Pope had diverted his attention and that mad young fool Carstairs had knocked the light out. Something equivalent to a ton of rock had fallen on him and he had simply collapsed. When he came to his gun had gone, there was utter darkness and silence, his head ached vilely and he was deadly afraid. Where was Claus Jensen who should have had the diamonds, where was Henry Higginsbottom, where was Pope? Had they all gone and left him here, perhaps dying for all they knew? He was lying in water, too. As his head cleared he was conscious of the chilly wetness against his skin. The tide was coming in. It rose to a height that covered a man's head in these caves, Henry Higginsbottom had said. Somehow, in the dark, he would have to find his way out before it rose too high. Even now he could hear the faint swish of incoming water and its gentle liplipping against the walls. He would have to get out without wasting a minute.

He had lost his elegant three-cornered hat and

his beautiful coat was soaked through with sea-water. He was a complete wreck, lost and panic-stricken and half drunk with pain. It only needed the Laughing Ghost to complete his demoralization. At the thought of that possibility the Kitten stumbled to his feet and blundered out of the cave.

His feet splashed in the rising water. He moved a few unsteady steps, tripped heavily on a rock and fell. A flash of light stabbed the darkness. Something gripped his shoulder. The Kitten squealed and Pope laughed softly.

"Well, Kit," he said in his gentle deadly voice, "you look like the wreck of the *Hesperus*. Don't sit there in the water. Come inside here. It's drier. Look, there's even a door to shut to keep out drafts. And sounds."

As Pope spoke he propelled the shivering Kitten through the doorway and clanged the massive door shut. It wasn't for a moment that his sinister last words penetrated the Kitten's consciousness.

"What do you mean, sounds, Kiff?"

Pope had set his torch on a ledge so that its light illuminated the cave. The damp walls shone with a glowworm brilliance. The floor was covered with a couple of inches of water. The Kitten was a big, brilliant, terrified figure in his bedraggled finery and Pope—Pope stood in the shadows, the glint of an automatic in his hand.

"What I mean," he was saying softly, "is that you have bungled everything so beautifully that I am going to kill you."

The Kitten's breath left him. He tried to swallow and couldn't. The black shiny walls of the cave went around dizzily and Pope's face, pallid as a corpse, went around with them. The water lapped at his ankles. He stood rooted to the ground, helpless with terror.

"Fortunately," Pope said, "I averted complete disaster. I've got young Higginsbottom and the girl locked up until I deal with you. You see how wise I was in coming down here to watch things. I've had time to explore the caves, and I knew the exact whereabouts of the one where I've locked them. I guided them to it—very skilfully, I might say."

The Kitten was stuttering with excitement.

"Did you say Higginsbottom? Listen, Kiff! Henry didn't show up. That's not him. That's Lynn Carstairs."

"Lynn Carstairs!" echoed Pope, for a moment shaken out of his composure.

"Yes. He hasn't got the diamonds. He hasn't even seen them. So you've bungled it yourself, Kiff."

Pope moved in the shadows. His voice was deadly.

"Whether I've bungled it is no longer any business of yours, Kit, because you're still going to die. Any last words you would like to say? I'm not an unmerciful man. I'm prepared to give you ten seconds."

There was a distinct lifting on the Kitten's scalp, as if his hair were standing on end. He was shivering all over with cold, although the perspiration ran down his face and dripped off his chin. His mind was an incoherence of fear. Already he could see his own body, repulsive with decay, lying here in this cold dark cave, with the figure of Pope, the devilish pitiless figure forever standing over it. Escape! How could he escape? His little, wild, terrified eyes roved around the cave, and suddenly, in the gloom of the ceiling, he could see the rafter with the three stout blackened hooks protruding from it. From nowhere that familiar mocking rhyme came into his head. *Kiffin Pope is afraid of the rope!* And he performed the first brilliant impromptu act of his life.

"Look, Kiff!" he cried, in a wild compelling voice. "Above your head! Hooks in the rafters! *This is where they hang men!*"

Involuntarily Pope glanced upward. He couldn't help himself. His gaze was drawn magnetically to those sinister hooks, and as he looked someone invisible laughed in his ear and the cave was filled with horror. In the split second that his gaze left the Kitten, the Kitten leaped. With his amazing agility he was on Pope and the two of them were on the ground, struggling in the chill salty water. Pope was no match for the Kitten. He was less than half the size and his shut-in luxurious life had left his muscles as flabby as an infant's. The Kitten had the unwieldy terrific strength of a rhinoceros. In less than a minute he had wrenched the gun from Pope's grasp, had slid off the silk scarf knotted around his waist, and sitting astride Pope's helpless figure had slipped a noose around his neck. He felt drunk with power and triumph.

"There you are, my lad," he gloated. "So you'd kill me, would you? Well, you just made a slight mistake. Just a very slight mistake. You should have chosen a cave where they didn't hang men. See?"

Pope struggled and the noose around his neck slipped tight. In the dim light the Kitten didn't notice his protruding eyes and ghastly face. Drunk with triumph he continued to sit astride Pope's prostrate body. He had the gaiety of an urchin, an enormous urchin in bedraggled finery playing at pirates and victorious after a fight.

"You've had this coming to you for a long time, Kiff. Ever since you got your reprieve. I'm going to string you to the rafters. See?"

The rising water lapped gently at Pope's face. The Kitten, suddenly aware of what was happening, hauled him to a sitting position.

"Here, this won't do. Keep your head above water, Kiff. You're born to be hanged, not drowned, do you see? Now, hold your breath while I string you up. This'll teach you to stop interfering in my plans, Kiff."

As easily as if he had been a child, the Kitten swung Pope's limp body erect. The rafter was very low. By standing on a rock it was child's play to tie the silken sash around the stout hook in the rafter and swing Pope up until his feet dangled. He made no sound at all, only swayed a little as lightly as if he had been made of paper. It was not until the Kitten splashed down into the water, retrieved the torch and shone it on Pope's ghastly face that he realized the man was already dead.

He could have wept with disappointment. It wasn't fair! Kiff hadn't deserved to die so easily. He had deserved hours of torment. Why, he didn't even know he had been hanged.

But there was no use wasting time lamenting. He would have to get out of here before the water was too high. It was rising with incredible speed. Already it was almost as high as his knees. Now at least he had a torch with which to find his way back through the passages and up the flight of stairs that led to the garden door. Once he was safely out of here he would shake the dust of St. Simon off his feet, diamonds or no diamonds. For that matter, after this experience, he would never want to handle diamonds again in his life.

But the Kitten's plans failed. He couldn't open the heavy oaken door which Pope had slammed shut when they had come into the cave. It was jammed. Probably it hadn't been shut for centuries and now its rusty hinges, fast closed, were immovable.

At first the Kitten wasn't alarmed. He felt a nasty little shock of fear, but he hadn't yet used half of his tremendous strength. Laying the torch on a rock he seized the iron ring of the door and tugged with all his might. It was no use. The chill of the water was creeping over his knees. Before long it would be up to his waist, then his neck. Higher than a man's head it rose, they said. And he was trapped. The door wouldn't open.

The Kitten pulled and tugged until his arms felt torn from their sockets, until his big, soft, clever fingers were in ribbons. But the heavy door remained closed and the water was reaching his waist. Pope's dangling feet hung in it, swaying ever so slightly as ripples ran across the surface. He watched the Kitten all the time, and his protruding eyes were dreadfully ironic. The Kitten, terrifed, distraught, despairing, splashed forward, torch in hand, to turn that slight shadowy figure around so that its horrible mocking stare would not torment him. But it swung as he moved it, as lightly as if it had been a scarecrow made of hollow clothes and a broomstick. Its knees thrust gently against his fat stomach, as if Pope, lacking humor all his life, had gained sufficient of it in death to give him a sly dig in the ribs. Overcome with horror the Kitten jumped aside, lost his balance and spluttered and struggled in the waist-high water.

He was nearly crazy with fear and horror. With the torch clutched in his hand he waded across the cave and clambered up the rocks piled at the side. There was just a possibility that the water would not rise as high as this. It was only lapping around his ankles now, and surely could not rise to his head. He had only to wait until the tide went out . . . .

An hour passed. The Kitten, clinging to his precarious perch, was like a strange gigantic bird with brilliant draggled plumage. The water, still rising, was as high as his armpits, and he was blubbering to himself in a hopeless desolate way. The lapping of the water and his hiccuping sobs were intermingled. It wasn't fair that Pope should die so easily while he endured this slow torment. Pope had a long ugly list of robbery and blackmail and murder to account for, while he had only petty thefts from the wealthy who had no need of the things he stole. Once he had had a wife to whom he had been good. Little Topsy. She had had bright eyes and black black hair. She had used to pinch his ears. She had said she loved him. But she hadn't had the patience to wait for him until he came out of prison. Perhaps she had died. He had never known. Surely the fact that he had once had a wife and had been good to her would count now, and stop this cruel water from rising as high as his head.

Pope's shadowy figure swayed slightly, and ripples ran to the walls of the cave. The water rose inexorably. The Kitten had a horror of being left in the dark. He held his stiffened arm with the torch in his hand above the water so that a wavering light shone across the roof. The torch was burning dim. It would not last much longer. As long as it lasted until the water began to recede it would be all right. He would be able to bear the darkness then. But the water still rose.

Half an hour later it was lapping against his chin. He had climbed frantically to the highest point of the rocks and could hold on no longer. A long ripple ran across the surface of the water and the cold salt taste of it was in his mouth. Funny. He could feel Topsy pinching his ear. Affectionately. He could hear her little soft laugh. Sweet Topsy. Sweet little kid to come to him in this vile place. Sweet . . .

The Kitten was smiling with his little buttony mouth as he slid down into the water. The torch went out and the cave was in darkness.

Lynn felt for Felicity in the dark. He expected her to be hysterical with fright, but when he felt the firm pressure of her hand and heard her small composed voice speaking in the darkness a rush of admiration swept through him. He might have known her better than to suppose that she would lose her nerve at the first sign of danger. She was Felicity Valentine, the greatest lady he knew.

"There's nothing we can do," she was saying quietly, "except wait until he comes back. I don't think that even one of daddy's elephants could break down this door."

"Have you any idea where we are?" Lynn found it a little difficult to speak. There was a stabbing sensation in his shoulder, and he felt unaccountably weak and tired, as if he had run a long way and his strength was ebbing.

"I think," Felicity said carefully, "that we're in Lynette Carstairs' dungeon. It's the only one besides Rollo's to have a bolted door. It was specially fitted—"

Her voice trailed off. In spite of herself she could no longer speak composedly. A sensation of horror crept over Lynn. He was seeing, as she was, that long-ago little figure imprisoned here, weeping and calling uselessly. He was seeing what he had seen that other day, the rough imperfect cross scratched in the wall, the last desperate prayer. He felt as if they were imprisoned with a ghost, the Laughing Ghost of Carstairs.

"I've got us into a mess," he said ruefully. "My idea was to get you away before there was a rough-house. I didn't anticipate just getting us locked up."

"You did the only thing," Felicity assured him, her voice composed again. "And it's all right. We've only got to wait until our delightful jailer comes back."

"Who is he?"

Felicity gave a little shudder.

"Ask me! He looked like the devil's own ghost. I haven't the faintest idea what's gone wrong."

"There's something about diamonds," said Lynn. "Henry Higginsbottom's mixed up in it. It looks to me, Felicity, as if you've got some particularly nasty crooks interested in your unlawful activities here."

"But how would they know? Henry may be a nuisance knowing too much, but I'm sure he wouldn't do a low-down thing like that."

"He mighn't want to," Lynn corrected, "but if you don't mind me saying so, Felicity, Henry hasn't much backbone or sense. He's probably been blackmailed into something like this."

"Oh!" cried Felicity angrily. "I don't know why we ever had him here. I've been crazy. Uncle Lynn was right. I haven't any sense of responsibility. But how was I to know smashing up a car on the London road would lead to this?"

Lynn had to speak carefully, because his strange sensation of weakness was increasing.

"Don't be sorry about it, Felicity."

"I'm not," she said swiftly. "I'm not in the least. You don't know how heavenly grateful I am. Lynn, where are you? It's so dark."

"Just here, Felicity."

"I—just want to feel you. Lynn! Your hand's wet! It's bleeding!"

It was funny that until that moment Lynn hadn't realized the pain in his shoulder would be due to a bullet wound. Of course! He had been hit as he ran from the cave. The blood was dripping off his finger tips. He moved sharply away from Felicity.

"Keep away from me! Don't get your dress spoiled! I must have got hit in the shoulder. It's absolutely nothing."

"Nothing indeed!" said Felicity distressedly. "It's bleeding like anything. I've got to bind it up. Oh, why is it so dark! I can't see a thing!"

"I had a torch," Lynn said vaguely. "I must

have dropped it when we ran. Felicity, you're not tearing your dress?"

"Of course I am," she said impatiently. "There's enough material here to bandage the British army. Oh, why haven't we got a light?"

Lynn had a peculiar sensation of sinking into a dark, cool, blessed sea. Felicity's agitated voice came from a long way off. She wouldn't hear him if he answered, she was too far away. But he would answer all the same because she sounded so distressed.

"Think there's a candle—in my pocket," he said. He had sunk so far into that cool sea he could scarcely hear his own voice. "Always candles at Carstairs . . ." The sea closed over his head.

He opened his eyes again later to the misty yellow glow of candlelight. Felicity was sitting in the circle of it, tearing a strip of silk from the white pool of her skirt. There was a ring of light around her hair. Her brows were drawn together in a little distressed frown, her lips set in a sweet seriousness. Lynn forgot his weakness and the throbbing in his shoulder, he forgot his plight, and was conscious only of a wild delight.

"Darling!" he said softly.

The color swept into Felicity's cheeks. She shook her head smiling.

"Wait until I start taking your coat off this shoulder," she said. "Then you won't be calling me darling. Set your teeth for a minute. I'll try not to hurt."

Lynn nearly fainted again during that operation. He tried to set his mind on the skilfulness of Felicity's hands and the candlelight in her hair. She talked quietly all the time.

"Thoughtful of you to bring a candle, dear. I shouldn't have been able to manage. I can just stop the bleeding now. You'll have to get a doctor as soon as we get out of here. I'll tell you about the smuggling presently. I would have told you long ago if they'd let me."

"And the ghost," said Lynn.

Felicity straightened the bandage. She looked delightfully mischievous.

"It's I," she said.

Lynn stared in incredulity.

"I knew it was tonight," he said. "That's why I came down. But the other time—"

"You might as well know," Felicity said. "I intended telling you in spite of what daddy says. It was a phonograph record of my voice, amplified. Uncle Lynn revived the old ghost theory to keep curious servants and"—her eyes twinkled— "usurpers from the cellars. Ingenious, wasn't it?"

"Damned effective," said Lynn. "And how long has this light-hearted smuggling been going on?"

Felicity chuckled.

"Oh, for years. The Carstairs have always been smugglers. Uncle Lynn didn't see why he should break the tradition simply because of modern times. He was partial to French wines and brandy. But he liked the element of risk most, I think. It was great pleasure to outwit the government. It was really his hobby. It was so important to him that he wanted to bequeath it to his heir. That's why he put that clause in the will about becoming reconciled to the ghost. Are you, Lynn?"

"If you're the ghost," said Lynn, "I don't think there's a doubt about it. Seriously, I think the whole thing's a damned good adventure."

"Uncle Lynn would say you're a man after his own heart," said Felicity approvingly.

"But why," asked Lynn, "did you have to be the ghost tonight?"

"Because you're so inquisitive, darling. Because in your explorations this morning you broke the phonograph record. That was the room where we had the amplifier. That's where I went tonight."

"And you were frightened?"

"I suddenly saw that strange man looking over my shoulder. I didn't hear him come. He was just suddenly there. I thought I'd seen a ghost."

Lynn was suddenly thinking of his own imagined ghost, Lynette Carstairs, bending over him in the uncertain candlelight.

"It was you this morning?" he asked.

Felicity nodded.

"I'd put on my dress to look at the portrait and see if everything was right. I just needed a fan. Mrs. Mell said you were in the ballroom so I went through the door in the library to see if everything was all right for tonight. I just meant to be a minute. But you saw me. If Peewee hadn't unexpectedly been there—"

"Wait until I get hold of this butler of mine!" Lynn said revengefully.

"You will," Felicity promised. "And now that's enough explanation. You know as much as I do. I think you ought to be quiet for a while. How does your arm feel?"

"Better, thanks. Fine," Lynn said, trying to fight the drowsiness that came from loss of blood. It was so pleasant just to lie here, listening to the vague far-off sound of the sea, looking at Felicity's hair bright in the candlelight, feeling the sweetness of her presence. He was in danger even of forgetting their predicament.

"I'm putting my shawl under your head," came Felicity's far-off voice. "We might have to wait a long time, so you might as well get some sleep."

"You, too," said Lynn drowsily, stretching out his hand for hers. "Put your head on the shawl, too." He saw her moving vaguely in the candlelight, but never heard her answer, for suddenly she had become too far away. . . .

He awoke later, his arm flaming with pain, to find the room in complete darkness. There wasn't even a glimmer of Felicity's white dress. He struggled up in alarm, to hear her quiet composed voice.

"I put the candle out. I thought it might be wise to save it. Shall I light it again?"

"How long have we been here?"

"Three and a half hours."

"But—God! Has the fellow forgotten us?"

Lynn felt Felicity's hand on his shoulder.

"Don't move, dear. You might start the bleeding again. It hurts, doesn't it?"

"Like Hell! But I'm all right, Felicity. Have you been awake all the time? Haven't you heard anything?"

There was a brief pause before Felicity answered.

"Only the sea. I'm afraid—Lynn, we'll have to face it. I'm afraid something's happened to that man, whoever he was. And no one else knows we're here."

Lynn moved.

"Darling! Light the candle—just for a moment. I can't see you."

Felicity fumbled with matches. The frail blue flame deepened and grew into a golden leaf of light that gathered thick shadows in the corners and over the ceiling. Felicity, with the undefeatable gaiety on her lips, smiled down at Lynn. But her eyes were enormous, and dark as the shadows in the corners.

"Have you been sitting here for three and a half hours realizing that while I slept?"

She nodded uncertainly.

"I wanted you to sleep."

Lynn sat up, the candlelight and the shadows dancing crazily.

"We'll shout."

"No one will hear us. Don't you remember? Lynette was imprisoned here so no one from the house would hear her calling."

A sense of doom began to creep over Lynn. He tried to dispel it.

"Someone will be here soon, surely. It's your turn to sleep, darling. I'll watch and keep the wild animals away. Lie down beside me. Put your head on my shoulder."

He pulled her until she had to obey. Her hair was on his cheek. She moved against him with a nestling movement like a warm soft animal. He forgot the pain in his arm and was suddenly wildly, unreasonably happy.

"Close your eyes, dear. I'm going to blow out the light."

Felicity sighed.

"It's funny. I feel quite safe."

The yellow light vanished and they were in the soft black darkness.

"You are safe, dear. You're my wife and we're in our four-poster. Safe from everything but the chambermaid in the morning. Did we tell her not to wake us early?"

Felicity chuckled.

"Yes, darling."

"Felicity!"

"Yes, darling."

"You will be my wife when we get out of this?"

He felt the movement of her cheek against his own, and she chuckled again, shakily.

"I've been throwing myself at you all the evening."

"Dearest! You've been so stubborn about it."

"Uncle Lynn throwing me at you like that made me stubborn," Felicity confessed. "I'd have gone on being stubborn too, if you hadn't told me today that you loved me. But I couldn't, after that. I knew I had to make you stay at Carstairs some way."

"I'll certainly have to stay now," said Lynn humorously. "We both will."

Felicity nestled against him.

"Someone will come soon. I'm not going to worry. Kiss me, Lynn."

Lynn found her lips and kissed them, then the little hollow in her throat that he had dreamed about.

"This is forever," he whispered. "In spite of dumb Yankees, dungeons and ghosts. Say it, Felicity."

"Forever," Felicity echoed. "Lynn, even if we die together, I'll be glad about finding each other."

Lynn held her closely. She was as slight and soft as a child.

"We're not going to die, my sweet."

"Well, anyway, we're happier than poor Lynette. We have each other. She was all alone. She must have fretted for Rupert. She was in love with him, I'm sure. In a way it's as if we're finishing her life happily for her."

Lynn sat up excitedly. Ignoring the pain in his shoulder he fumbled for matches and the precious candle.

"What's the matter, Lynn? Can you hear someone coming?"

"I've just thought of something," Lynn said, his voice unsteady with excitement. "Lynette didn't die in here, did she?"

"No. She escaped. No one ever found her again. She got lost in the passages. That's how the ghost story originated."

"She couldn't possibly have escaped through that locked door," said Lynn slowly, quelling his excitement. He struck a match, showing Felicity's face suddenly as white and tense as his own. "Therefore there's another way out of this cave somewhere —if we can only find it."

Day was breaking when the knock came at Polly's door. Objects in the room were taking shape and the gentle light flowing through the window was growing bright. It was a hot, still, colorless dawn. The sound of the sea was like distant tireless wind.

Polly sat up dazedly, rubbing her eyes.

"Come in," she called, thinking it was Mrs. Mell or one of the maids knocking.

But the door opened and Henry came in. He was still in his George Wahington costume, and the daylight made him look foolish and dishevelled. He was bleary-eyed from lack of sleep and his face was puckered up with worry.

"Good gracious!" cried Polly, scandalized, pulling the bedclothes over her shoulders. "What on earth are you doing in here? This isn't Chicago where you can go in and out of a lady's bedroom if you want to."

"Honey, I explained how that happened," Henry said aggrievedly. "I thought at least you would understand."

"Well, I told you last night I didn't," said Polly, who was cross and sleepy. "I don't see why you've got to wake me up at this hour to talk about it."

"But I'm not talking about it, honey. You started it."

"Then what *are* you doing here?"

"I just had to see you honey. I was so worried. Lynn and Felicity haven't been found yet."

Polly sat upright, forgetting her modesty and letting the bedclothes slip from her pretty shoulders.

"Good gracious! I was so sleepy I hadn't remembered. Is the tide out? Has anyone been looking for them?"

It was all coming back to her now, and she wondered how she could have slept. In that little conference in the library at half-past three in the morning after all the guests had gone and there was still no sign of Lynn or Felicity, Peewee had said they should all try to get some sleep. If Lynn and Felicity were in the underground passages there was no hope of searching for them until the tide had gone out, as half the caves would be full of water. No doubt they were marooned in some dry spot and would turn up in the early morning. Felicity knew the caves as well as anybody living. So Polly, so tired that she could scarcely stand, her mind a maze of bewilderment with the happenings of the night, had drifted disconsolately off to bed. And, incredibly, had slept. And now it was morning, with Henry, still dressed, looking like a child waiting for comfort, standing at the foot of her bed.

"Peewee and Mark have gone down now," he was saying. "Peewee's rung Scotland Yard."

"*What!*"

"I had to tell him everything," Henry said unhappily. "Why I wasn't down there last night, and so on. It's this fellow Jenkins he's worrying about. Says the police'll have to get him. He's not going to tell them more than he can help."

"It's probably the best thing," Polly said reflectively. "Where's Jenkins now?"

"That's what we don't know. Peewee thinks he's still down in the caves with an accomplice he's got with him. He's set a watch on the beach to see they don't get away that way. It's a nasty business."

"It certainly is," Polly agreed.

"I wish I hadn't got mixed up in it."

"So do I, but you're so dumb."

"Gosh, honey, I can't help it. One minute I'm wealthy and the next I'm broke. It'd make anyone feel as if he was standing on his head."

"Yes," said Polly. (He looked so shamefaced and pathetic she couldn't help relenting.) "I suppose it would. I suppose you have had a tough spin. (For that matter, so had she. Good-by, visions of Broadway.) But I can't help that. Now you'll have to get out of here while I dress."

For answer Henry came forward a step and sat on the edge of Polly's bed.

"Say, listen, honey, there's something I came to ask you this morning. I want to know if you'll marry me."

Polly's eyes opened wide with astonishment. Nothing, she thought, would surprise her again, not after last night and now a proposal of marriage at five o'clock in the morning by a very large young George Washington. But there was a creeping feeling of sweetness behind it all.

"Gosh!" she said slowly. "You've got nerve, haven't you? After last night and after that business in Chicago. And it's only two weeks since you were crazy with joy because Felicity was going to marry you."

"I know, honey. But Felicity isn't the sort of girl for me. I've discovered that. She's the sort of girl for Lynn Carstairs. And forget that Chicago business, will you? Besides, you mightn't believe it, but I'm just crazy about you."

Polly did believe that. It was the one thing she was clinging to in this suddenly topsy-turvy world. And it was surprising how sweet it was.

"You must care a little bit about me, honey," Henry was saying earnestly, "to get me out of that mess last night. And I'd be a good husband to you. You just don't know how good a husband I could be. We'd go back to the States and I'd open a little tobacco shop. And you could help."

"What'd you start it on if you're broke?" Polly asked skeptically.

"I'll raise a bit of capital some way. My father must have saved something from the wreck. I'll just be plain Henry Higginsbottom. After all, Polly, my father was just in a dry goods store to begin with and look at the fortune he made. We could think of some snappy slogan."

"Like 'A smile a smoke' or something like that," suggested Polly eagerly.

Henry's face lit up.

"That's it, honey. Gosh, you don't know the help you'll be to me. You've got the right sort of head. We could be married in London and catch the next boat—"

"Wait a minute," Polly protested. "I haven't said I'll marry you yet. And it's dreadful of you to be thinking of things like this with poor Lynn and Felicity lost."

"I know, honey, but I had to ask you now. What with me having to get right back to the States and everything."

"Yes," said Polly reflectively. After all, in a way, this was a business proposition. She was the sort of person who would always be helping lame dogs. She had stuck to Lynn while he had needed her, but now he no longer did. He had Felicity, and, anyway, his need of her had been due to bad luck. Henry was so dumb he would always be a lame dog. Besides she was in love with him. There was no use in denying it. She was so much in love with him that she didn't even care any longer about Broadway so long as she could be with him and help him. But she wasn't going to let him see her sentimentality about it—not yet, anyway.

"Okay, Henry," she said, with commendable airiness. "I guess I'd better marry you to protect you from blackmailers, diamond necklaces and Chicago matrons."

Felicity said, "Put the candle out for a while, Lynn, and have a rest. There can't be a square inch of this wall we haven't examined. Let's sit down and think."

Lynn turned to look at her. Despite his weariness and growing despair, he grinned. Felicity's eyes were so wide and eager. There was a smudge of dust across her cheek and her hair was untidy as it had been the day he had first seen her in the garage. She had pulled up her dress at the waist and had tied her sash very tightly to keep her long skirts off the ground. She looked as slender as a child, and her eyes were as eager. It didn't seem as if his own despair had touched her at all.

"Not a very cheerful thing, thinking in these circumstances," he pointed out.

"Neither is scratching for an imaginary door in a wall six feet thick. It's six o'clock, Lynn. The tide will be out and if they're looking for us they'll be looking now. We might try shouting."

There was an inch and a half of candle left. It was all they had between themselves and perpetual darkness. But that grim thought did not seem to alarm Felicity. Or if it did she hid her alarm. She blew out the small flame and pulling Lynn down beside her in the darkness cupped her hands to her lips.

"Let's shout together. It'll carry further."

So they shouted. At intervals for the next half hour they shouted, but all the answer they heard was the echo, far off and eerie, of their own voices. Felicity paused for breath.

"It's no use, I'm afraid," she said, rather breathlessly. "We'll have to look again for a door."

Lynn said: "Yes," his despair growing. Felicity was too young, too sweet, too alive, to die like this. starving in the hostile darkness. There'd be another ghost, young and lovely, to laugh at Carstairs.

"But just let's sit here for a while," she said, snuggling against him. "I like to be close to you. Do you know, if I could choose whom I'd like to be lost with, it would be you, so it's really extraordinarily lucky." She gave a soft little laugh, untouched with despair, and rubbed her head up his arm. "Makes me forget about being cold and sleepy and hungry. I shouldn't complain yet because I suppose we'll get hungrier."

"They say you can live quite a long time without food," Lynn said carefully.

"Yes." Felicity sighed. Her sigh was the rueful resigned sigh of a child. "It's not exactly pleasant, they say, too."

Lynn pressed her arm.

"There could be nobody but God to give you your courage Felicity."

"My spunk, Uncle Lynn used to say," she replied lightly. "Remember Uncle Lynn's poem?"

"The sea is calm tonight, the moon lies fair
Upon the straits . . . ."

Her light sweet voice was like a charm in that grim place. Suddenly Lynn knew that death in any form could hold no terrors for him with Felicity, a smudge across her cheek, her hair dishevelled, undefeatably gay and courageous, at his side.

"You're wonderful," he said softly. "I'm all the time learning more wonderful things about you."

"Will you love me," Felicity whispered, the lightness all gone from her voice, "so that when I die you'll remember me as the nicest thing in your life?"

"You don't need to ask me that, Felicity."

"That's how it is with me, too," she said, on a long breath. "I've always wanted to be loved like this—so that when you come into a room you'll know I've been there, or when you hear some music you love or smell a flower, you'll think of me."

Lynn kissed her gently on the forehead. Even their desperate plight was blessed, because of this moment.

After a time he said, "Are you rested, dear? I'll light the candle and look again for this non-existent door."

Felicity laughed.

"If we escape through a nonexistent door we really will have become ghosts."

The small frail flame once more lighted their prison. Lynn found his eyes kept returning to that scratched cross in the wall, and the half-finished text.

"I wonder," he said thoughtfully, "why she didn't finish that. Had she discovered God wasn't her refuge, after all, or was she too tired? Or had she found the way out?"

Felicity searched for and found a sharp fragment of rock.

"Supposing we finish it for her," she said. "It might even help us. How she must have worked to scratch all this, the poor lost child."

Lynn, holding the candle, watched Felicity scratch at the uncompleted last word of the text. She was so like his imagined picture of Lynette, slender, bright-haired, absorbed, her fine small hands working patiently and despairingly at the writing, that he could not endure it. It was that old unhappy scene repeated. Was Felicity's fate to be the same?

"Don't do it!" he cried. "It's useless. I—"

Felicity interrupted him with a startled cry. Her face, white with excitement and triumph, was turned up to him. She had dropped the piece of rock, for where it had cut into that letter, unfinished by Lynette Carstairs two centuries before, a slit, indicating the presence of yet another sliding door, had appeared disclosing a black passage beyond!

Inspector Clayton from Scotland Yard tucked his thumbs in his waistcoat and strolled around the library at Carstairs. The whole business sounded fantastic to him. It would probably turn out to be no more than a job for the local constable (whom he had not yet had the pleasure of meeting, since his beat seemed to take him to some little-known spot). Young Carstairs and the girl more than likely had quietly disappeared for a week-end, or perhaps had eloped. And as for this wild story of crooks and diamonds to be got away through the caves beneath Carstairs, using the old method of smuggling which probably had not been in use for a century or more, the thing was incredible. His chief had sent him down because of the diamond story, saying he wanted a good man on the job. But then for the last three weeks the old chief had thought of nothing but the theft of the Windermere necklace of which no trace had been discovered, and the mere mention of diamonds made him as jittery as a girl. It wasn't as if this business could possibly have anything to do with the Windermere diamonds. They would be safe in Paris or Amsterdam long ago. The thief was no amateur. All he could do was to clear the matter up as quickly as possible and get back to London.

"There's one peculiar thing, Inspector," Valentine, the missing girl's father said. "There are two dungeons in the cellars. The doors of them have never been closed nor locked in my lifetime. Probably not for a century before that. This morning they're both closed. One is locked and the other, as far as I can see, jammed. We'll have to get them open somehow."

The inspector smiled indulgently. This fellow, hard-headed as he seemed, had apparently been brought up in an atmosphere of ghosts and ancient history. What did he think would be going on in an underground dungeon in these modern times? A spot of torture?

"All right, Mr. Valentine. We'll have a look at 'em later. We'll get on to the track of the diamonds first. They're something concrete, so to speak. The other stuff's probably sheer whimsy."

"I'd point out it's my daughter, Inspector."

"Yes, yes. Quite so. But youth nowadays—"

His observation on modern youth, however, was never made. At that moment a very large, excited and triumphant constable dressed in a muddied and wet uniform burst unceremoniously into the room.

"Begging your pardon, Inspector, they said you were from Sctoland Yard."

"I am," said Inspector Clayton shortly and sternly. (Who did this fellow think he was—the Commissioner of Police himself?)

"Well, I've found something that'll interest you, sir. In the river. I had to wait till daylight to see whether they're valuable or not, but they look good to me."

With this breathless pronouncement, the man opened his grubby hands and slid a wet but brilliant string of the most magnificent diamonds the inspector had ever seen onto the table.

The inspector knew enough about diamonds in general, the Windermere necklace in particular, to know that this thing that had happened was fantastic, incredible . . . .

"Well, constable," he said, speaking with unusual dreamy incredulity as he threaded the diamonds across his palm, "it looks to me as if this is the biggest fish you ever caught." His voice became crisp and sharp.

"What's your name?"

"Diver, sir."

Constable Diver seemed to have difficulty in speaking.

"Well, Diver, you've done a nice bit of work today. I'll report it to my chief, of course. No doubt you'll get a promotion."

"You mean the jewels are valuable, sir?"

"Valuable!" The inspector paused, looking around the room to see that his audience was appreciative before dropping his bombshell. "They're probably the most valuable diamonds in England. You've hooked the Windermere necklace!"

Guy Valentine started forward, and the big Yankee

by the fireplace, who had been as nervous as a cat all through the interview, gasped audibly.

The inspector smiled.

"Yes, gentlemen. We've certainly had some good luck this morning. You'd better tell us about it, Constable."

"I can't hardly believe it," he muttered. "You see, for one thing, just before I came here they rang me to say me wife had a son. Nine pounder at that. It all seems as if it's too good to be true."

"Congratulations, Constable. But about the diamonds?"

"There's not much to tell, Inspector. I've been shadowing a fellow here. Had suspicions of him for a week or more. Big fat fellow, shape like one of the pumpkins the Vicar wins prizes with at the horticultural show. Used to wear a ruby ring on his finger. I scarcely let him out of my sight. He acted suspicious all the time, but I couldn't pin anything on him. Then last night I took a look around Carstairs. Big ball here, as you've probably heard."

"Yes. Go on."

"I was down at the river just near where the private path from Carstairs comes out, when suddenly two people appeared out of the bushes—it was dark and I couldn't see who they were, but I had the impression of a very large man and a lady. The lady went close to the water's edge and threw something in. I was curious and investigated. I had my torch, but it was too dark to see anything. I had to mark the spot and go back at daylight. Of course if I'd known it was the diamonds they were throwing away I'd have followed them, but as it was—I'm afraid they got away, sir. I've been inquiring at the *Duck and Drake* this morning, but neither the big man nor any strange woman had come in."

"You think this man at the river was the person you've been shadowing?"

"I haven't a doubt about it, Inspector."

There was a clatter at the hearth as the big Yankee moved suddenly and knocked his foot on the fire-irons. He said "Sorry," in an abashed voice. The inspector ignored him.

"What was this fellow's name?"

"Jenkins was the name he went by. Probably it was an alias."

"Jenkins!" said the inspector thoughtfully. "Jenkins. The name's familiar, but a common one at that. There might be a dozen thieves called Jenkins. Wait! My God!" He suddenly leaped to his feet. "Ernest Jenkins, alias Bert Brady, alias Harry Thompson. Enormously fat. The Kitten! Of course! The Kitten!"

He swung around on the astonished company.

"Mr. Valentine, how many outlets to those caves are there?"

"Only one on to the beach, Inspector, and I've had a couple of servants posted at that since the tide went out. The others lead up through the house, and no one has come that way."

"Then we'll go down to those dungeons at once. If I'm right, you've got a nasty criminal at large. What are you like with a revolver?"

"I've killed a lion at twenty yards," Guy Valentine said briefly.

"Good. This will probably be more exciting even than big game hunting."

It took a charge of gelignite to open the door leading into Rollo Carstairs' cave. The inspector stepped through the jagged opening first. Guy Valentine had said that if there were anyone in there there could be no possible chance of his still being alive. When the tide was in the water reached the ceiling. But he went warily, for if the Kitten were in there alive he would be desperate. The man's brains were negligible, but he had the strength of a rhinoceros.

What Valentine had said, however, was true. There was a clammy wet smell and the walls as high as the roof oozed drips of moisture. The floor was still under water and in the center of it lay an enormous heap of bright sodden clothing. The inspector flashed his torch on that almost before he noticed the figure dangling from the roof. But in a moment, satisfied that no life remained in that elephantine bundle, his torch crept around and the ray of light flashed on that grotesque lightly swinging form with its ghastly protruding eyes and skeleton grin.

"Cripes!" he whispered, reverting to the jargon of the days before a native shrewdness and acumen had lifted him to a higher social level. "Must have been a little lovers' quarrel!"

Henry Higginsbottom, peering fearfully in the doorway, gave a subdued, irrepressible, surprising cry of relief which nobody heard.

Guy Valentine's ruddy color had paled slightly. It was a worse sight than any he had ever seen or expected to see.

"Drowned!" he said, trying to speak evenly. "That poor devil—with the water rising all the time. Looks like a thorough job, Inspector. Thank God it's not Felicity and young Lynn. We'd better get along to that other dungeon. It's at least dry and safe—provided nothing like this has nappened," he added, his eyes turning involuntarily to the swinging form.

The inspector, bending over the Kitten's body, was searching gingerly in the sodden clothing.

"I've an idea," he was saying. "Have a look through that other fellow's pockets, Valentine. If they're in that cave and we use gelignite we might dislodge some of the ceiling. My God!" he said fretfully, to the swollen grotesque face of the Kitten. "What's the use of me catching a dead crook. Pinching the Windermere jewels, you might at least have let me get you alive."

Guy Valentine gave an exclamation.

"You're right, Inspector, if this is what's in your mind. Key to the other dungeon."

He produced the rusty medieval key from the hanged man's trouser pocket. "Let's go."

But when they had unlocked the door of Lynette Carstairs' dungeon they found that it was empty.

"Search me," he said. "Why should he want to lock an empty room?"

Guy Valentine had flashed his torch on the floor.

"They've been here," he said quietly. "Drops of candle grease on the floor. Fresh."

"Then how the hell have they gotten out?"

There was suddenly a tense silence. The inspector looked baffled, Constable Diver alarmed and awed. Henry Higginsbottom was as white as his florid face could become.

"The way they've gotten out," Guy said slowly, "will be the way Lynette Carstairs escaped a couple of hundred years ago. And," he added grimly, "no one has ever found that."

CHAPTER TWELVE

THE MATCH Felicity had struck burned her fingers. She gave a little cry of mingled pain and horror, and whispered:

"Lynn, strike another match. Quickly! There's something here."

Lynn did so, although his stiffened arm made it difficult to hold the box (the candle had burned out long ago), and the fragile flame lit what Felicity had stumbled over in the darkness.

Bones. A small finely-shaped skull, long slender limbs, a fragment of clothing that crumbled to dust when Felicity touched it, a locket suspended on a gold chain still hanging around the fleshless neck.

Felicity was white with horror. She knew, even before her trembling fingers opened the locket, what these pitiful lost bones had been: a young and lovely girl, once anticipating her share of laughter and love, once gay and reckless as Felicity herself. The lost lady of Carstairs crumbling away to dust alone in this unknown passage. Yes, there was her miniature in the locket—Lynette Carstairs aged seventeen years. It must have been painted before she had married Rollo. There was too much happiness in the brilliant young eyes. And on the other side— Felicity gave a little gasp. The miniature face looking up at her was the lean, dark, proud face of Rupert Carstairs, or it might have been Lynn Carstairs, so alike were the two faces.

So it was true about Lynn and Rupert. And here were she and Lynn . . . The match Lynn was holding flickered out as Felicity dropped the locket.

It was the first time, during all their dark imprisonment, that she had given way to despair. But now she sobbed desperately.

"Lynn, I can't bear it! It's too dreadful! Dying here all alone in the dark. How she must have cried for a light! I can't bear it!"

Lynn put his arm around her trembling body and drew her away.

"That's not we, my sweet," he urged. "That all happened long ago. The same thing doesn't happen twice. We've only got to keep walking. She stopped walking. That's why that happened to her."

Together they stumbled a few steps in the darkness. Then Felicity collapsed, sliding down onto the dusty floor, sobbing, and Lynn could do nothing but slip down beside her, trying not to admit even to himself the exquisite relief it was to rest. The pain had long since gone out of his arm. It was merely stiff now and dead, as if there were no limb there at all. He was so weary that he could have died.

The atmosphere was heavy with dust stirred by their footsteps. There was no sound in the whole world but Felicity's low desperate sobbing. Lynn had never heard her cry like that before. He had scarcely ever heard her cry at all. She was not made for tears but for laughter and courage and gaiety.

"Stop crying, Felicity."

She trembled and continued to sob. Lynn knew that he would have to stop her before she exhausted herself. She would have to retain the remainder of her strength—though for what, he asked himself involuntarily, shaking off that black despair.

"Listen, Felicity, I hate to hear you crying. I can't put up with it. I'll go to sleep until you stop."

Felicity gulped.

"I can't help it."

"That's all right. Go ahead. But if you don't mind I'll sleep while you're doing it."

Felicity's sobs quieted. She tugged at his arm. He could feel her tears dripping on his face.

"Lynn, don't go to sleep. You mightn't wake up again!"

Lynn yawned.

"Have you stopped crying?"

He felt her head move in assent against his shoulder. His voice softened.

"Good girl. We'll rest five minutes before we go on."

"What's the time, Lynn?"

"Half past three the last time I looked. Mid-afternoon."

Felicity sighed deeply. Her voice was still tremulous with tears.

"I'd feel better if I wasn't so hungry. When I think of all the things I could have eaten in my life and have refused . . . . I wonder what they're doing at Carstairs now. I expect Henry's half crazy with worry and Mrs. Mell will be in a permanent faint, and I daresay even daddy will be perturbed by now."

"And that rascal, Peewee."

Felicity chuckled faintly.

"Shall we get a new butler when we're married, darling?"

"He really knows too much," Felicity murmured naughtily. "Lynn, what's going to happen to our illegal activities now?"

"They cease."

"Oh, but darling, you'll have to have Napoleon brandy for your guests. It's a Carstairs tradition."

"Then we'll buy it and pay the duty like good British citizens. Seriously, Felicity, I mean it. We'll have all these passages shut up. They hide too much tragedy."

Felicity shivered.

"Yes. I'd like to do that too. We'll bury poor Lynette's bones and lay the ghost forever. What will you be doing, Lynn, when you own Carstairs? Huntin' and shootin'?"

"I'll be becoming a famous author," said Lynn, "while you go about being the lady of the manor. How many children shall we have, darling?"

Felicity reflected.

"We'll have to have an heir, even if we have nine daughters first. Can't be having motor mechanics inheriting Carstairs!"

It was strange to be talking lightly like this in the haunted darkness. Felicity's laughter was all the time dangerously near tears, and Lynn himself was using all his self-control to keep the fatigue and despair out of his voice.

"Look," he said, "I've got about two dozen match-es left. Do you remember Hans Andersen's Little Match Girl? Shall we be very careful and use these one by one, or shall we strike them all and make a blaze as she did?"

Felicity cried with childish eagerness:

"Oh, let's make a blaze! It would be so wonderful to see the light. Let's be reckless, Lynn. We're all of us a reckless lot, anyway."

Lynn pushed the match box into her hand.

"You strike them, darling. You make the blaze yourself."

He wanted her to so that he might see her face in the leaping light—for the last time. After that there would be eternal darkness. Or surely the gods would be kind when they saw how pitifully young Felicity's face was in the light of a hand-ful of matches.

The matches lit with a small hiss. One or two dropped flaming to the ground. The remainder Feli-city held aloft triumphantly in a glorious blaze.

"Look, Lynn!" she chanted. "God said: 'Let there be light and there was light!' Isn't it magni-ficent!"

But Lynn forgot to look at her young triumphant face. He was looking beyond her to a door set at the end of the passage. At first it looked as if the passage came to a dead end. That was what Lynette must have thought when she stumbled against the wall and turned back to die of weariness and despair. But there was a door, with an iron ring high up.

"Keep those matches alight!" he ordered, breath-less with excitement. "Just as long as you can until I get this open. Don't hope, Felicity, but I think we're going to get out."

Felicity wasn't sobbing now. She was simply crying soundlessly, the tears running down her white cheeks unchecked, as, having carefully blown out half the blazing matches, she lit one from another and held them up for Lynn to see as he worked. The door wasn't locked, only stiff with age and disuse, and it took ten minutes and all his strength, which, with his wounded arm, was pitifully little, to drag it open. By that time the last match had burned Felicity's fingers, but they were no longer in darkness. A faint gray light flickered in the dreadful passage behind them, and before them was the familiar wet narrow way that led to the sliding door in the library. In the distance Lynn could hear Buddy barking.

Felicity was clinging to Lynn and looking up with her white wet face.

"For Thine is the kingdom, the power and the glory," she was murmuring unconsciously. "Lynn, to think how near Lynette was to escape and then she had to die. No wonder they could hear her laughing before she died."

It was too dreadful to contemplate that but for their reckless act in striking all the matches the same fate would have been theirs.

Lynn took Felicity's hand.

"Come, darling. Let's surprise them in the middle of our funeral service."

But there was no one in the library except Peewee. He was sitting at the table with his head in his hands. He was dressed in a well-cut tweed suit which he wore with assurance, and he looked, absurdly, more like the master of the house than the butler.

Of all the impossible rogues, Lynn thought wrathfully, starting forward. But Felicity was quicker than he. She ran forward and tumbled into Peewee's arms.

"We're found!" she sobbed. "Here we are, both Lynn and I!"

Peewee's light blue eyes, startled for once into gravity, surveyed the pair of them, Lynn grimy, blood-stained, hollow-faced, Felicity a slight childish bundle collapsing in his arms. He tightened his grip around her.

"There, my darling, it's all right now. Thank God! Thank God!"

Lynn didn't know whether wrath or indignation filled him most. He was too weary to feel a great deal of either. But this fellow comforting Felicity was intolerable.

"You might explain—" he began.

Felicity turned her tousled head. Her eyes, enormous in her white face, suddenly held a spark of impishness.

"Oh, Lynn, I'm sorry. I should have introduced you. This is my father."

"Your—your what?" Lynn was at a loss for more words.

"He's been playing butler," Felicity explained. "He wanted to be on hand. I hope you don't mind."

"Mind?" Lynn echoed. The thing was becoming humorous. Even he, in his state of intense fatigue, could see that. "Of course I mind. It's like his damned impudence. But what can I say since the blackguard's going to be my father, too?"

It was Peewee's turn to look startled.

"What's this?"

"Daddy, Lynn and I are going to be married," said Felicity.

Peewee looked from one to the other. His light eyebrows were raised disgustedly.

"I should think you would," he said, "after that weekend away. But what with Polly and Henry and now you two—my God, Carstairs won't be tolerable!"

"Polly and Henry!" exclaimed Lynn.

"Henry," said Guy Valentine, alias Peewee, ironically, "is sharing in the reward for the Windermere necklace. On condition he keeps quiet about certain other things that he shouldn't know about. I believe he's imagining himself the States' perfect tobacconist." He strolled toward the bell. "I'll ring for Mrs. Mell to put you youngsters in a couple of hot baths. You need them. Or would you rather eat first? After that I wish you any amount of married bliss." He pulled the bell rope and came back to pick up his hat and stick.

"Daddy, where are you going?" Felicity demanded.

Guy Valentine looked around, gay, casual, bland, indifferent.

"Back to South Africa to pick up that elephant spoor I left."

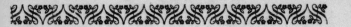

Don't Miss these Ace Romance Bestsellers!

_____#75157 **SAVAGE SURRENDER** $1.95
The million-copy bestseller by Natasha Peters,
author of Dangerous Obsession.

_____#29802 **GOLD MOUNTAIN** $1.95

_____#88965 **WILD VALLEY** $1.95
Two vivid and exciting novels by
Phoenix Island author, Charlotte Paul.

_____#80040 **TENDER TORMENT** $1.95
A sweeping romantic saga in the
Dangerous Obsession tradition.

D.E. STEVENSON ROMANCES

"Finding a re-issued novel by D. E. Stevenson is like coming upon a Tiffany lamp in Woolworth's. It is not 'nostalgia'; it is the real thing."

—THE NEW YORK TIMES BOOK REVIEW

ENTER THE WORLD OF D. E. STEVENSON IN THESE DELIGHTFUL ROMANTIC NOVELS:

AMBERWELL
THE BAKER'S DAUGHTER
BEL LAMINGTON
THE BLUE SAPPHIRE
CELIA'S HOUSE
THE ENCHANTED ISLE
FLETCHERS END
GERALD AND ELIZABETH
GREEN MONEY
THE HOUSE ON THE CLIFF
KATE HARDY
LISTENING VALLEY
THE MUSGRAVES
SPRING MAGIC
SUMMERHILLS
THE TALL STRANGER